TOTEM DREAM

TOTEM DREAM

ALEXANDER KNOX

The Viking Press | *New York*

TO ANDREW KNOX, MY SON

*The map reproduced on the endpapers is from a
Venetian reprint of D'Anville's map of Canada of 1755*

AUTHOR'S NOTE

My grandfather, Hugh Crozier, who lived not far from Toronto in 1850, told me that his mother had to prepare an emergency meal. She decided on a large pie. He collected fifty squab in ten minutes.

In the years 1917–18 I saw a great deal of a former Hudson's Bay Company employee named Mr MacLeod. He reported that his boyhood was filled with horror stories about Pontiac told by his uncle, who was born at the time of the trouble in Detroit, and his father, who was born soon after. Mr MacLeod in his turn took some pleasure in making my blood run cold by enlarging on Pontiac's suggestions as to suitable treatment for white men. I report this in Chapter One. Mr MacLeod, I found out later, was born about 1832 when his father was over seventy years of age.

It is a fact that I was hot and thirsty on the shore of Lake Erie some time before the First World War and that the natural thing to do at that time was what I did – I walked into the lake and drank part of it.

It is also a fact that every school child knows how dull the stories can be which History and Geography write unassisted. People familiar with the area inaccurately described as Western Ontario will see that I have not been lazy enough to depend on History or Geography to write my story for me.

I can go so far as to say that the only material in my story which I vouch for as being true is the substance, though not the situation, of Longhair's ecological dream recounted in Chapter Ten. Even this was dreamed, not by an Ottawa in 1770, but by a half Huron friend of mine in 1926. I've been able to report it very accurately only because so many of his phrases will never leave my memory.

AK

1

A Desperate Decision

*'The white Samson's strength was in his hair.
I'll cut mine when the last white man
leaves my land.'*

Longhair

CALVIN HEGGIE was terrified of Indians, whether dressed
in scraps of hide or in fine ranks of feathers. That was
the reason he found himself, in late May 1770, transcribing his own notice of dismissal. The inditement was loud
and came in bursts from his master, Mr Colethorpe, who
fumed and sputtered when the word evaded him. The
quill pen scratched and spattered. The ink was thick and,
in a canoe surging forward at forty strokes a minute, his
position was too awkward for Calvin to ask leave to trim
a new one.

'Where was I?'

'*– services not satisfactory –*'

Mr Colethorpe's anger cooled by half a degree and he
found his phrase. '*– services –* ah *– might be satisfactory
in a less wild factory or in a town or –*'

'Wait!' The pen scratched on. '*– in a town or –* Yes?'

'*– in a town or in a city, but he is not suited to the life
up here. He's frightened of the Indians. He's always asking for a book, wishing he was in a city and he's not
suited –*'

'You said that.'

'Write it down!'

' – *suited*.' There was a brief pause. 'It isn't fair to say that. The Indians don't frighten me – '

'You pissed your pants two hours ago!'

Calvin answered carefully. 'That was the noise. That was the shots, the yells, the arrows. You can't control your – I didn't even know! It was in- invol – it just happened. Oh, go on – *suited*.'

'*So I am sending him to you in Montreal via the Ottawa where he will fall in with some brigade or other. He is honest and hardworking, but – but he – is not – ah –* '

'*– is not suited to this life?* '

'Yes, say that. *So I hope you will find him a position for which his talents suit him better. Your obedient servant.* Beach this canoe! I can't sign in this bucket.'

The order was shouted. The big canoe was run up on the beach, the little one was hauled up beside it and the other five drifted off-shore. The signing of the letter took a long time because Mr Colethorpe wrote slowly and because Calvin hesitated over the address: was H. B. MacBain a Factor, a Superintendent or a Director, and should his title be included?

'Leave his title off,' said Mr Colethorpe.

The red seal took a long time to affix because Mr Colethorpe insisted on doing it himself and burnt his fingers repeatedly. He swore at the stub of wax, shook his fingers and the smoking lump hissed as it hit the dark water. Finally the crumpled and smudged missive was finished and stuffed into Calvin's pocket.

That was the moment when the last spurt of fury so unsettled Calvin's mind that it reached out wildly like the hand of a drowning man and took a decision. What had to be done had to be done in a hurry. The decision involved a theft and the theft was to change his life.

Quietly he closed and locked Mr Colethorpe's pretty

8

mahogany writing-case with the neat line of ebony inlaid along all edges. It contained a tiny folding knife, paper, ink, pens, correspondence, a ledger, stock-lists and maps. The maps were the most recent French ones and these were the fuse of the boy's decision. At a moment when Mr Colethorpe was otherwise occupied he laid the case beside the pile of duffle on the sand and threw over it, negligently, his jacket which the curious weather had made too warm to wear. As he did so he was sure that his Presbyterian father and mother turned over in their Berwick grave yard at this crime against property. His fellow-servants at the big house where he'd been a snot-nosed page probably felt a twinge. Maybe the distant male relative who'd apprenticed him to the Company listened, suddenly, to some unheard alarm.

A selection of supplies was piled beside the small canoe. Mr Colethorpe, red in the face and frowning, wet his feet as he climbed into the big one. There were grunts from the hired canoe-men as the brigade surged north along the lake. All six canoes rode high: the season had been bad. The boy glowered after them, sulky, full of wrath and terror. He'd denied it but there was too much truth in what Mr Colethorpe had said. He might get used to it but, at seventeen, and after only one confining winter, he wasn't suited to this country.

Then the sound of paddles could be heard no longer and the six gleaming shapes – the prows appeared to ride higher than his head – skimmed the black water silently and seemed to leave no wake. The surface of the water, bearing that weight of silence, was smooth as jet or black enamel. A kingfisher was a blue flash as it passed him but the terrible shriek, surprisingly, didn't startle him. He was beyond startling.

He refused to recollect the past few hours. He hauled the little canoe a foot higher on the sand. He moved two articles of baggage, preparatory to making camp. Then he stopped and sat on a rounded stone holding his flint-lock, a Brown Bess that had been loaded, primed but not fired at the capture of Quebec.

He sat in silence. What was the point? What was the point of making camp, of eating, of sleeping, of going anywhere, of doing anything? His shadow unfurled behind him. He pulled the brim of his felt hat lower and lower to shade his eyes. His dark hair prickled on his scalp. He waited. The world waited. Only the sun moved, dropping towards the saw-toothed wall of spruces. There'd been no sound since the kingfisher.

He wished that the cut on his lip would heal and that the big bruise on his cheekbone wouldn't ache so much. He moved his two loose teeth with his tongue. He felt feverish.

He caught sight of the incongruous mahogany writing-case. A theft. A deliberate theft. And an easy one. The flare of temper and resolution had been warming, even exciting. He would do what his boss refused to do. He would be a loyal servant of the Company. He would fill empty spaces on the map. And all the time he knew the decision was not exciting but fatuous. It was utterly hopeless and absurd. 'Think,' he told himself. 'Think! Face facts!'

There could be nothing ahead of him but the haul down the lake, through the river of the Frenchmen and into the wild Ottawa where, he'd heard, the section known as Rivière Creuse was black and bottomless. The thought of the Rivière Creuse being bottomless was an example of the kind of story, rumour and legend that left him fearful. He knew these things were not true, and he knew that they were told him partly to create the fear, but the knowledge didn't disperse the cold spot in his middle.

A pimple beside his nose was itching and he poked at it savagely, scratching and squeezing. He felt it burst. He looked at his finger and wiped the pus on his trouser.

10

He didn't bother to lift his arm again but let it hang inert between his legs. He slumped and got the sun out of his eyes. Why did all his teeth ache so? Quite a few had been loose, he thought, even before Mr Colethorpe hit him.

The water was black. The barricade of spruces was black as the water; and a depression quite as black – and as deep as the Rivière Creuse – enclosed him as in a jelly, slowly setting. His stillness could easily become permanent. He rather wished the night were already around him. He'd forgotten the brigade. It would be out of sight. He didn't look.

Not that any of this was unexpected—

He had known things couldn't have lasted with Mr Colethorpe, who was torn too many ways. He was greedy for whisky, greedy for trade, greedy for idleness and greedy for credit with the Company. It had been his greed for trade that had persuaded him to disregard his orders after the ambush this morning.

The ambush was intended as a joke. Maybe the joke would backfire. If he hadn't arranged the ambush Mr Colethorpe would not have heard the news that persuaded him to disobey orders. Would that disobedience have consequences? Would the Hudson's Bay Company—

What difference did it make? Whatever the consequences to Mr Colethorpe, he was here alone beside a nameless lake, sitting on a stone in his still-damp trousers.

He wouldn't have been fired if he hadn't pissed all over Mr Colethorpe's whisky-jug. He wouldn't have done that if Mr Colethorpe hadn't told the Frenchman that his apprentice was afraid of Indians. Mr Colethorpe wouldn't have known he was afraid of Indians if he hadn't woken him with his screams that night last winter. He wouldn't have had dreams vivid enough to wake him if he hadn't spent so much time with the quiet old men and women – Chippewas and Ottawas mostly – listening to stories.

And he certainly would not have listened to so many stories if they'd not been riveting to the point of hypnosis, told, as they were, in hushed voices in the half-warm stinking store-room of the cabin during the endless winter night. Most of the stories were about a bloodthirsty Indian named Longhair.

You could go on with cause and effect for ever. Very complicated. There were other reasons for talking to the old Indians every night; he wanted to understand and speak the language; and he wanted to avoid whisky, cards and conversation with Mr Colethorpe. It was complicated.

It wasn't; it was simple. If he hadn't been born he wouldn't be in trouble.

The afternoon was utterly silent. Three blue herons grew out of their frozen reflections just beyond a fold of smooth red stone – pierre à calumet – he could see that one jagged spot where little chunks were chipped and cut from the rock with knives and hatchets. The red stone reminded him of cheese. A few shards lay on the sand; someone had been at it quite recently. The Indians used the little chunks for carving peace-pipes. They made very pretty peace-pipes. They also made tomahawks.

At some point he stopped thinking. He was nudged towards a sounder sleep than he'd had for many weeks by the small things he began to see and hear, but mainly it was the spectacular sunset. Clouds built up to the east behind him and filled the valley with reflected light. The evening began officially with one of those gigantic North American robins fluting near him, and the liquid sounds were clearly echoed from the cliff of spruce across the glassy lake. Then a clatter of ducks wheeled past him, the iridescent heads a galaxy of emeralds flung against the dark. Four does trotted delicately between the distant stems to the water's edge where they spaced themselves and drank, four topaz flames—

At a sharp report – a beaver-tail on still water – they lifted their fine heads and listened to five separate echoes, then they drank again. The beaver trailed its arrow-head across the southern bay. As the sun, no longer blinding, sank behind the lace of spruce, one of the motionless herons croaked like a frog and all three unfurled their rounded wings, stepped, hopped and ran till airborne, when they banked and fanned their way over his head. His eyes followed and saw that the towers of cloud had turned to scarlet. The air itself began to glow.

He heard the breathy gasping of larger wings than the herons' and seven swans, pink as a strawberry confection, swung past him from the south. They flew so close to their reflections the wingtips seemed to touch at each downward stroke. He had the feeling the wings were saying words – 'just a while, just a while, just a while, just a while', repeated to infinity.

The evening was clamorous with song, beamed at him from every direction – shrill and almost beyond hearing from black swifts that sizzled in enormous arcs, woody and hollow from old frogs. Geese were brassy in the distance and two owls tried their tremolos.

The things he saw and heard were so distant, so unanxious and so unassertive that they caught his interest, and held it till he sagged to the sand and slept.

That day had ended quietly, and it had begun hopefully enough. But in between? Calvin could have endured the fright of the ambush, he could have weathered his own shame, but what he could not deal with was the anger he had stored up during the long winter with Mr Colethorpe. Still he shouldn't have lost his temper—

The orders, and the maps, had come to Mr Colethorpe

with the first canoes after the break-up. The Hudson's Bay Company was taking advantage of the new situation created by the capture of Quebec. Was the route via Montreal easier than that by Hudson's Bay? The French were cooperative and provided a great deal of information about the Ottawa route to the north-west, also the route through the big lakes to the Ohio country and the Mississippi. There was an island in between these routes and no one knew much about it. The Ottawa was north and east, the lakes were south and west. In this area memories of massacres were strong and lasting; the five nations had attacked the Hurons in French times. The Eries and the Neutrals were slaughtered on later raids. Five years before, Pontiac's great rising decimated the defenders of many forts and left them heaps of charred and tumbled logs to be quickly overgrown with rank burdock.

Mr Colethorpe was ordered to go south and to investigate this island in between the routes which many people reported to be a haven for mink and beaver, since permanent human occupation seemed to have diminished.

So their route was to be south along the shores of unmapped lakes and little-known rivers. The first days of the journey were upstream and arduous, though, since snow was not entirely gone, the rivers were full and the portages fewer than they would be later in the season. They reached the land of the divide. To the north the rivers fed the great and shallow bay. To the south the little streams grew rapidly to rivers that fed the lakes and the Ottawa. The huge turtle-shaped mountains heaved like sluggish tidal swells for many thousands of miles around them, slow and lazy as befitted immense age. The endless blanket of black spruce was torn here and there by a sharp edge of granite, or worn by a thrust of naked gneiss. The long lakes could not be counted.

On the morning of the day Calvin was fired they were

14

still in this country, but they were reaching its southern edge. Mr Colethorpe was trying to make out his order-list for the next season, a burst of industry that took him by surprise. His surprise turned to irritation when he found that Calvin had prepared a stock-list of his own which he kept consulting.

The boy had the writing-case on his knees, the ink-horn, unstoppered, clipped to the corner, and he wrote with difficulty. Splatters and cramped strokes were the result of uneven pressure on the quill. Bales of fur impeded the writing elbow as the two faced each other in the middle of the canoe. The feeling between them was resentful and Mr Colethorpe's temper fragile. With the long winter at an end he deserved a celebration. The crock of whisky that had given him a hangover was finished. The new one, held between his knees, was to cure the hangover.

'Axe-heads, cast, two boxes. Axe-heads, steel – how many did I order last year?'

Calvin grimly thumbed the ledger.

'A dozen.'

'Order the same.'

'But we traded them all!'

'We got rid of the cast ones too.'

'By lowering the price. They were still asking for steel heads when we left.'

'Steel heads one dozen I tell you.'

Then a similar argument over traps.

'Same as last year. One gross double-spring six inch. One gross single fours.'

'We traded only five dozen big ones.'

'If we've no traps to trade we can't get furs.'

'We've seven dozen big ones left.'

'Same as last year. It's my credit, not yours.'

'Credit? For how long? We could have traded a gross of Stroud blankets. We've ordered two dozen. We traded

one dozen white blankets. We've ordered six dozen.
We—'
  '*We* are not ordering these supplies, *I* am.'
  'All the coloured cloth is gone. Half the grey cloth's left
for the moths. The order's for the same again.'
  The jug was at Mr Colethorpe's lips. When it came
away he said, 'When you're as old as I am—' Then he
went silent.
  'Muskets? Meal?' asked Calvin.
  'Have a drink.'
  'No thank you.'
  'Have a drink!' The tone of his voice implied that if
he didn't have a drink he'd be outcast.
  So Calvin took a sip, remembering not to wipe the
neck since this action offended Mr Colethorpe. The spirit
made him thirsty. He leaned to reach the tin baler into
the lake and drank deeply. As he put the baler away a
few drops fell on Mr Colethorpe's knees and trembled
there on the oily fabric.
  Mr Colethorpe stared at these crystal beads, muttering
under his breath. The thunk, thunk, thunk of the paddles
made a rhythm, the repeated surges of the canoe were
rocking him to sleep. He made to brush the drops away
but instead he leaned back against a bale of the curiously
anaesthetic skins of skunk, took the sun on his face and
closed his eyes. Whenever he muttered the boy lifted the
pen, but the words and phrases were not dictation, they
came from long ago. At first they were barely audible.
  'Then they had bows and stone axes. Now they want
steel axes and firearms. How'd you like to run into Longhair on a dark night when he has a musket? They get
above themselves.'
  'They're just big children,' Calvin quoted placatingly.
  'You've never seen them burn a man alive. You've
never seen them skin him alive either. You've never been
offered a chunk of roasted leg.'

16

'Everybody's always telling these stories.'

'And you think they're not true?'

'People – people make the most of them.'

'Wait till Longhair gets you. He'll make the most of you.'

'Why does everyone tell stories about Longhair?'

'Because they say he's a wendigo.'

This word was supposed to frighten Calvin and Mr Colethorpe examined him for signs before he continued. 'They say he marches along looking for chances to carry out Pontiac's orders.'

'What orders?' Calvin couldn't help the question.

'Pontiac's orders. What to do about white men.'

'What—'

Mr Colethorpe assumed the word was a question. He answered seriously—

' "Rip their balls off", said Pontiac.' And Mr Colethorpe eyed Calvin closely before he continued. 'They're saying now that Longhair is Pontiac's nephew.'

'What does that mean?'

'It means he could be a chief among the Ottawas. I don't know, They used to say he was Pontiac's son.'

They listened to the paddles and the heavy breathing around them and watched the glittering water slide away. The sameness of the two riverbanks was confining.

Mr Colethorpe's head suddenly lifted and he raised his hand to shade his eyes as he gazed forward at the right bank. The gesture disturbed Calvin. Covertly he tried to see what Mr Colethorpe found so interesting. Then the older man relaxed.

'He's over six feet tall and his hair is ten feet long. He can bind a pack with it and carry it without a headband. Also he has yellow eyes.'

'Have you seen him?'

'He wouldn't be alive if I'd seen him. I saw what he did, though, at St Joseph.'

'What did he do?' Calvin asked the question as he was expected to. Mr Colethorpe's gaze was so inward and his voice so quiet that he compelled attention. Calvin felt the breeze suddenly cold on his left cheek. One of the Algonquin paddlers behind him had begun a hoarse, breathy chant.

Calvin knew Mr Colethorpe delighted in telling him horror stories. He knew he must listen and appear unconcerned. He knew Mr Colethorpe's greatest pleasure was to see a sign of nervousness. He also knew that, though the story had hardly begun, his pen-hand was already trembling. Over-actively he inserted the quill in its clip, raised the desk to the bale beside him and leaned forward, elbows on knees, one hand, white-knuckled, holding the other.

'Have a drink,' said Mr Colethorpe.

'No thank you. What did he do?'

'Have a drink!'

So Calvin removed the wooden stopper and took a sip. Mr Colethorpe's eyes didn't see the jug when he tried to hand it back; they were fixed on some vision on the right bank forward. Calvin tucked the jug on the slippery floor-planks beneath the split-ash stay he crouched on and held it upright with his raised heels. Floor-planks were always slimy: birch-bark is waterproof only if the seams are tightly sewn and well-stuck with hot resin. Mr Colethorpe spoke again in his hoarse voice.

'They say he spent an hour with the stone sharpening his hatchet. The five men were in a row. Their wrists were tied to a pine-log and it was hoisted – a rope at each end – and fixed against two trees. Their feet were separated and their ankles tied to another log – a heavier one. They were naked. But Longhair didn't let the women have them. He had another plan.'

Calvin was startled to see tears in Mr Colethorpe's eyes and he began to wonder if, possibly, this was the only true story Mr Colethorpe had ever told him. There was an unfamiliar note of conviction in his tone.

'The red fiends heaved on the ropes attached to the log their wrists were tied to, and raised it higher. The row of white men took the weight and the heavier log their feet were tied to was lifted from the ground. Just a few inches it was lifted. Some of them took more weight than others.'

There was a coolish wind but Calvin felt a prickling of his skin, like sweat erupting. He lifted his face and saw two hawks circling. From somewhere some creature he didn't recognise gave a long faint cry – it wasn't laughter. It wasn't a loon.

'So they were stretched out and their legs were straight. I suppose he started at the end. Ten straight legs in a row.'

'Yes.'

Mr Colethorpe glared at him.

'At least he's not like you. He's a man. He lets the women work on the privates.'

Calvin blushed till every pimple glowed. Mr Colethorpe continued.

'Longhair took his hatchet. He chopped once at each knee as he walked past. He'd sharpened it well. He hacked like an expert butcher. When he came to the end of the row and turned he saw ten legs with the knees laid open and the knee-caps dangling against the shin-bones.'

They were passing close to a high rounded rock. There was a shout and suddenly the rock was alive with fantastic figures. A flight of arrows whistled overhead and the yelling was more piercing than the wildest wind he'd ever heard. The colours reeled – feathers, streamers, embroidered aprons – painted men – gleaming hatchets – wild gesticulations—

The muscles of Calvin's eyes opened them wide till white surrounded the pupils. The muscles of his jaw gave way till his mouth fell loose and open, the tongue with

19

nowhere to hide. The muscles of his bladder opened and when he realised what was happening to him he couldn't stop. The trousers were worn thin and bulged as the hot stream dribbled through. Mr Colethorpe snatched his crock of whisky.

It was, of course, Mr Colethorpe's fury at the fate of his whisky that saved Calvin from the worst crowings over the evidence of his fear. You can't crow with delight when you're purple with fury. So when Mr Colethorpe greeted his friend the Frenchman who had staged the ambush he complained that it had been too realistic and that it was plain stupid to ruin good whisky. The Frenchman and his Indians hooted with laughter, partly at Mr Colethorpe.

But by the time fires were lit and the pot of stew was warming, scorn and glee had been redirected at their proper target.

'I said he'd piss himself, by God, and he did! He did! I didn't think he'd actually do it – actually piss himself, I mean, I just *said* that he would – and he did – and that's what I've had to put up with all winter. Holy God!'

'He did! He did! He pissed himself!' said the men who spoke English and it was translated into Ottawa, French, and even Cree.

Calvin found his bowl and knife, rose from his stone and got himself some stew.

'His stone's all wet! He did! He did!'

Hot and red, he sat on a log and chewed away. He knew what was coming; hours of joyful jokes and merry laughter. Hours, maybe days, of happy references to wet trousers. But he had a defence: dullness and lack of attention. If you pay no attention they go away.

But he was wrong. He was rescued, and by a piece of news the Frenchman brought. The Frenchman didn't

20

value the news highly enough but Mr Colethorpe did, once it had penetrated.

Two of the Frenchman's most trustworthy men had returned from the Abitibi country and told him that the Ottawa Walker was coming south with three, maybe four villages. Maybe two hundred men, with women, all peaceful, and heavy canoes, only two inches of freeboard.

'The Ottawa Walker!'

After the famous name it seemed to take thirty seconds for Mr Colethorpe's watery eyes to focus on the Frenchman. Then the executive took over.

He scrapped the orders he'd received. He demanded the use of the Frenchman's canoes and men. He overruled all objections to cutting short the meal. Speed. Speed. Speed.

There might be traders with a Montreal licence waiting even now. The season had been bad. He should have stayed in the north. Maybe the Ottawa Walker had gone to his factory, found him absent, and so decided to head south. The Ottawa Walker was a bastard. You never knew where he'd be. He always moved with hundreds of families. He was the richest Indian there was, but he was dangerous and too many damn tribes did what he said.

'I'm going north,' declared Mr Colethorpe.

There was the hurry of finishing the stew, the resentful grumbling of the men, the stowing of the canvas-wrapped supplies. Calvin was not permitted to help shove off because, as he climbed in, his wet moccasins would pour water over Mr Colethorpe's legs; so he was already in his place when the big canoe wobbled, scraped, pitched, came level and the regular stroke began.

After five minutes of paddling sudden doubts struck Mr Colethorpe and he called to the Frenchman, whose canoe crept up until only six feet of swift water separated them and they could talk easily.

'You believe your scouts?'

'Oui!' said the Frenchman.

He was questioned about their reports and eventually Mr Colethorpe's attack of uncertainty receded. He was satisfied that the Ottawa Walker wanted trade, not war. 'Best to be sure,' he said.

'Oui.'

Mr Colethorpe leaned back, 'MacBain told me the Ottawa Walker was seen last autumn on the upper lake with a thousand canoes behind him.'

'Peut-être.'

'I don't believe the thousand canoes.'

'Non.'

'But maybe, I suppose.'

'Peut-être.'

'No one knows much about him.'

'Le grand inconnu!'

'MacBain told me he was seen with a gang of Crows as far north as Churchill, in the same week he was sending food to Pontiac in Detroit.'

'Va vit,' said the Frenchman. 'Leger comme un oiseau. Il est deux hommes, peut-être, ou trois—'

'Talk English.'

'Mais oui, monsieur, je le parle.'

So the Englishman grew morose while the chatter continued; and the fact that Calvin smiled at some remark of the Frenchman appeared to exacerbate the gloom. Was the apprentice getting above himself again? When the Frenchman, with gestures, got going on the attractiveness of Ottawa girls before they began bearing children, a familiar line of play presented itself.

'You'd better drop it. You'll upset the boy. He's pure. He keeps himself for himself. He grows warts by the dozen'.

Calvin kept as still as possible. There was nothing else to do.

'Wake up three times a night with the cabin shaking!'

22

'Ah, le pauvre petit prêtre!'

'His poor little priest is worn away! Worn away!'

But there wasn't enough laughter and Calvin knew the following silence was sinister because of the calculating glances from Mr. Colethorpe's shadowed eyes – glances at him. His stillness was absolute. He fixed his attention on the row of tiny whirlpools passing under the bleached hickory of the gunwale. How neatly the ribs were bound to this bent sapling he thought absently, though in a better-made canoe these bindings would be cased in oiled leather to protect them from the rubbing of the paddles.

Mr Colethorpe finally spoke. 'You may as well get busy. Make out the list the same as last year. No more argument.'

'Yes, sir,' said Calvin. Then, unexpectedly, he was seized with a stubborn, grinding fury. Blood rushed to his face and he didn't care what he said. 'It's crazy. What do we keep accounts *for*? You learn nothing. You'll see. Whatever you've too much of, you'll have more. Whatever you're short of, you'll have less.'

Mr Colethorpe hit him. 'Keep your mouth shut.'

'What you need you won't have. You'll be piled to the roof with what you can't get rid of.'

Mr Colethorpe hit him twice, left and right. He bounced against the crate of guns and back against the muskrat skins. His lip began to bleed. The canoe lurched.

The Frenchman, who wanted to haul no dripping bundles from the water, roared across, this time in English:

'Watch out! Wait! Hit him ashore.'

Suddenly Calvin realised he had this advantage, and remnants of caution whirled away like a breath in winter. He pointed an inky finger at Mr Colethorpe and found himself yelling.

'You've got a dozen blankets from years ago! All moth-holes! You've a pile of old iron you couldn't get rid of to a tête boule! Why should they take your rusty bracelets when they can pick up copper on the nearest hill? Bent guns, chipped axes, knives made of lead or something—'

He'd been blamed all winter as an unpersuasive salesman, the implication being that if he'd tried he could have moved the goods. The list of the Factor's stupidities grew longer, louder and more furious as Calvin realised he'd gone so far already there was no turning back; but he wasn't good at getting angry and he was curiously weak. Sometimes no words would come and tears took their place, which made him angrier. Soon he became a bouncing kettle of bubbling incoherence.

When, at last, the heat dried him up his face was purple but Mr Colethorpe's face was white. The sobs and fulminations died away and a bubble of hate grew around them excluding everything. After a time Mr Colethorpe pricked it coldly by telling him to get his things ready. There was a letter to be written.

So Calvin Heggie was dismissed.

2

The Beginning

'The People die when their stories
are told no more.'

Longhair

'FIRST there was nothing, then the nothing became blue. This was sky and it was one blue. Then it became a mixture of pale blue and dark blue and the dark blue was heavier and came together, and it found it was water. Then the mud in the water came together, and it found it was an island. The waves in the water shaped the island like the back of a turtle and made it smooth. So it was learned that smooth things could be made of mud so why not make them? So, out of the mud of the island two people were made, smooth and good to look at. They were Wendet, people of the island. Everyone knows these people were made but who made them? No one knows. It was too long ago. Not even the spirit of the oldest tree, or a mountain, or the moon could tell you because even those old spirits are too young to have been there—'

The words were half dream, half recollection as he lay on the bank beside his canoe, slowly waking. Several voices spoke the words – male and female, young and old – and they were speaking at twilight times through the winter. Calvin didn't begin by being interested in the stories but by trying to grow more fluent in the language so he'd be a better trader; but the stories stayed in his mind. And now, waking to the world already busy, he knew he was on the island. This was it. This was where it all began. The island, the garden.

As he became conscious that he was thinking as well as dreaming he recognised ponderously that this heathen story had an unexpected resemblance to the truth as revealed in Genesis. It would be hard to make these people see the difference, of course. They were simple and could neither read nor write and didn't know right from wrong, and they were always fornicating. They were pagans, uncivilised, and savages.

Savages!

He was fully awake instantly but he moved no muscle except to roll his eyes. He was comfortable and in his field of vision everything was peaceful, so he lay still till his brain nagged at him that there might be savage dangers behind him. Softly, slowly, he rolled half over. With a wild chittering two quail shot towards the red rock, up the side and over. Long after they disappeared they repeated their exclamations, but he could see no dangers. Then he began to be conscious of the grass and found it cold with dew, so he raised himself slowly, wishing he were still asleep. His leather jacket was stiff, his moccasins were stiff, his homespun trousers were stiff and he was stiff. He slouched to the pile of duffle, thinking to sort it: he sat down instead. He slouched all day. He ate very little. At about eleven he launched the canoe and saw that the leak amidship would have to be closed, so he hauled it up the bank and sat down again. At about two he sauntered among the trees looking for drips and oozings of resin he could use. He found a few and his hand got sticky holding them so he threw them away and sat down again, scrubbing at his hand with sand and a bundle of grass. At about three o'clock he chewed on some biscuit but it was too hard so he just mouthed it, finding it unexpectedly palatable. He thought idly of spring. It was slow in Berwick. Here it was magically quick. Then he took off his jacket and went to sleep. When he woke his forearms and left side of his face were scarlet. His beard was much too thin to protect his white skin from the sun.

The only bit of purposeful activity came at about six o'clock when he cut some cedar boughs and shingled them down along a bulge of granite. Then he spread two blankets on his bed. On several occasions he found himself crouched, a cedar switch in his hand, doing nothing, absent, out of thought. It was the strangest day he'd ever spent. He spent the day not thinking.

He was, as Mr Colethorpe said he was, terrified of Indians; but all day he had done nothing to protect himself; he left Brown Bess leaning against the canoe. He'd done nothing to conceal himself; his baggage was spread wide in the open. And he'd done nothing to prepare for his long trip. The white men he came with were miles away by now. The Sault, Michilimacinac, Detroit, Niagara, Frontenac, Montreal – he was hundreds of miles from any of them. He was alone.

The only moment of real consciousness came with the dark, when he held a prolonged debate. Was his day-long idleness caused by exhaustion, or by a fear of loneliness and Indians so powerful as to throw him into a paralysis? He didn't light a fire. He drank great draughts of the cool lake water, sucked some maple sugar, mumbled another rock-hard biscuit, huddled between his blankets and gradually stopped shivering. In the listening before sleep engulfed him he was almost on the point of discovering, several times, just what it was that the anaesthetic smell of cut cedar reminded him of – a memory so full of peace it was a drug. And the voices – but they weren't voices – nor were they phrases recollected.

These people were Wendet, people of the island. Who made them? No one knows. Not even the spirit of a very

27

old tree, or of the moon. What about the Wendet? People of the island can't tell you because there aren't any. A thing happened no one talks about. And anyway, when they were made whatever made them went away, so they never saw who – or what—'

It was the same two quail that woke him on the second morning. They carried their two-note hysteria away on a racket of wings as Calvin turned over and sat up out of old melancholy into a crystal, active world. He was hungry, so he made a fire and cooked three slices of salt pork – tough and somewhat rancid. He might run into trouble. There'd be white men travelling down the Ottawa. He'd be less a possible victim there than here.

The leaky join in the bark of his canoe had opened in yesterday's sun. He could stick the sheets of bark together better when they were dry. He cruised the nearby trees picking lumps and bubbles of gum and melted them in his spoon. The gum caught fire and he smothered the flame with a flat stone. The resin thickened up quickly so he eased the flap of bark back and poured the resin under it. Some was glutinous and he poked it in with a stick. He pressed the layers of bark together. They were too dry and sprang away tackily. Quickly he took a hard, thin strip of the salt pork skin and made a stitch which he held until the two layers adhered. He melted another batch of gum and smeared the join before he lifted the stern and slid the bow into the water. A drop or two came through, but the bark would swell again. He began to stow gear amidships, then shifted the whole load forward. He'd be heavy in the stern. The canoe wouldn't be towed, he'd have to paddle; and he'd probably go in circles.

He was certain to go in circles. He hadn't had enough time in the canoe on his own. Paddle on the right, the bow swings left. Lift the dripping paddle over, change hands,

28

paddle on the left – the bow swings right. There was a trick but he didn't know it. He'd been out in canoes a few times last autumn but the winter came so early. It would be a slow trip, and when he reached the end of it his hopeful HBC career would be at an end. He took the letter from his pocket, resisted an impulse to tear it up, and slipped it into his canvas bag which he lugged impatiently to the canoe.

There was only the mahogany box to load. Why was he hurrying? He liked the mahogany box. It was expertly made. He sat down on the sand to examine it again. It was a luxury to examine it without Mr Colethorpe's bloodshot eyes on him. He removed the papers and put stones on them. He didn't bother to look at the French maps. He knew them by heart. Even the best, by the Sieur D'Anville, showed little detail of this particular country.

On the clean wood inside the box was pasted a paper label. The maker's name was torn away but the remaining spidery writing indicated that his workshop was in St Martin's Lane. He didn't consider it necessary to specify the town.

Calvin knew he should be on his way. Why was he wasting time? Delay wouldn't help things.

The dovetails were so perfect you couldn't find them. You couldn't slip a hair between any two pieces of wood. The hinges were strong. When the box was opened the writing-table, inlaid with fine leather, sloped flat and firm. And it closed as neatly as a good book.

As usual, the thing that interested him most was the secret drawer, a compartment which, he suspected, Mr Colethorpe didn't know about. Even the placing was ingenious. You would assume that the six-inch strip of smooth mahogany was intended to strengthen the fixing of the handle. The placing of the heads of the two brass bolts, neatly sunk in the wood, made this obvious. But one of the flush brass heads was a fake and the other was the button which operated a tiny interior latch. When the drawer was pulled out it offered a compartment measuring $\frac{1}{2}'' \times 1\frac{5}{8}'' \times 6''$.

By peering into the shallow cavity it was possible to see how ingeniously the handle had been secured without allowing the cavity to lessen its strength. A great deal of careful thinking was involved, which Calvin admired. He thought of putting his letter of dismissal in this secret place, but it seemed a shame. The wood was as fresh and clean as the day it was made. The letter was mean, dirty and unfair.

But he'd given up all notion of trying to execute Mr Colethorpe's orders himself. Exploration would be valuable to the Company but it should be done by a proper expedition, not by someone with rudimentary ideas of map-making and none of the necessary equipment. Of course the French maps indicated the large features but the spaces between were blank and distances were inaccurate. One map suggested that Detroit was two hundred and fifty miles from Niagara, another that the distance was less than a hundred miles. D'Anville's map was not much better than Popple's, though it was French and fifteen years later.

Mr Colethorpe, of course, was a fool. He might meet the Ottawa Walker, he might even make a profitable trade: but, however profitable, detailed maps of 'The Island' would be more valuable. If the HBC, with the law on its side, were to stamp out trading from Montreal or New York, maps would be necessary. As a sort of gesture he marked his guess as to his present position on one of the French maps. Then he drew a large-scale outline on blank paper, using his compass to fix the bearings of features which he knew. But, eventually, the Company would have to send someone – someone adequately trained – to map this 'Island'. 'People of the Island'. He was thinking of it as 'The Island' all the time now.

All this was sheer waste of time. He'd have to go to the Ottawa and present his letter to MacBain in Montreal. Hanging about would make it no easier. He crammed everything back in the mahogany box and put it under the canvas in the canoe.

The canoe was loaded. His fire was scattered. He was no longer foolish. He shoved off, stepped in and paddled on the right. Five thrusts and he was moving south, parallel to the shore. Five more and the bow scraped sand. He changed over, dripping water on his canvas sack. It was too shallow to paddle so he poled. The canoe went higher on the sand, so he poled backwards.

He reached deeper water but the bow kept swinging left. Now the canoe floated slowly south, the direction he had to take, but the bow pointed due north. He could paddle round here in a circle till he was frozen in next winter! He was glad there was no one to see how awkward he was.

Or was there? He peered about anxiously.

What difference did it make? There were Red men everywhere. If he were going to be killed he wouldn't have to hand the letter to MacBain. So he'd paddle in a circle, and he did. He was filled with a foolish fury. He paddled on the right and went round and round, thinking of his many troubles. Round and round—

Then it happened.

It was ridiculous, but he was going straight! And with no particular effort except the slight twist at the end of each stroke which they'd told him was the secret.

He was doing an outward twist. He had been doing an inward twist. He'd work it out some time – it had to do with the motion of the canoe through the water, the motion of the blade through the water and the angle of the blade.

He was going north. He paddled without the twist and swung left. He used the paddle as a rudder and the canoe

31

tilted, sliding over the water. When the bow was pointing south he introduced the twist again and his course straightened. He churned on looking for the mouth of the little river that would conduct him to the Ottawa and Montreal.

He began to paddle more violently, digging in and pulling with his back, not just his arms and shoulders. His speed increased till he could feel the cool wind. This stirred up a sense of triumph absent in his life since the previous August, when he first saw, from the deck of the stinking ship, the long hills of Hudson's Bay.

The canoe was so sensitive. It felt the pull of the stroke, the wind and even the little waves. His heart beat faster. He pumped furiously and saw foam at the bow. Maybe this was one of the things you do by instinct and not by taking thought. He couldn't imagine why his ability suddenly to be able to do a thing that any savage could do should lift his spirits into such joy. His back was aching, his arms were tired but he was the first man ever to learn to paddle straight. He'd solved a problem of the universe, which was triumph. Was he feverish?

Was it his triumph which made him suddenly weak when, at noon, he saw to his right an arm of the lake opening south-westward, very wide and inviting? He stopped paddling. The canoe continued south – straight, smooth, steady.

Then, racing in from the left he saw white water where the swift current of the little river piled up on the lake waves. That was his route. To Montreal. To humiliation. He rested his paddle across the gunwales.

He wouldn't go to Montreal. He'd carry out the orders given to Mr Colethorpe. He had the pens, the paper, the compass and the maps. He had Brown Bess, powder and lead. If savages could harvest the wilderness with bow and arrow he could do it with Brown Bess. He had no limits of time or space. He had the whole of summer,

which was just beginning. Of course he would be purposeful and shrewd.

Rather complacent in the back of his mind was the
feeling that if he could do a decent job on the maps the
mean letter might be disregarded. He could explain that
he'd been feeling peculiar, that he'd lost his temper, that
he did not intend to be impertinent.

(The thought also crossed his mind that the sudden
acquisition of skill with the paddle was an omen.)

He put the paddle in the water again, turned his back
on the route to Montreal and headed south-west.

The avenue was wide, blue and brilliant. The lake of
the Hurons, Detroit, Sainte Marie, Bruce Factory, or
south into the mysterious island. He'd find out on his own
whether he was 'suited to this life' or not.

He was so excited that he forgot to eat. At about three
o'clock he noticed a grassy terrace and a sort of path. He
recollected from the sketchy chart a place where a river
made a long loop. He might save twenty miles by doing
a brief portage. He beached the canoe and started to climb
the path.

The only thing that disturbed him on the steep climb
was a sound which might have been the sizzling of an
alarmed rattler. He examined the ground carefully. The
slope was in shadow. He could detect no movement in the
young grass. He went on. It was hard work for stiffened
knee joints, and when he burst through the scrub-pine at
the top he was red, hot and sweaty. What he saw, quite
suddenly, froze him, drained his colour; and the healthy
prickle of sweat became a cold slime on nervous pimply
skin.

Gently he moved behind a boulder. The ridge he was
on came to an abrupt end a mile to the south-west and
the lake or river bent sharply to round it. He'd have met
the four canoes he saw directly below him at that bend.
There'd have been no warning, and no escape.

He was high above them. He could have hit them with a gob of spit, or a small stone. He moved his feet with great care till he had retreated far enough, then he plunged back down the path, leaping from ledge to log and sliding where it was too steep to run. No rattler would have stopped him. He untied the line with trembling fingers and pushed the canoe into the water.

Had he time to make for the opposite shore? He did it with arm-wrenching strokes. The tiny bay he aimed for was even safer than he expected. A spur of rounded granite half enclosed it and tall reeds were growing on the inner side. He thrust the canoe among them and waded to the shore. Keeping low among the sunlit trunks he climbed the marvellously dappled slope, slippery with needles. A fallen log, half in shadow, gave him his look-out. He lay on his belly behind it.

The stillness was so absolute he thought he could almost hear two columns of ants that passed each other over a flat fungus growing on the log. The air was rich with the smell of rotted wood and there was a sharper smell which might be the fungus. Was it edible?

The four canoes rounded the bend; they looked small and peaceful and un-dangerous.

At that moment he realised two things, one as potentially disastrous as the other; he'd made no effort to conceal his visit on the other bank, and, far more disturbing, he'd left Brown Bess in his canoe. The four, moving towards him, were suddenly sinister again.

They took almost an hour to cover the distance. When he thought they must by now be far away he heard a couple of shouting voices. They were close enough to enable him to recognise a few phrases: a discussion, he thought, of where they could camp for the night. They were Ottawas and, therefore, presumably friendly but—

He was beginning to be ashamed of his panic, but he argued that it would be foolish to reveal himself now.

They would be curious as to why he had concealed himself. Such weakness could give them ideas. Better wait. The voices had ceased. He heard no sound of paddling. He was about to raise his head when the slight wash from the canoes ran lightly along the shore. Why hadn't he waited for that, knowing it must come? The sound meant that they had passed him, that they hadn't seen his canoe, and that they were not going to choose as their camping-site the grassy platform on the other shore. The marks of his landing would remain unseen.

He raised his head. They were out of sight. He waited for five minutes and crept towards his canoe. He peered through the rushes. They were setting up their teepee on the other bank, half a mile away. A couple of dogs ran the bounds and he could hear the high, thin yelping. The dogs might cause trouble. They couldn't see very well at night but they could hear. He'd move when it was dark. He couldn't crouch in wet rushes or lie prone behind a rotting log indefinitely.

It was dark by nine o'clock but streaks of reflected brightness near the horizon proved the moon was rising behind a bank of clouds. The cloud-bank reached the zenith and where it ended the stars were dimmed by drifting haze. He had to wade into the water too slowly for comfort. It grew colder six inches below the surface and the chill increased as it crept up his legs to shrivel his privates. His belly writhed away from it. He reached the stern of the canoe and pulled slowly – slowly.

There was a hissing against the rushes but no sudden noises and the hiss could have been produced by the faint breeze. When he was beyond the rushes and out of the tiny bay his progress was soundless. He smelled wood-smoke from the Indians' fire. He couldn't see it – he was too low in the water – but he could catch a glimmer of light cast on the brown teepee and on the leaning skein of smoke. So what wind there was came from them to him. He moved the canoe towards the shoreline, found a reef of granite he could use and, with infinite care – though there was nothing he could do about the sound of water running from his clothes – he put a foot and a hand in the bottom of the canoe and gently transferred his weight. He was in, though crouching, and it took time to change his position, but he'd chosen the place well and was able to give a tiny push to the canoe which, with the breeze, moved it to deeper water. He let the breeze do the work for some time before he ventured to use the paddle. The water was black but the pine-clad hills were blacker, so he was able to keep in the middle. He touched the paddle to the water as delicately as a brush to canvas and after several hours of absolute caution he reached the ox-bow bend. As he rounded it the moon rose above the bank of clouds and he thought himself a woodsman, and lucky. Pride in the success of the operation diminished his shame at feeling the need for it.

A couple of days passed. He saw no more Indians and he travelled slowly south. The weather began to change and when a steady downpour set in he found a bulge of granite with a hollow under it, filled with dry sand. Two saplings helped him to rig a canvas wind-break to stop the driving rain. Here he took time off from travelling to perfect his map. He was not a surveyor but he'd had the sense to mark down the bearing of each prominent feature he saw and to estimate and note the distance. Then, when he reached or passed the particular tree or cliff or hill, he'd correct his estimate.

When he finished transcribing his notes it was evening. The rain had stopped but it was chilly, and large drops fell from the trees. He tried to light a fire but all the wood he found was wet so he gave up and huddled between his blankets. Maybe he shouldn't light a fire anyway.

36

In the quiet evening he felt a sudden access of deep shame. Why had he been so desperate to avoid the Indians in those four canoes? There had been women and children in that party. Here he was, making maps, doing Colethorpe's job, setting himself up as an explorer, and he couldn't bring himself to meet and talk with a peaceful band of people whose language he knew. It was worse than his behaviour at the dreadful ambush. There he'd had the excuse of surprise. He made himself into a ball.

Those Indians could have told him about this country. Maybe they knew it well. Maybe they lived here. Maybe the whole incident was cowardly and he was utterly disgusted. He shook his head violently, partly as a declaration, and flopped over on his other side.

He was barely conscious of the world outside his shelter where pine-boughs bent with the collected rain and large drops splashed on sodden needles. The smell of cedar enveloped him. The sound of occasional winds, tentative and changeable, seemed human at times, like a voice he had once heard and nearly recognised. He was suddenly asleep. His dream was familiar and half cultivated. It concerned things warm, comfortable and female, though the individual images of breast and waist and inevitably escaping thighs were not as powerful as the subtler, undefined sensations they were part of. Suddenly his back arched and he straightened out, straining and pressing – pressing – His breathing grew harsh. He gasped and the sound woke him. Taut-voiced Presbyterian warnings of warts, pimples, impotence and madness had fought a losing battle with congested glands. He was hot. He panted. He was desperate for a companion; nevertheless when sleep resumed it was deep and long. He woke late and decided the mist was heavy enough to hide a column of smoke, so he lit a fire and made bannocks. He was proud of them till he tasted the first one and found he'd left out the salt. He could split them and sprinkle a little salt on the white interior, but it wasn't right. He'd remember next time. It was a pity he'd made so many, though they were less painful to chew than salt pork.

It continued misty on the fourth day but he decided he was moving too far west so he followed a small river that came in from the south-east. He could find no such river on any French map. He noticed that there was a fringe of young grass underwater on both banks. Maybe the river was usable only because it was in flood.

Through occasional gaps in the mist he glimpsed a massive rise of land to the south and west. It would take him a day or so to reach it, but from its summit he might survey the country to the south and choose a practicable route.

He brought his chart up to date. He saw no Indians. He kept recollecting with shame his panic at the sight of the four canoes, but the mood of his recollection changed subtly from shame at cowardice to shame at a foolish decision. The change may have come about partly because Mr Colethorpe was fading into a memory, and partly because he was now able to argue himself into the realisation that the stories that caused his anxiety were, in all probability, just stories.

So, about noon the next day, the meeting with the three old men produced a startled pause, but nothing that could be called terror. He was, in fact, rather proud of his reaction. The meeting occurred at an easy portage. He had beached the canoe where the river shelved to a riffle and had climbed to a point high enough to enable him to see a reach of placid water that lay above the wide rapid. He piled his baggage well up from the flooded grass. The water was clear so the spate was probably dwindling, but you never knew. With the line in his hand he threaded his way up the middle of the run. The water didn't numb his knees as more northerly streams had done. He saw more hardwoods breaking into leaf on a southern slope. The canoe bucked and bobbed but the flow was deep enough to float the lightened vessel, yet not swift enough to tear the line from his hands. He was glad to see that the expanse of still water stretched to the south. It was almost big enough to be a lake and he must mark it down. He heaved the bow of the canoe to the grassy verge and went back along the shore thinking he should have brought Brown Bess. He was stupid and he should remember, not for fear of Indians, but he might see game.

On his way back from his second trip he had great luck. Beginner's luck? He saw two prick-eared rabbits on their haunches, one slightly behind the other. Softly he lifted the guard. His priming was neat. He cocked the hammer, raised the musket and shot both rabbits with the one charge. His aim must have been perfect. He had a distinct impression that the rabbits heard the snap of the flint, glanced towards him as the priming hissed and were already on the move when the charge fired and the bird-shot peppered them. He skinned them at once, turning the skins inside out. It was silly to take such care with rabbits but he might find the skins useful, and he'd keep in practice.

So his last load consisted of the rabbits and his forty-pound sack of food. He stumbled on the three old men without warning. They were sitting in a row on the ground across his path. His canoe was five yards behind them. They must have been watching his approach, maybe for a hundred yards. Their eyes were fixed on him. He stopped dead a few feet away, too close for comfort. They must have heard the shot. The silence grew. Calvin found no spit to swallow.

He noted several details quickly. They wore the painted blankets favoured by some northern Algonquin. They would probably understand the language he knew best. They were not armed and very poor, having no moccasins, leggings or jackets – only the blankets. They didn't wear many decorations. The middle one had a headband decorated with black and yellow quill-work and around his neck he had two leather thongs, each supporting a small, carved, greenish stone figurine – some elongated animal. The two carvings were almost identical, intricately cut and highly polished. Calvin had seen totems often enough, but why two? And so similar?

He thought the silence had gone on too long. His shock was easing. They were poor, no danger to him. He must behave with ease and not be frightened as he'd been frightened of the other Indians. After all, he had his rifle and they were not to know he had not reloaded it since the shot.

He must say something. He couldn't stand there staring. The three old men were very still but they smiled slightly so he could see they had nearly all their teeth. Their faces were seamed with deep-cut lines and the flesh around their eyes was folded heavily. They were thin. They looked hungry, and their gnarled legs were bare, stretched out before them.

'Ah,' said Calvin. Three heads lifted slightly and six eyes widened politely. Of course they couldn't know his heart was thumping. And next time he spoke his voice would be steady.

They weren't in the least uncertain. They were utterly relaxed. They seemed calm, more at ease and sure of themselves than any Indians he'd met in the north – in spite of their obvious poverty. Why? When they were so old and thin? (Though their legs were stringy as twisted rope.) The most peculiar thing about them was how clean they were. They didn't smell at all.

Calvin began to sniff his own rank smell, or maybe it was the two rabbits, and he found the reek offensive.

'That's my canoe,' he said firmly, his unloaded musket prominently held. His voice had not trembled.

'He can speak,' said Two Totems pleasantly, and the others smiled. Grey Blanket turned,

'How old?'

'Hard to tell,' said Yellow Blanket.

'Fifteen?' suggested Two Totems.

'I'm twenty-one,' lied Calvin.

'Life is a fishing-line,' said Two Totems in his deep voice. His intonation, not the words, indicated two things: that what he had uttered was profound, and that a question as to its meaning was required. He had the quality that pulled questions out of people.

'A fishing-line?' enquired Calvin, much against his will.

There was a faint smile and a grateful nod before the rich voice continued.

'A fishing-line. When you're ten it stretches ahead of you and it's very long and straight, with a happy light at the far end. When you're twenty-one you're in the middle and it's a tangle. When you're a hundred it trails behind you but it's long and straight again with a happy light at the far beginning.'

Rather impatiently, Calvin thought, the one on the right observed, 'He has a skimpy beard for a white man.'

'Maybe he doesn't need a full one,' said the one on the left.

There was a satisfied chuckle, then a silence. Then Grey Blanket hitched his privates from between his legs where they'd been squashed and Two Totems pulled a small steel knife from the hem of his blanket and began digging at a callus on his left foot. When Calvin had mentioned his canoe the remark implied that they weren't supposed to touch his canoe and that they were sitting in his way. Neither implication had been noticed.

The sight of the knife crashed through his uncertainties and he realised how badly he'd prepared himself. He should have had some tobacco for the poor man's knife to cut.

'I'm going south,' said Calvin in an effort to appear easy. 'For the Hudson's Bay Company.'

'I told you. His musket is English,' said Grey Blanket.

'Far south?' asked Two Totems.

'Quite far.'

'There are no white men between here and the big lakes.'

'No.'

'And now – not many of The People either. Have you met many?'

'No. The country seems empty though I'm told that once—'

'Would you like to be the first man?'

That question was peculiar. Did it have some other meaning? Calvin took the obvious meaning and answered it.

'Well, I'm sure there've been many other white men here before, but—'

Two Totems turned to the others, left and right.

'He doesn't need a full beard,' he said.

Again the chuckle.

'What's funny?' asked Calvin.

'It's an impolite saying.'

'What is?' he insisted.

'About the beard.'

'Well – tell me.'

After a slight hesitation Two Totems went on, 'The beard hides the colour of the face. We say, by way of a joke, and to explain the difference in colour, that a white man is just a frightened Indian.'

'Oh,' said Calvin.

Very positively the old man declared, 'He's brave to go scouting by himself.'

Then, after a pause, 'Especially in this country.'

42

'And now. And such a distance,' interposed Yellow Blanket.

'And towards Detroit,' said Grey Blanket.

'I hope he hangs on to his balls,' said Yellow Blanket grimly.

'Oh, no doubt of that!' said Two Totems, laughing in his chest, 'He's one of us. Two rabbits!'

And the three of them began to laugh.

'What do you mean?' asked Calvin.

'Two rabbits.'

'With one charge,' explained Two Totems. 'Your luck is very good.'

'They were sitting up in a row,' said Calvin.

'Like us,' said Grey Blanket and they laughed harder.

'Oh, I'm not going to shoot you,' said Calvin, feeling suddenly rather grand as his nervousness left him and he circled round the three old men to reach the pile of duffle near his canoe.

Everything in the pile had been moved – blankets, tarpaulin, and the mahogany box. You couldn't trust them an inch. They meant no harm. They were children, but you couldn't trust them. Satan's children. Nevertheless he must not get angry, and it would be foolish to reload his musket. All that would accomplish would be to make clear the fact that now it wasn't loaded. Also he might learn something. These were peculiar Indians, but they might know the country. There'd been a real flicker of interest in the eyes of Two Totems when he had mentioned The Company. He wouldn't even comment on the interference with his supplies. He saw that the mahogany box was still locked and undamaged. He turned slowly.

The three had swivelled round on their shrunken shanks and were examining him just as seriously and amiably as before. There was, however, one difference and he'd no idea why he noted it – Two Totems now wore only one totem. Calvin had his eyes so fixed on the thick, corded neck that he could not be mistaken.

'Did you make that box?' the old man enquired in his remarkably memorable voice.

'No,' said Calvin. 'And there's no tobacco in it.'

Then he felt ashamed. He hadn't eaten. He found himself saying all in a rush, almost as if the three old men were not savages at all, 'I've two rabbits and I'm hungry, and I'm going to cook them and I can't eat them both. Would you like some?'

He was at first offended when the old men made a great effort to keep straight faces but couldn't. They grinned. The grins became smiles and all offence vanished and Calvin smiled too, though at what he couldn't tell.

The rabbits seemed young enough to joint and cook on pointed sticks. Calvin gave each of his guests one of the bannocks he had made. Grey Blanket and Yellow Blanket examined the bannocks with interest but nibbled cautiously. Two Totems bit his at once and said accusingly:

'No salt.'

'I forgot it,' said Calvin.

'This isn't maize,' said Grey Blanket.

'No. Wheat.'

Grey Blanket peered closely at the bannock Two Totems had bitten into. 'Very white indeed,' he said.

'White food for a white man,' said Calvin, and smiled at his joke.

The three of them exchanged glances. They didn't smile. Two Totems was suddenly very serious.

'There are some Indians you should avoid,' he said.

'This boy comes from the north,' protested Grey Blanket. 'And his hair is black!'

'Would those things matter?' asked Two Totems.

44

'No, probably not,' Grey Blanket admitted sadly.

'If there's something I should know I wish you'd tell me.'

The old men were uncomfortable. After a pause Two Totems stopped eating long enough to make what sounded like a brief speech he'd made before. Calvin realised later that he should have listened more carefully. Maybe his attention wandered because the utterance sounded so like a set speech.

'The People in the south are foolish. There are more white men there but not that many, and the white men don't want to kill The People because then they'd have no one to gather furs for them, and furs are what they come here for. There's plenty of country, but The People in the south are soft and don't want to move about the country. Some of them have become so crazy that they want The People there to kill men of The Company, which would make things inconvenient for us. There is one in particular. He's crazy—'

Calvin saw the strong hand rise to hold the green stone totem.

'He now says he's the nephew of – of a Great Man. This could make him a Chief. He says he is obeying the orders of this Great Man but – all he wants to do is kill white men. And not in his own country but in country belonging to other Peoples. This Great Man became a drunkard and is now dead. He was, in his day, very wise and a member of – of important Societies. Also he could laugh. He was serious but he could laugh. This young man can't laugh. This young man, who now calls himself his nephew—'

'Longhair!' said Calvin, a distinct chill tickling his spine.

The deep voice stopped. Maybe Two Totems was offended at the interruption. They told him no more. The name 'Longhair' seemed to have stopped conversation, though they went on eating till the rabbits were white bones.

Then, 'Think! Think!' thought Calvin and decided to pick their brains. He got the box, unlocked it and took out the maps. He tried to show them to the Indians but they weren't interested in the maps, only in the box. Everything was removed.

Two Totems – and Calvin was close enough to verify the fact that the old man now wore only one totem – fingered the hinges, the lock, the writing flaps and smoothed his muscular hand over the polished wood. He held the box upside down. He closed and opened the hinges and showed their construction to his friends. He was delighted with the metal handle and examined the inside to see how it was attached. He touched one metal button on the strip of mahogany, then the other. Calvin was astonished when the old man discovered that the buttons were slightly different. The second one moved. Two Totems, deeply absorbed, pressed it and heard a click. A sharp convulsion ran through him and his knuckles went white as he gripped the box. He looked at Calvin searchingly from beneath frowning brows.

'Is it a trick or have I broken it?'

Calvin showed him the secret drawer. If the old man had been interested before he was now engrossed. The drawer came out and went in, the button was pushed – out and in.

At one moment Calvin thought he'd finished and reached for the box but the old man took his arm firmly and moved it out of the way. That was the only moment when his concentration was broken. His hand closed round Calvin's arm and he looked at what he gripped so firmly as if he didn't believe what his hand had discovered. He moved his hand and gripped again. He poked Calvin with his finger. Then he put his hand on Calvin's shoulder and turned to his friends. His voice was full of astonishment.

'This white man is starving – and he gave us his food!'

Then he went back to the box and the fascinating secret drawer.

When he had satisfied himself about the box he consented to examine the maps. He knew at once that they were pictures of the country. He indicated that the height of land Calvin had seen was half a day's journey farther than the pen-marks suggested. Calvin corrected the sketchy chart.

While he did it the three Indians discussed him almost as if he weren't there, but their voices were relaxed and kindly. The meal seemed to have made them somnolent.

'He has a fever,' said Grey Blanket.

'Possibly we could tell him things it would be better not to do in this strange country.' This was said by Yellow Blanket but the answer was firm and came from Two Totems.

'He's quite polite. He doesn't seem ignorant. How many young men know enough not to ask questions?'

'Not many.'

'He hasn't even asked our names.'

'He's sensible for his age.'

'Or is it the fever? The spirits tell things to people with fever.'

'He hasn't that much fever.'

'The spirits, because they've been neglected here, are very anxious, very nervous.'

'Not as nervous as he is.'

What a strange world, Calvin thought, a little dizzy while he marked his map, with a cool breeze, a warm sun, the sound of running water and three wise men from the north who felt themselves familiar with spirits.

'His nervousness is spring sickness.'

When Calvin put away his maps and began to gather up his duffle he found the old men curiously melancholy, and they spoke as if finishing a conversation begun before he'd met them.

'I don't think the spirits here are nervous. They may be lonely,' said Two Totems, 'but that's because they've been here so long in an empty country with no new friends to meet.'

He turned to Calvin and explained patiently, 'This was prosperous country once, with a prosperous people who were all killed by The Adders from the south. These people believed this was where the world began. This was the first land, the island, where the first man was made out of clay, and his wife, and then they had children in the way now familiar to us. All that was very long ago but it is a pity when old speculations about the causes of things are forgotten.'

Then, a moment later, he observed almost as if it were an unavoidable threat – 'the weather is too warm for so early in the season.'

There was a portentousness in his tone that caused a short silence. Calvin tried to think of a way to break it. He was standing. They were sitting. Then he thought of the disappearing totem. He was curious. He'd never find out if he didn't ask.

'That's a good carving,' he said with a gesture.

'Very smooth. Feel it,' said Two Totems, so Calvin stooped and took it in his hand. It was an otter, carved as if swimming, the long body curving slightly to the left.

'When I first saw you—'

'We've said it is unusual to find a young white man who is polite,' said Two Totems slowly, coldly and with utter finality, taking the totem from him.

When he had his canoe floating and loaded the three old men got to their feet. He said goodbye in English. Grey Blanket nodded, Yellow Blanket nodded and Two

Totems smiled. When he was ten feet from the shore and looked back they half saluted him, not impressively, like Indian-imitators, but tentatively, like children ('They're like children, you see'), but not children in that way. Friendly, rather; and contented: self-contained and interesting. This was a discovery.

'Any man who's any good thinks he's a first man,' said Two Totems, quite loudly.

What did he mean? Was the remark intended as an encouragement? Calvin made his turn into the lake and looked back again, ready to wave. They were walking slowly away, their backs to him, discussing and laughing, the voices low but distinguishable over the water. He corrected his course and when, with a faint hope that they might once more be paying him attention, he looked back a third time, they had disappeared. He was startled, it had been only a few seconds. There was no swaying branch or shifting bush to mark their path. The absurd notion crossed his mind that he had been dealing with spirits.

When he was half a mile down the lake he realised the whole world had changed. He was at some kind of a divide. It wasn't just the stillness or the disappearance of the old men, there were visible changes – fewer pines, more maples; more earth, less rock; paler colours in the water; and a million little invisible birds twittering or fluting rather quietly and far away.

But these little changes, even when added together, were insufficient to explain how peculiar the country was, and how disturbingly new it felt in the bland light. Nothing important had changed, yet everything had changed. He was conscious of an increased awareness that brought with it an increased tension and his thoughts were hardly under his control any more. Fever?

The old men had spoken of this being the first created land. Or was it rather a land that hadn't been created yet

– a land that, like the old men and the whole noon-tide meeting, hadn't yet happened and didn't yet exist?

He paddled steadily enough, but underneath his curious anxiety he was conscious of an inexplicable excitement.

He was still congratulating himself on his behaviour with the three old men. He hadn't panicked as he had with the four canoes. A day and a half later he found the rise of land, and the way to the top was a long slope of sparse, light grass pranked with a few fat single birches, many clusters of birch saplings, dark shrubberies of sumac and elder, the great panicles forming, and low prickly tangles of blackberries already in bloom. The soil was loose and full of little round stones. Where the summit curved off a few large stones, so smooth they were almost polished, thrust up through the grassy gravel. Thick lichens grew on the side from which he approached. The climb had taken all morning. He was out of breath but a little exalted. He wished he felt less weak.

The air was crisp and clear, the sky deep blue, the single clouds were very near him and unbelievably white. They formed a splotchy pattern on a lacy parasol that swivelled round a pivot beyond the south horizon. Only above his head could the movement be detected. There the great bales of sunlight dozed slowly eastward. He patted his pocket; he had his telescope. Before him was a single great stone, the shape inescapably suggestive of a woman's breasts.

He flung himself down in the smooth cleavage and gazed at the widest prospect he had ever seen. It was like watching waves at sea. You thought you'd come to the horizon, then shadows would shift a little and a new rank of hills would be revealed, and another, and another. At the edge of the sky, where, because of the angle of view, the layers of white cloud were closely crowded, there was a curious elongated gleam – a narrow shining band that curved round a third of the horizon. It looked as if the clouds at that enormous distance were lit from beneath, by reflection. They might be. It could be sunlight glancing upward from the brilliant surface of the southern lakes.

A river curved away from him to the east, then hid itself behind a range of hills. When it reappeared farther south it was diminished with distance, but seemed magnificently wide, meandering into a grand valley, rich with a hundred shades of green. Farther to his right there was a silver line that indicated another river, and from the shapes of the long westward-sloping hills he thought it flowed in that direction. Three clusters of lakes glittered like spilled diamonds on crumpled velvet.

By one of them he saw a thin column of blue smoke sloping slightly eastward. It didn't rise very high. How far away? Fifteen miles? Twenty? Even thirty? Very hard to tell in such crystal clarity. And the glint he saw from the blue mirror-surface of the wide river? It was much farther away. Only an occasional flick of light. A new white bark canoe? Then closer, only about six or seven miles away, he saw a very long line of steely blue detach itself from the forested crest of a low hill, rise slowly, wheel with a million minute scintillations, each far tinier than the distant glint of the canoe.

He took out his difficult telescope and tried to focus. Finally he found them; a flock of pigeons, the sun gleaming momentarily on metallic feathers as they swerved. The field was much too restricted to hold more than half. The flock was thick, two miles long and two miles wide – so wide it concealed a lake, so dense it cast on the hills a moving shadow, blacker than the shadows of the clouds. The immense flock settled slowly and was swallowed by the tree-tops.

They might have been stimulated to flight by their own whim, not a human disturbance. But the smoke; that was human. And when he swung the glass to the river he thought he found the one canoe; a short white line with a dark bump sitting on each end. Indians fishing? He focused on other points. There was no sign of lodge or clearing. One wisp of smoke and one glint of birch bark in ten thousand miles? An exaggeration? Well – a hundred times a hundred—

Then he looked up. He couldn't feel the breeze though a few birch leaves twitched nervously, but from somewhere—

He couldn't believe it – he was back in Berwick, walking past the iron gate of the barracks and he heard the faint sound of a fife! Was it a phrase of the 'Lass of Richmond Hill'? He was in the middle of a delusion. It didn't recur.

He resumed his survey and found one triangle of a tan colour which could have been a teepee, but it could as easily have been a rock. Near it was a patch of something different – a sort of tremble in the air – it could have been a shimmer of specks of light invisibly small, like the pigeons, but it stayed in one place. No. He'd moved the glass and couldn't find it again. A fish-rack?

So in that whole vast panorama there was evidence of the existence of three people. He didn't count the illusion of the fife-notes. And, of course, he was there – four.

There was a loud cawing, two crows landed on a branch very close and at eye-level, the female crouching, wings half spread. Then she slid down the air mewing like a cat and crouched in the wide clear space, fluttering. The male followed, trampled her, croaked and switched his tail. She switched hers the other way. They were finished. He cawed and hopped off limberly and stood watching her, his beak open, as she juggled and preened her feathers into place.

Flies were at it too and zoomed in couples past his nose. As long as the crows were performing Calvin was fascinated. When it was clear that they were finished for the moment a surge of Presbyterian disdain caused him to close the telescope with a snap and sit himself straighter on the rock. The two crows, startled beyond belief, clacked noisily into the air. He left that place. Why should the sight of two crows affect him so?

Two gawky crows!

He hurried down the hill again and was panting when he reached his camp. He smelled his sweat, and the sour smell of underclothes removed only a few times in the whole winter. He gathered some wood ash and mixed it with sand in his bucket. He took the dirty clothes from his duffle-bag. He undressed and squashed his flannel undergarments, socks, shirt and britches into the bucket where he stirred them with a stick. His weathered hands were brown, the rest of him a pale and mottled grey. Bruises seemed to last a long time. He wished his jaws weren't so sore.

He took the bucket to the shore of the river where the water sparkled over clean gravel. He spread the garments on the bottom and weighted them with stones. The sun glared at his back, unbelievably hot. He decided to swim to a sandbank opposite. His dog-paddle didn't move him very quickly. The river wasn't deep; it would have been more sensible to walk. He was carried farther downstream, but there was another bank of sand where he grounded and sat in the sun, scrubbing himself. The sand was fine and left his skin tingling when he rubbed it, taut and pink. He was fascinated at the amount of skin that rubbed off his feet. He rubbed till his feet and his fingers were wrinkled and very white.

Suddenly he smelled something that filled his mouth with saliva – mint. He followed his nose farther along the river till he found a swampy stream coming in from the east. The whole heavy crop of sun-splashed leaves moved constantly, sinuously, sensuously as the unseen current swirled the plants. For some reason he was uncontrolled. He pulled up handfuls, the black roots trailing clear water. He crammed his mouth with the tender tops and chewed till his tongue was hot. He flogged himself with the long square stems till the mint smell filled the little glade and he was camouflaged with stains of black and vivid green.

The notion of being naked disturbed him, but only distantly since there were only three other people in ten thousand miles. Indians? Well, these fears jumped out at you from some dim space, but now, he was convinced, they were controllable. For some reason he hoped – he thought – his meeting with the three old men had made a difference. He didn't know why, but he felt freed forever of all irrational fear, and his fear of Indians was irrational.

He headed back to his camp, removed the stones from his fluttering, stream-washed clothes and wrung the water from them. They were much cleaner, but he was stained with mint and mud. He spread the clothes on a spiky pine-log brought down and stripped of bark by some old flood.

He felt the itch again to swim. He wanted to learn to float properly. There was a deeper pool below the mint-bed. He lay in the water – it had turned curiously cold – and bumped his way down the current till it gentled and flowed down and – it was sudden and unexpected like paddling the canoe properly – he was floating easily, with no fear, looking at an eagle clearly visible against a cloud.

He thought about it. The secret of floating was to bend your head back as far as it would go so only your face stuck out. It stood to reason. Your head was heavy. If your head stuck up its weight would force you down.

A grotesquely gnarled maple branch stretched half way across the pool. There was a circular current and he passed under the branch three times. Two crows watched him as he passed, making sounds he couldn't hear because his ears were under water.

Hundreds of two-inch minnows nibbled at his fingertips. Some larger fish swam up, bumped him and drifted away. He was delighted when a beaver swam past him, very swift and purposeful; it didn't look at him. Maybe it didn't see him.

He couldn't drift for ever. He waded through the shallows, thousands of silver slivers flashing through the water from his splashing feet. He started back along the open, park-like shore. Probably it was flooded every spring and little trees had no chance to root. His clothes would be dry by now.

Wendet. The Island. The first man. The first woman. Adam and Eve. The Garden. He was naked but not ashamed. He thought of childhood and church and being good and utter safety and a curious awed delight. The world was big and wonderful, and it was his. He had a sudden access of holiness. He was washed, and pure. The feeling was intense but short-lived, because he couldn't help but find it absurd. Maybe he wasn't holy, he told himself – what *was* 'holy', he wondered – but he did feel different. He felt light and free as the warm airs dried him and the blood tingled back to the surface of his skin. Maybe he'd fish this evening. Maybe he'd make some bannocks too – and remember the salt. The world was a good place. The miserable winter in the north was washed away and, with it, all uncertainties were gone. Old Colethorpe was gone. Old fears were gone; his foolish fear of Indians was gone; and, when he reached the spiky pinelog, he found that all his new-washed clothes were also gone.

3

A Mark in the Sand

'The People kill their enemies.
White men kill only their friends—'

Longhair

AT FIRST, even in this wilderness, Calvin took the disappearance of his clothes to be a joke; but there was no
one here to play a joke. He stepped closer to the silver log
and touched a couple of jagged spikes which his fingers,
if not his mind, had recognised. There was no mistake, it
was the right log. His thick grey shirt had flapped from
this knot to this bleached bar. His heart lurched and he
turned at a rustle in the grass. The absurd, in the circumstances, notion of modesty occurred to him and was
instantly drowned in the stronger fumes of danger. He
had heard something, not imagined it. He was very still.
Only his eyes moved, glancingly, and wherever they
looked they saw nothing to fear, yet just beyond the circle
they covered, something waited for his attention.

The ordinary life of the forest and the stream was
suddenly loud and smothered the sounds he thought he
heard. Bees thrummed past him. A few ducks flew overhead. Three quick splashes hinted that fish were rising.
Small birds twittered. An orange butterfly clung to a grey
twig and waved its wings. At a distance he heard the
drumming of a woodpecker.

Quite suddenly, out of the tan earth, the brown bark

57

and greening shadows, not ten feet from him, there materialised a half-grown fawn. His eyes had seen it before, yet he had not. Maybe he heard it when it rose to its delicate feet. It moved into clear sunlight and was aglow with tawny light, small head high on its column neck. Each circle, dark and light, of its marking shone like stained glass. The head stretched towards him and the little tongue cleaned the nostrils. It came forward, walking, then trotting a few steps, and Calvin couldn't move. The black nose nudged him above his right knee and the cool tongue licked towards his groin.

As suddenly as it had appeared, the fawn leaped away, but there was nothing mysterious about this as there had been about its appearance. Like lightning it was there, then gone; but, though it was beyond direct sight, Calvin could hear the thudding of its progress for a quarter of a minute. His heart pumped blood three times to each bound and his brain sifted explanations. The fawn had made a mistake. It had approached with confidence. His taste or smell had been so wrong as to galvanise the startled beauty into panic.

Like the noon meeting with the old men the episode had simply not happened. The appearance of the fawn was so strange as to belong to an unreal world. The disappearance of his clothes was, maybe, as unreal. He tried to use the fawn to argue against the terrifying presence of Indian thieves but it didn't work. The clothes were gone and his groin still tingled.

He relaxed a little and paralysis diminished. Among the thousand tiny sounds he strained to hear he heard a faint snort which could be laughter.

Naked you were vulnerable. Clothes made you safer. From some deep store he dredged up anger to douse terror. He strode firmly to his encampment. Everything was as he left it – canoe, supplies, Brown Bess.

Then strangeness assailed him again. He didn't have to

cock his head to listen, he heard it and recognised it – the fife. It wasn't close by but it was clear and cut cleanly through all other sounds. He recognised the tune. Then it stopped.

His hat was here, his jacket – too heavy to wash – and his moccasins. The moccasins were big and loose without socks to fill them. The jacket felt stiff and metallic without shirt or shift. The hat was—

There was a flash of white fabric waving and a burst of unmistakable laughter. He raced towards the place and tripped on the thong of his moccasin. He went forward into swamp on hands and knees and the tail of the jacket, the pockets heavy, surged forward inside out to flap over his head. The position displeased him and the peal of laughter made him angrier. He stumbled to his feet, tried to fasten the jacket, but gave it up to chase after the elusive hyena again when he caught a glimpse of the short tan figure threading swiftly through the birches twenty yards away.

The fact that it was a girl stopped him cold for some seconds and he lost ground. He put on a burst of speed. There was a more open space ahead of him. He was catching up, though she still slipped tantalisingly through the white saplings. He hadn't had a clear glimpse. He'd see her soon.

He reached the edge of the glade and she was gone. In the time it was impossible for her to have reached the two great elm trees on the other side. He heard running feet behind him. He turned. He was close. She was an Indian, young, wearing a supple tanned doe-skin tunic and two braids of black hair fluttered after her as she ran.

He was closing on her and she made an error. She half dropped the bundle of his clothes. When she recovered them he was ten yards closer, pounding fast. She dodged left. He cut the corner. She plunged down a slope and was brought up sharp on a grassy overhang, a bow of the river quite deep before her, and so close she came within a step of plunging in. She screamed.

'Moonluck! Moonluck!'

'Here,' said a voice behind him and he heeled to a stop in the moist grass.

The bundle of clothes soared over his head and he followed it with his eyes. It was caught by another Indian girl, taller, more slender, and far faster on her feet. The first girl had been pudgy.

They were off and Calvin found it far more difficult. This girl – he supposed Moonluck was her name – took longer strides and could turn on a silver penny. She wore a similar tunic but her hair hung in one braid which had been plaited with scarlet thongs or bits of yarn. He lost her and stopped, listening. Not a sound. They were back among the birches and he peered carefully from both sides of the patch of berry-canes he found in his way. He went left. No sign. He went right and stopped again, listening intently.

He opened his mouth wide to breathe more quietly and improve his hearing. The sunlight slanted in at a low angle. It would soon begin to cool off. He wasn't sure he could find his camp again, although the river would lead him to it. His camp—

Why hadn't he brought Brown Bess? This game with the stolen clothes might be a trick to get him far away so more deadly creatures than these girls could steal his gun, his food, his blankets.

If that were the idea why hadn't they stolen them before, when he first went swimming? The noisy birds announced the evening – or was it something else? Three jays rose into the tree-tops to his right grating and screeching. He moved silently in that direction. The jays flew away, still screeching, and he stopped. There were grackles and robins, a thrush at a distance, a busy wren nearby and the undertone of twitters that seemed sourceless. But he knew that the melodious babel – bird-song sometimes sounded curiously like bells – could not hide the rustle or snap of movement.

It was the fife again, loud and quite near. It was a song popular some years before and he remembered the words:

'Four beautiful maids
Were all in love with me.
They said that I could have but one
So I went off to sea.'

But before the lilt of the chorus was well into its happy rhythm, two female voices protested loudly

'You've spoiled it.'

'He'll hear.'

The voices spoke in Algonquin but the melody was Scots, or British at least, or maybe New England.

Calvin drew himself up, set his jaw at a resolute tension, pulled down the corners of his mouth and his jacket, and marched towards the sound. He knew he should have been more cautious. As the distance lessened his feet sounded loud among the grass. The fife began again. He should wait, turn about, find his camp, and return with Brown Bess. That's what he should have done, but he didn't.

He came to another glade. There was a large round stone to his right and the foot of it was set in a small pool. A tiny trickle of clear water glittered down a slope towards the river. Near it was an arrangement of three logs marked with the vivid black and white of a dead camp-fire. The two girls sat beside it, their arms across each other's shoulders. In front of them, between the fire-logs and Calvin, a red-headed young man lay on his belly and elbows. His fingers fiddled with the fife. Calvin stopped. The sun was lower and the tiny camp was vividly lit. They all looked at him. Calvin was about to shout at them furiously when he saw they were all three smiling. Then he noticed a slight movement and, from behind the man, the spotted fawn stood up briskly and looked at him too, with eyes that were luminous as large garnets in the warm light.

'You've lost your drawers,' said the red-headed man in English.

Calvin marched up to where the bundle of his clothes was lying, picked it up, tried to say something – he'd have said almost anything if he could have thought of the words – gave up and marched out of the clearing as formidably as he hoped he had marched into it. It wasn't too difficult to find his camp. He sat down. When he left those three they'd been laughing at him – not loudly, but he'd heard them. He dressed himself properly.

Many weeks later he remembered that evening as silence before storm, or tense waiting, rather, before the start of a race. The race was to be so full of mixed and violent emotions that he was to wonder if he'd ever been really alive before. There were terrors more extreme than the petrified despair of sick and savage beatings in childhood, than the wilderness, than the Indians, than the ambush of a week ago, or than the night-blooming bogles steaming up into his time from the mediaeval pit itself. There were delights that transported him to high, steady over-worlds where he could survey perspectives of rapture he'd never before suspected could exist.

And the evening contained hints of both ultimates. He didn't take the hints. He was, instead, doleful, irritable and filled with his usual ferment of corroding self-contempt. Three more pimples were sore and swollen. He had two blisters on his gum. He felt the threatening sensitivity and numbness of bad sunburn. Listlessly he cut, fried and ate two slices of salt pork. The evening was still light. Rather sadly, remembering his pleasure on the gravel hill, he got out his writing-case and did more work on the pages of his map, entering the features he'd seen from that high point. When he opened the case – which he had not locked – it occurred to him that the papers were in an unexpected order. Hadn't he left them with the more distant, less detailed sheets at the bottom of the pile? Here they were at the top. He must have made a mistake.

He slept restlessly. At midnight, though the night was not cold, he was shivering and his shoulders were aching and painful. He couldn't find a comfortable position. He rolled over and the pain flashed along his back and side. In the morning he undressed enough to see large areas of scarlet. The backs of his legs were angry streaks. He held his hand an inch away from his shoulder and could feel the radiated heat. He felt feverish and not very hungry. Following a dull routine he picked up twigs and branches, enough to light a fire and fry more pork. His teeth ached as well as his shoulders.

As he gathered wood he saw the mark of the canoe. It was close to his own canoe but it was a different groove, the cut of a sharp keel. He hadn't seen that mark last evening. Had he missed it? Had it been there?

What did those three want? He wondered if any of his supplies were missing. He felt nervous at the notion that they had come and watched him while he was asleep. Strange, because he'd slept so little. He recognised his own disgruntlement. With all sorts of fresh food available – and quickly – why did he fry slightly rancid salt pork?

As he finally swallowed the much-chewed, last, fibrous lump he saw the little round girl looking at him from the other bank. She carried her moccasins in her left hand and her right forefinger was hooked in the gill of a two-pound trout. They eyed each other for a while, then he stood up. She waded across the sparkling riffle and put the trout on the log where he'd hung his clothes to dry. It was a brilliant jewel on the silver log, but Calvin paid it no attention.

'I've had my breakfast,' he said.

'Red sent it,' she said. Then she wandered round a bit, glancing interestedly at his things. She was young, maybe an inch over five feet tall, and her expression was child-like and eager. Her round lips were parted. Her bunched cheeks crowded her quick round eyes. No belt constricted her knee-length tunic of tanned soft deerskin, and she had left off the sleeves. A pattern of long points, embroidered in blue beads and outlined in white, rayed out from the round neck. A similar pattern, but more web-like and delicate, less encrusted, bordered the hem. Soft as the deerskin was, it was stiff enough to focus attention on bits of the brisk body beneath that fought against confinement. Calvin's eyes flicked from haunch to crowded breast.

She was bending over the writing-case, touching the polished wood with an enquiring finger. The plump hand glittered with tiny scales from the trout. She didn't look at him.

'Where did you learn to speak?'

'In the north.'

'You speak like the Ottawas.'

He answered with a little of a Chippewa dialect, 'I can speak Chippewa too.'

She giggled. 'It sounds funny.'

'Don't you know any language but your own?'

'English. I know English.'

In English he asked her if the red-headed man had taught her, but she looked blank and he said 'Ha!' with mild contempt.

'I'll cook your trout for you.'

So she became all bustle, rearranged his logs, built up his fire with small twigs, and, while it was flaring to usable coals, cleaned the fish with a small steel knife which he had not noticed. She wore it in a sheath strung on a thong round her neck. She cut a wand of poplar, peeled it and

64

slipped it neatly along the backbone, then she began to turn it just to one side of the little steeple of lavender flame and faint blue smoke.

While she did these chores Calvin sat and listened to her chatter, his appetite slowly building as he smelled the fat fish.

'Moonluck has left her husband. His name is Speechmaker. She's going to her father. His name is Coppertooth. We found Red. He's taking us there. I've no husband yet but I'm going with them. My father may be angry. His name is Firepouch. You look lonesome sitting there. Why are you alone?'

But Calvin wouldn't be drawn.

'Are you rich? You have a fine gun. It looks very fat. Is it heavy?'

'Yes,' he said.

'Does it make a loud noise?'

'Yes.'

The trout was sizzling and turning the colour of her tunic. She made two vertical cuts in a birch trunk and peeled off the square of aromatic bark. She trimmed it neatly and put the trout into the clean tan hollow. His lips were puffy from the sun and he burned them when he tried to bite. He took his knife. The fish was hot, moist, fresh and slightly flavoured with wood-smoke. Unexpectedly he found himself ravenous.

'Do your teeth ache?' she asked suddenly.

He was startled. 'Yes,' he said.

'Red says maybe you have scurvy.'

Why hadn't he thought of it? Was that why he was tired?

'Goodbye,' she said. 'I'm going now. Moonluck will make you some tea.'

He sat with the half-eaten trout in his hands, watching her. She took a short-cut through a deeper part of the river, lifting her tunic to her waist. As the cool water tickled her privates she gasped, jumped and tried to run. Calvin watched as she moved into shallower water and kicked the drops from her sturdy legs. They were so round, such a beautiful colour, and so smooth – and he was off into the shameful and feverish vision. He couldn't take his eyes off the bushes where she had disappeared until a whiff of the trout brought his attention back to another appetite.

Calvin spent the morning on his maps. The trout had improved his disposition and his careful work pleased him. He kept in the shade and moved as little as possible. The sunburn was a fever, an ache lit by flashes of pain, but he knew it would go. After thinking about it for some time he took off his jacket and shirt. He wondered if bacon fat would ease the pain but did nothing about it. The cool air helped and he was finishing his map when he heard a shout.

It was the red-headed man coming along the river bank wearing wide raw-hide breeches and a fringed leather jacket. He carried the longest gun Calvin had ever seen. The red-headed man waved. After a second Calvin waved back. The brief delay was caused by a slight shock at the top-heavy loom of the man's shoulders, his height, and the glare of his hair and beard as he moved from shadow into a beam of sunlight. Even his walk was outsize, demonstrating with no ostentation a power and purpose not subject to laws such as, for instance, gravity. The man had been prone and still when Calvin had seen him before. In motion he was – Calvin knew the thought was silly but it jumped vividly to mind – both bodyless and brawny; there ought to be wings somewhere and a high, free range of air.

The man's quiet voice scattered the fantasy as he came close, looked Calvin over and said in English, 'You need goose-grease or something.'

'I stayed in the sun too long.'

'Yes,' said the man, and sat down.

They talked about guns.

'Brown Bess used to be longer,' said Red with an interested glance at the bulky weapon.

'Look at it if you want to,' said Calvin, so Red picked it up.

'So light!' he said. He spun it round. 'So short!' He examined the lock. 'Grice,' he said, 'London. I wonder how many he's made.' He looked in the barrel. 'This one's nearly new.'

'It was at Quebec.'

'Oh.'

'Then it went round the world and was never unpacked. Then it was sold in London and shipped to Port Churchill and brought to us as trade goods, but it was too good for the Indians so I bought it. I had eight pounds owed to me.'

'Hudson's Bay Company?'

'Yes.'

'Where?'

'Rupert river fort.'

'A long way north from here.'

'Yes.' And Calvin hesitated. Then, pompously because he was lying, he explained at length that he had orders to explore this country between the main brigade routes.

'Then north again?'

'No, Montreal.' He blushed as he said it and felt ridiculous. Why should he care what this man thought? And why should he think anything? It was none of his business. Calvin wondered why he was always answering other people's questions. Why did people always find out all about him and he never found out anything about anyone else?

'That's one of those rifled muskets,' he said, pointing. The man patted the chased and delicate lock and the stock ornamented with ivory, so much more lovingly made than fat Brown Bess.

'Pennsylvania,' he said, 'Philadelphia.'

'It shoots a tiny ball,' said Calvin.

'Big enough.'

'Could it stop a bear – or an Indian?'

'It's killed two dozen bear.'

'Indians?'

'Six years ago.'

'Loaded with ball, mine will stop anything,' he bragged.

'If you hit it,' said the man.

'Mine will kill a man at fifty yards,' said Calvin.

'If you hit him.'

'You ought to be able to at fifty yards!'

'But where? You'll knock him down if you hit him in the arm but you won't kill him.' And the man shook his head slowly.

'They tell the soldiers to fire at that range.'

'I know. I've watched them. I watched Braddock's army. Brown Bess – at least the old long one, I've never tried the short one – will hit a target six feet tall and six feet wide at fifty yards. That's about four men standing still in a row. Can't help hitting one of them!'

'Can you do better?'

'I've killed a rabbit with a bullet at a hundred yards.'

'Anything left of it?'

'Shot him through the head. Didn't hurt the meat.'

Calvin watched the man closely. He couldn't believe him. Colonists were full of tall tales. They took pleasure in fooling people from the old country, yet the man seemed serious – and there seemed to be no malice – and the Indian girl had—

'May I – may I heft the – rifle?'

The man handed it over. It was twice as heavy as Brown Bess. The barrel was half an inch thick all round the hole: a strong, octagonal bar with a tiny bore, not a thin-walled pipe like Brown Bess. It was carefully and beautifully made but surely difficult to use. The butt seemed too slender and delicate. Calvin rose and put it gingerly to one sore shoulder. The man watched him. He could barely hold it in position long enough to aim at an elder-blossom across the river: his arms began to tremble.

'It's best to use a stick or to lie down,' said the man. 'We'll try it sometime, and yours.'

For a second Calvin wasn't listening. Fear sprang out at the most unexpected moments. When he'd pointed the rifle at the elder-blossom it had moved! And a second later another branch three feet away had waved briefly and become still again.

'There's something there,' said Calvin, whispering.

'The does are moving about more,' said the man, so casually that Calvin was ashamed of his nervousness and put the rifle down assertively. 'It must be heavy to carry.'

'It evens out. Martha's twice as heavy as Brown Bess, but I don't have to carry half the lead you do. And with half the lead you carry I can mould four times as many bullets. And they go farther, and faster, and with less powder.'

'If an Indian was coming at me I'd rather have Brown Bess.'

'What if a dozen came at you? I could start scaring them off at half a mile or better.'

'You couldn't kill one that far off.'

'It's been done.'

Calvin hesitated, then he asked the question, blurting out, 'What happened six years ago?'

The singularly pleasant and open expression on the red-headed man's face gloomed over. He shook his head slightly. A ripple ran around the fringe of his jacket as he shrugged his heavy shoulders and changed the subject.

'Kittypet said you were drawing maps. I'd like to see them.'

So Calvin reached for the writing-case, and the man went on.

'I like maps – might know something useful. I've been in this country a year. Mostly south.'

Calvin handed him the carefully marked sheets and was pleased that they received concentrated attention. He was surprised as well as pleased at the generous admiration the man expressed when he handed them back. And why should he feel so warm and confident when he was addressed as Mr Heggie?

They talked a bit more but never, Calvin noticed, about the red-headed man, or his interests, or his allegiance, or his life. When he rose to go Calvin felt a slight desperation.

'What are you doing here?'

The man paused. Maybe the question was too bald.

'You said you'd been here all winter.'

'Farther south,' and again the man turned.

'Which of these squaws is your wife?'

Calvin asked the question quickly and as quickly the man laughed.

'Do you want one of them?'

'No,' said Calvin, and, as if some explanation were required, 'I'm travelling too. And fast. I have no time.' Then a terrible thought occurred to him. Was he talking to an enemy of the Company? He must find out. He bubbled on. 'Are you licensed in Montreal?' he asked.

'Licensed to do what?'

'Trade.'

'No.'

Calvin, though somewhat relieved, was even more desperately curious. 'Well, what *do* you do?'

'I've a few skins if you want to buy them.'

'You're a trapper?'

70

'More of a farmer.'

'Here.'

'Farther south.'

'There aren't any farms till Detroit or Niagara.' Calvin was positive.

'Only mine, I reckon.'

'But what about the Indians?'

'What about them?'

'Don't they – don't they—'

'They don't bother me. There aren't very many in this country now. And this month they've gone. Don't know why. Goodbye, Mr Heggie.'

Then the man went. Calvin didn't even know his name.

'Mr Heggie!' How did he—? Oh, that was easy: the two finished sheets of his map were elaborately signed and decorated – though really flowing scrolls were difficult to do unless you had a steady table.

Then another curious thing – the mark in the sand; the keel-mark of the canoe last night. Yet today the man had walked. So had Kittypet with her trout.

Was there one more to come?

A stream of visitors where he thought to see no one. Well, they were harmless, even friendly. But he didn't like mysteries. He glanced quickly along the river-bank where the man had disappeared. No one. Nothing. Yet a canoe had moved up that still reach of the river just about twelve hours ago.

He felt constricted and feverish. He ached in many places but it would be better to move. He did a circle round his little camp and found himself thinking again of Kittypet and her round legs. He climbed to a terrace parallel to the river and found older, nobler trees. On the ground was an enormous silver log, all bark long stripped away. Two round curved roots had been pulled from the ground and they rose into the air above his head.

What was wrong with him? The roots and the thick

trunk of the tree were cleaned and scoured by decades of rain, wind and sun. The trunk was hollow and the roots were legs – thighs. The space between was shaped to cradle him. He turned away. It was the fever, the inactivity, the round legs of Kittypet.

One more to go. Moonluck.

He'd no sooner said her curious name in his mind than the world grew darker. He peered up between the leaves. Then he heard it. Was it the same flock he'd seen from the gravel hill? They were still quite high and the sound didn't deafen him as it would if they were close, but they cast a dark shadow as they wheeled, and he could hear the curious, distant, heavy but thin thunder of the million wings. Round they went in many tiers – so many levels or layers of flight, and each layer so crowded with birds, wing-tip to wing-tip – you could catch few flecks of blue between the birds. Then, as one, with that strange hissing thunder, they wheeled the other way and headed east, the whole flock taking many minutes to pass over him. When the sun came back Moonluck was at his camp watching and listening too. He'd been conscious of her presence for some time, but the wonder of the monstrous flying shadow kept them still. When it was gone a tension eased, Calvin moved towards Moonluck, and the small green leaves danced in and out of sunlight.

Moonluck was as tall as Calvin, and he noticed, now he had time to look, that her features, unlike his own, were very definite. The single heavy braid pulled the black hair away from a high forehead. The brows were strongly marked and they shadowed richly luminous eyes. Her nose was aquiline, her jaw strong, her teeth white, her lips – but she was talking to him and he switched attention from the lips to what they said.

'Red told me to bring it in his cup, and when you've drunk it I have bears' grease for the burn.'

It was a sort of tea, still warm and aromatic in the

72

pewter mug, greeny-brown in colour, and it tasted faintly of wintergreen. He thought it tasted too of slippery elm – a curious dry, bland flavour. She explained in Algonquin that the tea was for the scurvy and it worked a cure in twenty-four hours. His teeth would be firm in a week. He must make the tea himself. She'd tell him how.

Her voice was low, but definite like her face. She used many Algonquin expressions he didn't recognise, but he got the sense. She was persuasive and easy. It was several minutes after he took his clothes off before he felt surprise at finding himself naked on the grass while she smoothed the soft grease on the reddened patches of his skin. She found the whiteness here and there 'just like Red'. She found his stringy stomach pathetic and too hollow. She also found his chest too thin and bony. When she was finished she closed the leather flap on the bark container, wiped her strong hands on the grass, and leaned back on her heels.

For the first time Calvin was embarrassed, for her neat privates were exposed. He hauled his gaze to her eyes again.

'All your pimples will go too,' she said, 'and you won't get angry any more.'

It was incredible. It was all so easy. She'd been standing in the shadow with him, listening. Then the shadow went, and he did what she said, and she told him what would happen and he believed her – already the pain of the sunburn was less.

And, while there was something about her that reminded him irresistibly of Red – something still, grave, fated almost – there was also something dangerous, and dangerously alive.

This was not, of course, because she was Indian, he told himself.

Who were these three? Why were they here?

They came for him in their canoe and gave him supper. It was a pinkish mess he distrusted, picked at till the taste grew on him, then he ate ravenously; a mush of ground maize but savoury, not sweet, and it was filled with the tails of what he imagined to be tiny lobsters. A few of the bigger ones, say four inches long, were boiled in their shells, but most chunks were just the pinkish tails. He ate until his belly was distended and he joined the chorus of burping. Red could articulate words on a long burp. They drank a tea made with wintergreen and something else, sweetened with a little maple sugar.

Next day the sunburn had gone, and by evening he forgot his sore teeth till he put his tongue against his palate and felt only a roughness. They were all very interested in his blisters. He was sad when he learned that they were on their way north while he was going south. But no one was in a hurry. The weather was grey, not too hot and a steady breeze blew in from the southwest. The breeze kept the few mosquitoes moving.

He developed the foolish feeling that he was being born, that his life was beginning and that everything that preceded these few days was a bad dream. He grew stronger and was much troubled with lust.

When his sunburn was cured enough to peel, Moonluck sat on the silver elm-log and did his back. He wasn't able to control himself any more, apparently. It was the tickling of the skin or the touch of her fingers. He grew the most painfully throbbing erection he'd ever had and felt he must sit making conversation till it relaxed. The skin of his back reached out to her like a limb to be caressed, a spirit to find home. In those days messages from senses that had been rigidly censored were suddenly heard and understood.

He recognised that, improbable as it might seem, he was beginning to feel a sort of personal attachment. They weren't Indians any more they were – people. Astonish-

74

ing! Red, of course, was not an Indian, and he was easier to communicate with because he spoke English. But, amazingly, he lumped Red with the two girls and had begun to think of them as of a happy family.

This family picture, he thought, probably sprang from Kittypet's long account of Red's childhood, and how cheerful and warm it had been, and how much Red liked his seven brothers and sisters. Red was the eldest. They all loved each other very much and sometimes Red told stories about them which showed how carefully they looked after each other. Red came from Pennsylvania and was probably a Quaker, Calvin decided. Quakers, of course, were not Presbyterians, but at least they weren't Papists. Quaker. The Algonquin word Kittypet used was the word for 'ally', or a friend who would go with you in war. Calvin didn't know much about the curious sect but he knew they declared strong opposition to military service. How, then, did Red know so much about guns?

Calvin learned more from Kittypet than from the others because she chattered more. Details of her curious life came out in bursts which were hard to fit together because she assumed that the ways of her people were the ways of everyone and, since he could speak the language. . . .

He decided she was jealous of Red's childhood. She had only one brother.

'He's the only one I miss,' she said. 'He's funny. He asks riddles like the Miamis. He marches into an important political meeting and asks my father, "How many eyes has a four-eyed bear?" "Four," says my father. "None," says my brother. "There aren't any four-eyed bears."

'Every stranger gets cheated once and there are a lot of strangers because my father is always talking politics. My brother will bargain for tobacco and agree to pay as many strings as he has fingers. The stranger measures out ten strings' worth. My brother wins because he has only three fingers on his left hand.'

All three of these people, Calvin decided, were misfits. Late in the previous summer, Kittypet had found Moonluck walking, all by herself, along the reedy shore of the shallow lake not far from Detroit. (That's where her people lived, not far from Detroit.) It was so peculiar to see a girl – and a foreign girl – alone, that Kittypet had followed her, talked to her and found they had many things in common. That evening the interesting stranger had agreed to stay with Kittypet for a while. The villagers were curious about the scandal of an unconnected woman but Kittypet's immediate family were not upset since food was plentiful. They had become great friends.

Then the story became confusing. Kittypet explained that she too was running away from her husband and that her father was probably angry. He was probably angry at both of them because if it hadn't been for Moonluck she wouldn't be running away. He would have to pay back the musket, the blanket and the jar of French brandy he'd been paid for her. Except that he hadn't yet been paid so he wouldn't have to pay them back yet. And since she wasn't there to be taken, her husband would probably not pay for a wife he couldn't find, so no one was any worse off. The main reason she didn't want to go with this husband was that he didn't want to take Moonluck and she wouldn't go without her.

Kittypet's husband-to-be had had an interview with Moonluck and afterwards reported three things wrong with her: she talked differently, she wore her hair in one braid, and she didn't like men. He also said he couldn't afford to keep two wives yet, but this was absurd because he could get Moonluck for nothing. He said that no man wanted a wife who could be had for nothing. The fact was, Kittypet explained, her husband-to-be was frightened of Moonluck.

76

'So you're not married yet,' said Calvin.

'Oh yes, he married me about ten times but he hadn't paid for me. He married me very nicely too – just as well as any other men – but not as well as Red.'

(Different language, different customs, different meanings!)

Anyway, they'd run away, the two of them, very early in the spring, and after about two weeks they'd found Red on his farm, and he liked them, and they liked him, and they were going north to find Moonluck's people.

All the time he talked to Kittypet he was interested in what she told him, but he had to fight against being half-drowned in the sparkles from her eyes, her smooth legs and the curves of her breasts. He reminded himself of a blear-eyed drunk trying to get the bottle to his lips. No. Not a bottle. Everything about the girl was like a round of yeasty dough. It cried out to be smoothed or pressed or moulded or lifted or patted or stroked or gathered up or folded – her tawny round legs as she sat on the elm log, arms round her knees, made his voice quaver. She didn't notice but his hands reached out, half-cupped, right and left, and they were going to fit themselves one to each round thigh and lift her like a bowl of cream.

He went away quickly and she was, he knew, startled and a little hurt. He was sorry. Her chatter was warm and kindly and full of interesting things, and it wasn't her chatter that drove him away.

Something was wrong with him. The purest thoughts could be instantly transformed into visions of joined bodies.

But the real tearing crisis didn't happen till a week later when even his pimples had disappeared. Everything was wrong – he knew that. Whatever he did he would regret – he knew that. His mind was a midden for the Devil to crow on – he knew that. On the other hand, curiously, he'd never felt so well. The two busy girls gathered things from the forest and fed him as he'd never been fed before. He remembered orphan days in Berwick; fancy, untouchable food, and a watering mouth. This food was better.

Brown Bess was loaded with bird-shot and he was looking for squirrels. Moonluck wanted the tails to trim the neck of a dress she was making and Kittypet said she'd found a large patch of doe-head and the blue-green leaves of doe-head went well with squirrel stew. Usually there were a lot of black squirrels, but not today. He wiped some sweat from his forehead.

He'd heard a twig break in the shadow of a big beech, then breathy sounds, like cursing. He went to investigate. He found a porcupine rubbing itself on a log. It was light grey and dark grey. Its eyes were black but each had a diamond in the middle. As he watched it the rubbing sounded less like a hoarse-voiced man, and, when the porcupine was finished rubbing, it lowered its spines and waddled away. Calvin was never quite convinced that the original sound he heard had been the rubbing of the porcupine.

He moved his camp nearer theirs.

The best thing, he thought, was the mysterious incense of cedar and the sleep it wrapped him in – eight, ten, twelve hours; maybe the others wakened or kept watch, he didn't care. He slept. And he would wake, every nerve alert, to a crystal morning.

The waterfall was magical, and so near. It was curious he hadn't heard it, but the sound was muffled by great hardwoods and tumbling torrents of wild grape vines growing where the sunlight shafted through. A ten-foot terrace of limestone crossed the river. Near the middle the terrace was heaved and folded into a hump, tufted with two tall pines; an island that split the stream. On the left it was pebbly and shallow and poured a transparent curtain over the ten-foot drop. On the right of the island the water had worn a smooth channel five yards wide, which dropped the ten feet in fifty. The flume, about five feet deep, was fast, clear and a challenge to trout. With sinuous vigour five or six big ones tacked upstream, beating their way across the eddies at the sides; then a few would turn and launch themselves into the current crowding down the middle.

Naturally the humans imitated them, at first in the canoe, moving so swiftly they felt the cool wind pour round their faces. Then, almost with one accord, though Calvin was the last, they dropped their clothes and plunged in naked where the stream sucked into the sluice. All the way down they wrestled the powerful water as its light-distorting whorls coiled round them – turning, lifting, swirling and falling – to spill them into the wide whirlpool at the bottom. Though it was all over in ten seconds, it was a ride well worth the breathless climb to the top again through fern and cress and mint, over moss and sun-warmed, swelling rock, well carpeted with lichens. Then a few chest-straining breaths and in again, where the water took and ravished every inch of skin.

Tunnelling the water they seemed lithe as the trout that bumped them once or twice. Splashes of sunlight rippled on the clean stone channel and fine curls of white sand formed marvellous patterns as they passed. One deep breath was enough, though they panted when they surfaced. The half-grown fawn grew nervous. She came close to plunging in when Red dived. She leaped straight up in the air and teetered like a rocking horse bucking in agitation. Then she saw, through flare and shade, where the flaming head was going and in seven curving bounds was testing with nervous hooves the water in the lower pool. Then back to the top again. Red invited her in but she backed away, trembling. Her tail, such as it was, was up, down and sideways, a blur of light. Her speed on the downward slope tore light to tatters. She never seemed to touch the ground. She was always at the poolside, waiting, long before the humans flashed into sunlight.

Every person Calvin had met in his life before that afternoon had somehow neglected to tell him that joys could jump out at you in sunlight as unexpectedly as bogles in the dark; and that the range of wonders and of high delights was no more limited by bounds of common sense than fears. And further, he was beginning to suspect, misery has a limit but joy has none.

They did too much and flung themselves on grass to dry and slow their breathing down. They dozed a little. Calvin closed his eyes, believing closed eyes captured delights and held them captive, but he didn't sleep. This dream was not a sleeping dream. He heard Red breathing very slowly and snoring slightly. He opened his eyes. The two girls were giggling as they sat up and looked about the grass. Each pulled a single curving blade. Quietly they inched their bottoms towards Red and ran the grass-blades lightly over his chest. He moved his thick right arm to scratch. The shoulder was limber and heavy with muscle. The biceps wobbled as he scratched. He eased his cock and balls to flop on his bent left leg as he straightened his right. His cock was big but – of course it was shrunk by the cold water. Calvin was astonished at the size of his balls. Each of them was like an egg, heavy and strongly distending its half of the neat sack that held them.

The girls tickled his chest delicately again. It rose as he heaved. The slabs of muscle were cut straight, like thick tiles draped from his shoulders. The brilliant head went back, the mouth opened and the snore grew louder. The two girls covered their mouths and shook a little. Red didn't have much hair on his body but what there was gleamed gold on light bronze. The muscles of his flat belly were bunched in two rows and faintly bulged the taut skin. They tried to stick the grass-blades upright in his navel but there wasn't enough fat to make a fold so, when the blades fell, they blew them off lightly and turned to his calves. They had too much hair. The tickling felt like a fly walking and Red kicked. This time the giggle was not quite inaudible.

They moved to consider other places to tickle. His thighs were so long they seemed graceful but the circumference of each was much greater than that of Moonluck's waist. Tree-trunks, he thought, or posts, or pillars.

Moonluck's waist! Though she sat on the ground her belly made only a little bulge and her waist was long, a stem to support her ribs which swelled to hold breasts which the sun lapped warmly, making a curve of shadow – the most delicate and tantalising line Calvin had ever seen.

And Kittypet too, so different and so alike and so crammed with places that cried to be touched and smoothed – and the places more crowded together since she was shorter. And not just touched because everything was curved so wonderfully to fit his hands— The space between her lightly bouncing breasts was deep enough to smother in; her waist was a handle; her bottom two loaves for squeezing.

His concentration on what he saw – he'd never really seen a naked woman before – was so complete that he was utterly unaware that his mouth was open, he was panting, his eyes were staring—

Something – some gasp or movement – attracted the attention of the two girls and they turned away from Red, nudging him as they did so, to look at Calvin. His cock, like his gaze, was fixed and aimed directly at them. It was a divining rod, hard and quivering. It had found its object and it pulsed towards them with every beat of his heart. Red was awake and the three of them looked and laughed.

'He's better,' said Red.

Calvin leaped to his feet and raced into the aspen thicket, making them laugh again. He cared nothing for the fallen twigs that cracked under his tender feet. His up-reared cock, expecting another treatment, hurt as it swung in front of him, heavy and blind. He went far into the wood before he thought of clothes, then he circled back to pick them up at the point where the river split into two. The others' clothes were there, so they were still on the grassy bank below the fall. He dressed and started in the opposite direction. Then he slowed, stopped and turned, drawn and ashamed of being drawn. Finally he crept to a high point where he could watch them.

The fawn and Moonluck were watching too, lying near each other on the grass. He was very quiet in his hide, but even if he hadn't been the other two wouldn't have noticed.

They were in a shaft of brilliant sunlight. Red, feet spread apart as wide as his shoulders, was two triangles balanced one on the other, apex to apex. He held Kittypet by the waist between his hands and lifted her till she put her knees on his shoulders and he rooted his bearded face between her belly and her breasts. He had to lean back to lift and hold her, and his knees were slightly bent, thighs smooth as the back of a dolphin. His truncheon, up-curving with pressure, was proud as a sabre and gleamed like steel in the sun. He put his head back and licked her breasts, then lifted her again, grinning with effort and groaning with pleasure.

His feet were planted in sand at the edge of the water, so that rippling reflected light was added to the shaft of sun they bathed in and they became one golden marvel. Red was powerful, but to lower the girl slowly enough to aim his cock correctly, took all his muscle and his concentration. Kittypet moved her reaching thighs at tiny hints from the big hands. Down she came, and moaned as the hot knob found the searching mouth. He held her

82

there, just touching. They didn't breathe. His juice mixed with hers, and she was impaled so slowly that, when the probe was home and totally enclosed, they were breathless and gulped great lungfuls of air.

Her hands began moving from his hard square buttocks to his lumpy shoulders. He lifted her again, his neck a column of hawsers, and swung her round, and let her down again, and lifted her—

Calvin was frantic. He ran a mile. He walked three more, half way up the hill and down again and round and over and up, and he dared not stop. He'd never known anything like it. He was whimpering with desire. Whenever an aching erection was subdued by violence it grew again – and so on through the evening, till the moon rose and he found himself by the elm log where he had talked to the girls and, for some reason, this was too much.

He dropped his trousers and flung himself into the thighs of the log, between the two fat silver limbs that once were roots. The log was hollow. A bear might live there, or a wolverine or a wolf or – it didn't matter. His cock was sore with pressure and with waiting. His face caressed the moonlit log. He was half crying. He grabbed his cock and battered and bent it and groaned—

A week ago he'd been stunned into gibbering surprise when he stood naked, alone in an empty land, and looked at the place where his clothes should have been. For some reason a far more surprising event on this frantic evening didn't startle him in the least.

He resented the work he was doing and stopped when he felt one warm, plump hand cradle his balls and the other smooth and soothe his convulsing bottom. It was all quite normal and as it should be. This was an occupation that shouldn't be pursued alone. He stopped trying, staggered back, tripped promptly on his dropped breeches and thumped to the ground. Kittypet was down beside him. He kicked his legs out of the breeches. She was so wet that when he rolled into place between her legs his misused cock found refuge without search. She held him. She was the first woman and he was the first man. Wendet. The Island. The island lurched about, churning his teeth, bones, brains and guts, and erupted into what he recognised quite clearly, even at such a time, as the creation of a vast new life. Nothing as small as a baby, or himself, but a whole new universe.

As one day followed another and they stayed in the same place it *was* a new universe, the Island, a garden just created, full of new joys, fresh as dew each morning. The only hangover from the old universe was a sentiment familiar to Calvin: the sadness brought by the knowledge, a deep knowledge springing from a sombre racial memory, that it was too good to last. Anything so full of pleasure must be too good to last.

The girls had to go north and he had to go south. He had decided to go south and he must carry out his decision. The start could, however, be delayed.

Moonluck kept surprising him. They were lolling about after a good meal. The girls were quiet. Red and Calvin discussed Indians. 'That man talked to his snowshoes,' said Calvin.

'They think there's a spirit in everything,' drawled Red.

'They think some weird things.'

'They tell good stories.'

'Yes, they do,' said Calvin, remembering the winter.

'They, they, they—' protested Moonluck, suddenly spitting like an angry cat, 'You're crazy! You're all crazy! The French admire a Jesus who inserts himself in a biscuit and they eat him alive! Yet they say we're savage because in a savage winter a starving man might eat a dead man. The English admire a Jesus who says

84

nothing but "Don't fuck", yet they do it every day and twice on Sundays. They, they, they – you're different, we're different.'

But she soon forgot her irritation.

Calvin was repeatedly surprised by the amount of work the girls did and the fact that they appeared to enjoy it, chattering away as they pounded maize, or cleaned a fish, or sewed neat double seams with strong well-soaked, translucent threads of gut. They had four steel needles of different sizes which they kept dry and treasured in a leather folder. They chattered so rapidly that half the time Calvin didn't understand them. Some of their conversation concerned the likelihood of their being followed. Moonluck said that her husband, Speechmaker, wouldn't demean himself by following her. She'd been away from him ten months now. He had other wives. They'd be glad to be rid of her since she was sometimes lazy and walked about instead of doing her work. Also he wouldn't worry about getting back his bride-price. He hadn't paid much. Bride-prices in the north were low. Besides, he didn't like her. He'd never made her pregnant. Why should he want to take so long a journey to recover a barren bride he didn't like, or her small bride-price? But one overcast morning she was agitated about Kittypet. Kittypet's father – and Calvin learned he was a very important man – had not yet received his bride-price. Kittypet would be a good wife to any man so both her husband-to-be, who had no wife yet, and her father might be expected to chase after her.

Moonluck was deeply agitated for a time but she calmed down when Red pointed out that they'd travelled very slowly, that they had stayed a week at his cabin and no pursuers had turned up, that the hill was a good place from which to detect pursuers and no signs had been seen, that Kittypet's father had nieces to get rid of, that her prospective husband had not been a man whose

alliance was necessary to the tribe, and, finally, that nobody wanted Kittypet except Calvin and himself.

'I can be nice to any man if he's nice to me,' Kittypet
bragged. Calvin liked her spirit but found it shocking.

'Which of these two do you like best?' asked Moonluck.

'Red,' said Kittypet, without a second's hesitation. 'But
he doesn't need me as much as Calbn.' She had difficulty
pronouncing the 'v'.

'I like you too,' said Red.

'You fuck me because you know I want you to. Calvin
fucks me because he thinks I'm the best and the only,'
and she laughed because Calvin's face went scarlet.

'He's a helpful man to have in camp,' said Red.

Moonluck laughed softly. 'You have enough to keep
seven women happy seven times a day,' she said. 'Maybe
it's the spring.'

'I like to enjoy myself.'

'But how did you spend the winter alone?' asked
Calvin rather desperately, having spent seventeen winters
alone in that former half-life.

'Same as you. Same as anyone.'

'Don't you think about women all the time?'

'No.'

'I do.'

'You won't any more.'

'Yes I will.'

'Oh, I think about Moonluck and Kittypet when they're
here. I can't help it, and they want me to.'

'I don't understand you,' said Calvin. He thought for a
moment, then burst out, 'Would you mind if I chased
after Moonluck?'

'If you fucked her?'

'Well – yes.' Calvin was defiant. Moonluck and Kittypet laughed.

'Does she want you to?' asked Red.

'I – I don't know,' said Calvin.

'If she wants you to you'll know.'

Calvin shook his head seriously, and his face was so screwed up with bewilderment that Moonluck and Kitty-pet went on laughing. Red explained to them that white people were brought up differently and had some strange ideas. 'They think,' he said, 'that only men enjoy fucking and that it's wicked of them. Women are supposed to hate it, and to be ashamed, and to suffer, and to do it because it's their duty.'

'Do the men like to make the women suffer?' asked Moonluck, unexpectedly serious, unexpectedly interested.

'Some do.'

'Are the men supposed to hate it when the women have a good time?'

'It isn't proper.'

'What isn't?'

'For a white woman to have a good time.'

'But can the white man have a good time when the woman doesn't have a good time?'

'They think so.'

'The men think that?'

'Yes.'

Moonluck considered the matter for some seconds and her voice was sad when she spoke. 'No wonder they leave home. No wonder they wander all over the world for no reason.' Then a little later she said something that stuck in Calvin's memory, partly because he couldn't understand it and partly because, curiously, he did.

'I think they invented guns because they couldn't use their pricks properly and politely.' Moonluck was very definite. That point was now decided. No argument was possible. Calvin was amazed, distrustful, but interested.

Kittypet was predictable and understandable; Moonluck did and said strange things from time to time, and unexpectedly. How, for instance, he thought – how on earth do you use your prick politely? What a curious phrase! In English it had the connotation of ceremony, propriety and public good manners. How could you even talk about using your prick in that way? The universe *was* new. It was also shocking. It was also becoming so friendly and unbelievably serene that the thought of their impending and unavoidable separation must, quite suddenly, be stamped out, dammed up, thrust back into darkness.

So he tried to do these things though he knew the effort was useless.

The time came. They'd spent the evening packing their few belongings. They'd made one big cedar bed against a log. They'd make an early start. Moonluck must find her own people to the north. Calvin must do his map-making to the south. To help himself be manly and decisive he'd been building up his credibility as if he were a sort of official map-maker for the Hudson's Bay Company. He had to explain away his confession that he didn't know much about making maps. He also had to counter a certain amount of teasing from Moonluck, who kept asking when the Hudson's Bay Company had begun to employ boys as map-makers. (She knew more about the Company than the others, having come from the north.) Calvin's knowledge of the letter that lay sizzling like a fused bomb at the bottom of his pack made him lie harder, and the more he lied the more the letter leered at him until his lying developed a sort of desperation. The more desperate he became the less the others were impressed. So he had to go south to prove something. Red was no help. He knew the importance of maps but he just sat there smiling. Did he know Calvin was lying? Did he enjoy the bickering that went on?

'We don't need maps,' said Kittypet.

'You use signs on skins or birch-bark.'

'We keep the maps in our heads,' said Moonluck.

'You can't give those maps to someone else,' protested Calvin.

'Who?'

'Anyone.'

'Where does he want to go?'

'Anywhere.'

'Why?'

'Any reason.'

Moonluck shook her head. 'He should stay where he is.'

'You didn't,' said Calvin, triumphing.

Red laughed, but he leaned back against the elm log and put his big left arm across Moonluck's shoulders.

They were sitting on their wide bed in a row reading from left to right Kittypet, Red, Moonluck and Calvin. The little fire was twelve feet away. They were just at the edge of its dome of warm light. The fawn lay nearby, watching them, not the fire. She was alert. They could see the pale outline of the large sound-gathering ears and when the head rose, turned, and was held at a particular angle the fire glowed red in the wet, large eyes. If they paid attention to the fawn they needed no watch-dog. They'd heard distant wolves and the fawn trembled strongly at the singular, sourceless note curving towards them as if on the whining orbit of some racing spirit.

Kittypet said she'd heard that the Ottawa Walker needed no maps, knew every people everywhere and could talk to each people in its own language.

'Like Calbn,' she finished. Then she took Red's upper arm in both her hands – her fingers couldn't meet around it – and wrote circles on it with her short nose, finally burying her face in the hollow of his elbow where she blew and made a flapping sound.

Red tightened his arm, lifted his elbow and she somersaulted across their knees. Calvin had her calves to play with, Moonluck her middle and Red her head. She was blissfully happy.

Calvin wondered if the fawn was jealous. The creature staggered to her spindly legs and trotted towards them, then made a lovely leap to the log and lay down on it behind Red's head. Though Calvin was immensely contented, full of good food and lapped in friendship, he remembered an old suspicion that he was always the unwanted. It didn't worry him in the slightest.

Two owls fluted softly across the little clearing.

Kittypet slapped and killed an early mosquito on Red's shoulder, and they heard two quick echoes of the slap. They heard the soft hiss as the fawn licked salt from Red's armpit and Moonluck's shoulder.

'Play your whistle,' said Kittypet, sleepily. Red was brushing his knee with the tip of one of her plaits.

'I need two hands for that.'

So they sat in silence. The fire didn't crackle now; the flames were lavender. There was no breeze. Only a few stars could be seen through the high lace of leaves. Then there was a slight change. A star would wink. The fawn moved its ears. A flock of small mouse-coloured bats flickered darkly into the light of the fire and out again, repeatedly changing direction. In and out. In and out. The humans listened intently and thought they heard the dusty flutter of the wings. The fawn lifted her head, hearing something else. The bats were a cloud of withered leaves in a wanton breeze and they swirled in the clearing for a full minute before, as suddenly as they appeared, they were all away and no one had seen them go.

Calvin couldn't help the remnants of superstitions that he'd brought, unwittingly, to this mysterious Island. These scraps of mediaeval terrors linked so closely with more recent dangers, and with Colethorpe's relished

90

efforts to chill his spine, that his thoughts flew to the grimmest of the bogles.

'Why does everyone talk about Longhair?' he asked.

Kittypet, though sleepy, was prompt. 'Because he's a wendigo. He haunts people and eats them,' she explained.

'Some people like to be talked about,' said Red, and so solemnly Calvin had a notion there was special knowledge in his head.

Kittypet was full of information. 'My father met him. Longhair is a very tall man,' and she reached her left arm to pat Red's springy hair. 'But not so tall as you. He used to tell everyone he was Pontiac's son. Now he says he's Pontiac's nephew as well. My father says this isn't true because his mother was a good woman and wouldn't fuck her brother. But Longhair says she had special permission from an important spirit. Longhair says it was the spirit of the twin rivers who are brother and sister but marry together. My father says that Pontiac was drunk most of the time so it was no use asking him. He says that once Pontiac was almost as wise as the Ottawa Walker, though not as clever at lying.'

She paused. 'My father says if he had been as clever at lying he'd never have been fooled by the Senecas or the Tuscaroras who are all poisonous snakes. As you can tell from their names, says my father, in many languages – Nadowa, Iroquois, Kwe—'

'Stop talking now,' said Red, and she stopped.

So silence flowed in from the forest and Calvin thought of the morning, and how he would never see these people again. It was unmanly to cry but his eyes were pricking.

'Two weeks,' he said. 'I was in a temper when you stole my clothes.'

They laughed, Kittypet the most. 'You ran about like a blind rabbit. If we'd been thieves we'd have taken your baggage '

'Men,' said Moonluck with disgust.

'What's wrong with men?' asked Calvin, pleased rather than otherwise.

'They get excited.'

'It's women that get excited.'

'You didn't see yourself! Pale as snow. Red as blood. Jumping about. Trying to hide. And every now and then holding something in front of your little prick! Men!' Moonluck was a strange person and Calvin changed the subject a little.

'How long would you have kept it up if Red hadn't stopped you?' he asked.

'He didn't stop us.'

'He played that song.'

'Oh yes,' Moonluck remembered. 'He spoiled it. We wouldn't have kept it up long.'

They were all conscious of talking about old times, of an interlude now about to end. There was regret to be detected even in the voice of the forthright Moonluck.

Calvin was curious. 'Who was it who came to visit me that night? Was it Red? Was it all of you?'

'None of us,' said Red.

'In the canoe.'

'When?'

'That night. I saw the mark, beside mine. I didn't think I slept that soundly. What time did you come?'

'Next day, we came. We paddled up next day.'

'I saw the mark in the morning. I thought I did.'

'No,' said Red. 'We came in the afternoon.'

But talking about old times was a melancholy diversion. They were sleepy. They were going to make an early start. Kittypet rolled off the couch of their legs towards the fire. She put two biggish logs on to keep it going and picked up a blanket which she flung at them. Then she took her old place beside Red. The smell of cedar searched their lungs but only Red fell quickly asleep.

Calvin felt Moonluck's buttocks in his lap. Suddenly

she turned her head half towards him as if to speak. Her lips parted but she held the position saying nothing. Calvin, in the shadow of her head, examined her profile against the reddening light. The lips were full, with clear-cut edges. Chin, nose and forehead all showed determination and a ruthless, untouchable reserve. The details of her face were in shadow except for the fine fiery outline, and it was so close that his eyes couldn't focus properly. It was possible to look through the outline at the dark trees and the stars. When he focused on the stars the outline of her face became a constellation on its own, distant, glimmering, vast and delicate, with a hint of a power not quite normal in human beings.

Her sudden voice shattered his nebulous reverie. She spoke softly, but with characteristic finality, everything thought out in advance.

'Wake up, Red.' She nudged him and he was instantly with them again, no slow return to consciousness. 'We could go with Calvin in the morning. I don't have to go north till autumn. We know the country and could help him with his maps. Kittypet wants to. I want to. You're only going north for our sake.'

'Why not?' said Red, and took her left hand, pulling her against his back. The profile disappeared.

'Why not?' repeated Kittypet. 'Why not.'

Calvin, of course, thought it would be wonderful, but he was too surprised and relieved to say much. His left hand found the hollow of her armpit, which he pressed. Moonluck clamped her arm down, holding his hand there. Not long afterwards everything dissolved in the smell of cedar.

Calvin woke once more when the fire flared. Moonluck was also awake. She was sitting up and she had her soft medicine bag in her hand. She took from it an odd object; a slim stick eight inches long, feathered and nocked at one end like an arrow. The other end was fixed to the centre of a wooden disc. She was drawing a hair across the flat bottom of the disc and it made a faint scraping sound. He sat up to see more clearly.

She was startled but gestured for quiet and, after hesitating, showed him the mock arrow. Dozens of porcupine quills were thrust through small holes in the thin disc. They were fixed securely and the butt ends were neatly trimmed. The invisibly sharp points projected about an eighth of an inch.

Calvin couldn't figure it out and he glanced his bewilderment. She lifted the blanket slowly with her knee and placed the disc lightly against the slope. The thing stayed where she put it. You'd have said an arrow had pierced her leg. She put her mouth close to his ear.

'I've a little bag of blood too,' she breathed.

'Real blood?'

'Duck-oil and red earth. Go back to sleep.'

Calvin did as he was told. Only the fawn had lifted her head at their whispering.

Calvin did, two weeks later, recollect this evening in some detail and there was one fact about the sequence of events which was then to disturb him with a sudden and painful illumination.

4

Cases of Odd Behaviour

*'A man whose spirit is killed is deader than a man
with an arrow through his heart'*

Longhair

THEY SLEPT late. They were in no hurry so they didn't
travel fast. The days passed cool and pleasant but they
were, to Calvin, a continuing riot of curious, small surprises at his new friends and at the country they passed
through. Some of the impressions were contradictory.

The fawn, for instance. She was growing quickly. Once
she would ride contentedly on a bundle of reeds in Red's
canoe. Now she was impatient and, since birch-bark is
thin and grained, a sharp hoof could pierce it. They tied
the four feet together but the struggle was so violent –
Red got a two-inch cut on his leg – and showed such
hysteria that they tried it only twice. After that she
followed the two canoes along the bank. This relieved
them of the duty of cutting grass and leaves for her because she could easily graze for a quarter of an hour and
still reach a shallow place in the river ahead of them. As
the shallow places became more frequent they were often
warned of a stretch of rapid to come by seeing the active
little flame bucking and dancing near the bank.

At dawn one day Calvin had marked on his map a low
hill topped with big pines, and he estimated the distance
at two miles to the south-west. When they made camp at

about five o'clock the same hill was two miles to the north-west. They'd followed a deep ox-bow which curved for eighteen miles and landed them only three miles south of their previous camp. Along this dark water hardwoods, unlike the pines and spruces, leaned and trailed low branches into it. Beneath the cloud-shaped forest the shadow was a black tunnel through which, sometimes, they saw the fawn streak by.

When they made camp Calvin went to collect kindling. The girls both said it was their job but Calvin wanted to stretch his legs. They knew he was white and young. He didn't know any better. Like Calvin on this trip they were finding that customs were not physical laws. Calvin was somewhat oppressed by the heat and quietness of the day, and he was glad to be alone for a minute where he could be watchful without exciting derision. He snapped dead and brittle twigs, well dried in the air, from standing trees. He'd collected enough when he came to the small clearing where a black log lay and its companion tree, almost as large and even blacker, leaned over the sunlit patch of grass. It was a tree he didn't recognise; round leaves bigger than dinner-plates, most of them at rest, a few side-slipping left or right apparently independent of any wind.

In the middle of the patch of grass he saw another movement. He called the others. The four of them stood in a row and watched where he pointed. Sure enough, a leaf of the huge dandelion that grew there lifted its arrow-tip into the air and swayed it two inches above the rest of the circular cluster. No breeze had lifted it; at that moment, Calvin thought, the air was very still. Another leaf lifted.

The cluster had not been crushed but its vivid green showed a few white streaks radiating from the centre. Nearby there were areas of grass that appeared flatter than they should be.

96

Then the whole glade was buffeted by a sudden gust. The places which had seemed flattened were now hard to find.

'Two deer,' said Red.

Two, thought Calvin. So Red had seen the flattened grass.

'Or bear.' Kittypet liked bear-meat better than any other.

Calvin said in a rather laboured manner, as if ashamed, 'If people had been following us they could have crossed the neck of the ox-bow while we took the long way round. They'd have been here before us.'

But they found the hoof-prints of deer near the basswood tree, and short reddish hairs were caught in the black bark.

'A couple of deer,' said Red again.

'You scared them away,' said Kittypet, taking his bundle of dry twigs.

'Why should anyone follow us?' asked Moonluck. 'And if he found us why shouldn't he show himself?'

The hoof-prints of deer they'd found looked old. Of course the ground was hard and new prints might not show. Calvin took his canoe and scouted both banks of the river. There were no marks of human feet or of canoes, other than their own.

He was moved more by remembered panic than by present fear. These people he was with were satisfied. If there were a pursuer why should he be unfriendly? The girls weren't frightened and they, just possibly, might have some reason to fear pursuit. Next day he forgot the dandelion leaves that moved by themselves.

A day later they made a portage to a small stream, flowing south-east. The carry was short and mostly downhill. By the end of the week they paddled on a slow grand river curving steadily south through rolling country with the many greens of heavier hardwoods – maple, beech, ash, elm, hickory and oak – interrupted more often by grey willow.

They followed the deep water by a six-foot clay bank topped with sumac. It tapered to a muddy point, and to the west was a mile-wide swamp. Their sudden emergence frightened a thousand ducks. They squawked and rose clattering from the flat plains of water-lilies, threading expertly between four moose, fetlock-deep on a mudbank. Some of them arrowed neatly underneath the wet bellies and between the long legs. Only then did the moose raise their heads, mouths chewing and trailing pale green streamers, to watch the real disturbers of their peace. They went on chewing.

They had legs like sticks – the two canoes could, like the ducks, have paddled underneath their bellies, and with room to spare. They had humps on their backs and faces that hung to their knees. The tallest carried horns that spread more than three feet on each side of the doleful eyes. Two preachers could have stood securely, one on each horn, high above their congregations, as on pulpits or the palms of almighty hands, and preached in all directions. The notion was as fabulous and as ludicrous as the beasts which, still chewing, watched the canoes till they were out of sight.

Then they came to Red's farm, and Calvin wondered why he'd ever left it. The corn was three feet high and the wheat was swelling at the tips. They ate young carrots and very young potatoes. The garden needed weeding and the girls went at it busily. Calvin, now having a table firm enough to work on, brought his maps up to date. The few cleared acres in the forest seemed marvellously civilised. The cabin was dry and light when the door was open. But Red wasn't like himself.

Calvin watched him. The big man was examining the

log shelter he'd built for his cow and he slouched around it, disconsolate and impatient. At one time, obviously, he'd worked hard at the farm. Now he shot some rabbits, carried water from the spring, and wandered about.

On the second evening Red told them about the calf and the cows and bull. He'd waited, he hadn't bought them too soon. The farm was ready for them. He'd driven them in for a hundred miles, and carefully. The bull was, he admitted, too young, but the cows were in calf. The bull broke his leg in a fox-hole and had to be shot. One cow was drowned crossing the big river. The cow that was left had its calf in February. As soon as the snow cleared the calf ate some plant that disagreed with it and died bawling. After the calf died the cow bellowed for three days and was hard to milk.

Maybe the continuous bawling attracted the wolves. Red knew the den was near and had set a few traps to protect the calves he was going to have.

'I didn't set many. Just a few.'

It was at that time that he found the fawn. He felt responsible because the doe had blundered into a trap he'd set for the wolves. Four high-wheeling hawks and a chorus of crows had led him to the trap before the wolves had finished eating the body of the doe. One slender fore-leg was still in the jaws of the trap.

How the wolves had missed the fawn he'd never know. There was a big enough sheet of the doe's skin left to conceal his own smell so he was able to approach, touch, lift and carry the fawn. Her nose rested contentedly enough on the doe's skin spread over his shoulder. She was still unsteady on her legs but she'd already begun to nibble a little grass in imitation of her mother. Cow's milk disagreed with her only when she had too much of it. A birch-bark container with a rag through a split in the bottom made a successful udder provided he held it himself. The fawn wouldn't suck if the contraption were just hung on a bush. She learned to graze earlier than usual, of course, because she'd lost her mother.

'Where's the cow?' asked Calvin, and Red took a long time before he answered. He didn't seem bitter, or angry, but he was disgruntled. It happened about a week before the girls had arrived.

He found the cow bellowing on a riverside meadow half a mile away one evening, its belly distended. He didn't shoot it, he watched it. He had no medicines. One by one its legs gave way. It sagged and subsided. The big muscles wrenched. Gusts of gas and jets of green shit shot out. For a brief time it quietened and gurgled up a cud which stained the lips with green and bloody froth. Convulsions began again and it couldn't swallow. It stretched its neck out straight, tongue lolling, mouth open, chest muscles clamping and heaving with no sound of air rushing through the tubes. Quite suddenly the muscles relaxed, the head dropped awkwardly to the tough sod with a loud thump. It was dead and flies walked over the pupils of the eyes. Maybe the same plant had killed the cow as had killed the calf.

For two nights Red could hear the big wolves feasting. That year's cubs were with them. Once, he thought, a bear lumbered in and chased them temporarily away. Foxes took their turns, and many crows. Late one evening he sat with his rifle watching the five grey shapes materialise out of the shadows to growl and wrestle with the large bones. He didn't shoot.

'Why?' asked Calvin.

'Oh—' and Red fumbled for words. 'I'd have to bury her. They saved me the trouble.'

There was, even now, a note in his voice that indicated an expectation of disaster – even a melancholy acceptance of it – which Calvin found bewildering, though this disappointed feeling seemed to explain how he could bring himself to leave his nice farm when the girls came and asked him to go with them. But Calvin never understood how Red could sit watching the wolves eat his cow without taking a shot at them.

Then the garden was weeded, the maps were up to date and Red's restlessness eased at the prospect of more wandering in the south. The morning they left was windy. Cloud shadows raced back towards the fields, the raw little buildings and the new split-rail fences left to guard them. Red refused to look back.

A day later they ran into rains, not heavy enough to stop them, but frequent enough to urge them into sheltered places at night. A high bank and a tarpaulin could become a cave with a fire in front.

Cuddling close became a nightly habit. Calvin was surprised at how calmly a cuddle, by mutual recognition, became most comfortable heat, then tension, climax and release; but he was more than surprised at the limitless range of feelings the same gestures could express. All this with Kittypet, not as avid as he was, but not slow to be aroused; and astonishment was repeated. Their encounters were full of unexpected moment of affection.

Moonluck was quite different. On the two occasions when proximity could have warmed into affection and affection deepened into sexual feeling she would, at a definite point, become cool, nervous and apt to laugh. Calvin, lying awake, argued idly, though in the manner of a sermon, through three possible explanations. 1. She didn't want him and despised him. 2. She thought Red might be jealous. 3. She thought it right to save herself for Red.

The third implied that savages have Christian impulses. The second was complimentary but, judging from Red's attitude, unlikely. The first was the least flattering but the most probable.

Calvin knew that popular opinion would demand that he resent this last conclusion but he didn't. Popular opinion demanded attitudes towards 'savages' and towards 'women' which he was also coming to distrust. Not that it mattered. This universe was all new and you couldn't expect to understand it.

For instance, the girls laughed at him every now and then. Once he found this offensive, now it made him curious. Was he being seduced into savage ways? Was that letter correct? Was he 'unsuitable' to life in the north? Mr Colethorpe insisted that savages must 'respect' you. Laughter didn't indicate respect. But they laughed at Red too, and Red was beginning to seem not only more amiable than Mr Colethorpe but far more admirable.

And this was curious too. What was admirable about a man who was unassertive, who was a Colonial without the slightest social distinction, far from rich yet lacking in ambition, over-familiar with savages, loose in his morals, certainly a non-conformist and probably an atheist? Most disturbing was the impression Calvin gained that Red was a deserter from the army.

Didn't he know too much about Bouquet at Fort Pitt, Gladwyn at Detroit, Wolfe at Quebec and even General Braddock at the frightful massacre near Fort DuQuesne, as Fort Pitt was then called? Especially considering that what he knew was not just recent history as it might be learned from reports; it sparkled with little details such as where Pontiac's yellow pipe came from, or where the Virginian Colonel Washington found his second horse after Braddock was shot; not important, but interesting, with a ring of truth. And if Red puzzled him, Calvin was finding himself more puzzling still. When he left Berwick he'd considered himself reasonably well-informed. He was now becoming aware of blank spaces in his experience which were completely unmapped. When he left Berwick he thought of himself as, though possibly a coward, a virtuous, religious, hard-working, ambitious and intelligent young man. Now he was – though probably still a coward – immoral, irreligious, lazy, not very ambitious and stupid.

Though he kept telling himself to 'Think! Think! Think!' he didn't care much. He began to wonder if carelessness could actually clear your mind.

He would never forget the disturbing sight of Moonluck among the white, unfamiliar flowers. There were no flowers like that in Britain.

After days of shivering in mist and a cold rain they came to a broken area of limestone hills and caves and gullies where vines, cedars and hardwoods were richly mixed. Tall ferns grew in damp hollows and a million violets patched the torn fells with blue. And the curious sloping glade! The ground between the widely-separated beeches was white and the white moved with the wind like water. The flowers were innumerable. Each individual blossom, some three inches across, swayed at the top of a slender, pale green stem about a foot tall. Each had three blanched petals. Each petal was beaded with raindrops. They glimmered with light as ghosts are supposed to glimmer. A little beyond this pearly parkland, which they skirted a little nervously, they put down their canoes. Again they skirted the slope when they brought their baggage. The wind changed and they were suddenly enveloped in steam. It was tepid and it smelled faintly of rotten eggs. Presently they stood on the edge of a crusted basin at the mouth of a cave. Hot currents of air moved around them. Kittypet tried the curiously black and steamy water with her toes. In half a minute they were soaking in it, warmed as by an embrace. They tasted the water and spat it out. Kittypet said that it was a bad idea to drink too much of it, but they lolled in it for hours till fingers, toes, palms and soles of feet were wrinkled and newly sensitive.

An old bear with a grizzled snout shuffled up and watched them, sitting back like a fat dog with worms. When Red went towards their pile of duffle the bear sauntered into the concealing spruces but reappeared when he came back. Red now had his pewter cup, which he began filling with scrapings from the crusted rocks. The warm water lapped around his waist. 'Where's Moonluck?' he asked.

She'd disappeared and they were so dopy with warmth that no one had seen her start back along their trail. The sun blazed suddenly from behind them, the wind changed and the steam was momentarily lifted. They could see the slope of white flowers. Gold and black in the middle of the flowers Moonluck stood, her hair unbraided now and falling about her tawny shoulders almost to the swell of her long thighs.

Their three shadows lengthened towards her. Then, parallel to their shadows and like a shadow itself, Calvin noticed a stain, a patch of the same flowers but the colour of clotted blood. Why did this crimson variety grow all in one place?

Red called, Moonluck waved and began to thread her way carefully towards them. She was curiously lit by light reflected from flowers, steam and mist. Seven bluebirds swooped across, the blue so rich it left an after-image on the eye.

Again the light wind changed and the whorls of vapour shifted, condensed or disappeared. Moonluck was now half visible, now half obscured. As branches of the beech trees lifted letting shafts of sunlight through, scraps of rainbow formed and faded all about her. Some tatters of colour were brilliant, some vague and broad; some floated behind her and others fell before her like a curtain. The luminous mist lapped round her like the atmosphere, Calvin thought, of some other world entirely. She waded through rainbows. It was not a sight to be forgotten. She came to the crumbling edge of the basin and eased into the warm water where she luxuriated with the rest of them.

Kittypet, for some reason, suddenly fell forward on the water and threw both arms round Red's waist like two constrictors, fingers hooked to opposite sides. She hugged him so tightly he could breathe only with his chest. She trailed out from him, floating, and rubbed her wet face bumpily across the long muscles of his back. Red looked round at her and carefully set the pewter cup of sulphur scrapings on the pitted rock. He swung his shoulders and reached his right hand under her floating waist. He side-slipped her slowly through the water. Her face moved smoothly round his flank to his navel, up his ribs, over his chest, along his neck and at the same time her legs encircled him. He sat slowly on a rather slippery rock so deep that only their heads, each now hooked with a half turn to the other, protruded above the surface. Their arms were round each other. Their two heads described small circles.

Calvin, with mixed feelings, watched them. He felt a firm hand on his arm. When Moonluck spoke she was forthright as usual.

'Kittypet likes both of you. She told me.'

'And you?'

Moonluck smiled cheerfully and the smile included Red and Kittypet as well as Calvin.

'I'm different. Kittypet knows what she wants and she's getting it. I don't. But I know that when everything is changing it's best to want what's coming.'

Then her eyes swung slowly to look across the slope of white flowers towards the trail they'd come by. Calvin looked too and waited for a second before he asked:

'How far back did you go?'

'To the top of the hill.'

'With no clothes?'

'There's no one there.'

Calvin was watching her. His next remarks surprised himself as well as Moonluck. He stumbled over them awkwardly.

'You spoke as if you were sorry for Kittypet,' he said.

'Yes, I did.'

'Maybe it isn't Kittypet you should be sorry for.'

Moonluck looked sharply at him, frowning. Calvin had the distinct and shocking impression that her black eyes were probes, scraping the inside of his skull. Then suspicion disappeared and she smiled warmly, although her words and voice were grave.

'You could have valuable dreams,' she said. 'I think you could have very valuable dreams, and I don't believe they come for the asking.' And a moment later, 'Don't get too old too soon.' She still examined him through a long silence, then she changed the subject. 'What a good man Red is. I think we'll be safe.'

Then she told him she'd found mushrooms. They dressed and went to collect them, hurrying to keep warm. Moonluck had a mortar made of iron-wood but here, near their camp, she found a clean natural kettle in hard limestone with its polished stone ball still inside it. She wiped it out with a piece of moistened skin and the hard maize was ground very quickly – so quickly that she ground enough for a couple of days.

The narrow sulphur stream poured blackly into the river. Above this place she filled the bark bucket with fresh water and brought it back to the natural mortar. It was difficult to lift the ground maize into the bucket because the mortar was a foot deep but she managed with two scoops of thin bark. She stirred the water and the meal grew moist. Sand and rock-dust fell to the bottom but the paste floated. She lifted it out, squeezed it, and spread it on a slab of bark. To the milky liquid that was left she added a little maple sugar and it made a bland drink, which the others were dressed in time to share. Some Indians would leave this liquor to ferment; but the mildly alcoholic drink was sour, said Kittypet, screwing her face up.

For a little while they watched the old bear. He had kept his eye on them till they were out of sight but they found a good hide. Maybe the bear was a little deaf. He inserted himself into the steaming water with deliberation. He tested various depths. Finally he found a place where his back was supported against a great boulder. He patted the water with his paws and lowered himself till only his jaws, eyes and ears projected. His eyes rolled up to contemplate the sky and his jaw fell open. They could hear him slowly breathing. Kittypet wanted bear-meat but Red pointed out that this bear was certain to be tough. They'd look for a younger one.

They didn't see any until two days later when they'd travelled almost forty miles south and reached a point where the stream they followed was joined from the east by another of the same size. The united stream flowed to the west through a most beautiful valley of dark, fine loam that produced a tall crop of hardwoods.

They found evidence of former clearing at the top of the rise that separated the tributary streams. At some time there'd been a village there and little fields. There were no signs of a palisade. The cleared ground was now thick with quick-growing soft maples and wide sunlit tangles of raspberries. The saplings grew incredibly straight in their reach for the sun. Some, though they were no more than three inches through at the base, stood thirty feet in height.

Red and Calvin left the girls to make camp at the crest of the rise while they did a circuit. They'd seen bear-tracks. They weren't hunting with any determination but they took the trouble to load. Calvin was slow and awkward. Red was swift and careful. His powder-horn had two brass releases, one for the main charge and a smaller one for priming.

They argued as they walked. West with the main river or east, up the tributary? There was an indication on a French map which could be the mouth of the main river. The tributary from the east would be less travelled. They'd gone far enough west already. They came to a patch of ground that was thick with flies and speckled with the wings of butterflies. The patch was elongated to their right. They didn't stop to see what the insects were interested in because they saw tracks of bear in a low place near the river.

They were circling the camp at a distance of about a quarter of a mile, and on the side opposite the first patch of insects they came on another, which fixed it in their minds. They heard a distinctive hum in the direction away from the camp. When they investigated they saw it was a chunk of rotten wood with beeswax adhering, bees coming and going purposefully, straight as arrows. It was just a small piece of honeycomb. A bear might have carried it.

They went back to their argument as they continued their circuit. They decided against following the main river which would be on some map or other; less would be known about the tributary. The main river would be much easier to follow but Calvin insisted that new ground was more important. They swung back towards the camp, still talking. The fawn rushed up to them, bucking and trembling. They went on, and they went on talking till they stopped in mid-word—

There *were* bears about, three of them, and they were talking too. They found one object of interest after another in the camp and their grunted comments were quite audible. They were a little over a year old, about as big as a medium-sized pig. They were doing some damage but not much. One was sniffing and tapping at Calvin's

108

writing-case. The girls were sitting on a branch of a tree. The bears turned as Red and Calvin approached. Red raised his rifle and fired. Two of the bears took off in a hurry. One was wounded and ploughed in a circle, shaking its head and squealing. Red was reloading.

'Shoot,' he said, and Calvin did. The bear was knocked off its feet and lay still. From the twist of the heavy neck you could tell it was dead. Moonluck and Kittypet were down in an instant and Moonluck cut the bear's throat so that a great pool of blood was forming when the men joined them.

The skinning and butchery was expertly done, Calvin looking on. He cut and brought platters of birch bark for the others. That was all they'd let him do. They set aside the fillets. The best of the lean meat that remained was cut into strips for drying, and Red's big brass pot was full of melting fat: no fat was so good as bear fat for making pemmican. When the fire died to coals that evening they grilled chunks of the fillet on sticks and their bellies were steadily distended until they could hold no more.

The south branch was shallow. There were rain-clouds in the sky that might raise the water level, so the girls spent a day preparing the bearskin and the meat they intended to carry with them while Red explored and Calvin worked on his maps.

But there was no rain, the water level remained low so that they made only ten miles the first day. They had to portage three times. The river was snake-like and kept doubling back. Round the next loop was a long fourth portage. They were too tired to tackle it so they made camp.

The spit of land was a garden jutting out from the high-sloping promontory. Three patches of rushes edged the river curve. Wild roses poured over the high bank into a tangle of blackberries, all in flower. Under the blackberries was a deep shadow. An old choke-cherry tree, the fruit clumps of small green gems, grew from this

shadow and it was into a crotch of this tree that Calvin
slipped his writing-case that night before he slept. The
fawn, he thought idly, was unusually alert.

'She wants to meet a buck,' said Red.

On the following day they learned that there were
other Indians about and – it was both curious and worry-
ing – that these Indians seemed to be following them.

It was Calvin who made the discovery, and by pure
accident. The accident would never have happened if Red
hadn't had a notion to try something new – new, not only
to Calvin but to the girls who thought Red a genius.

Normally on a portage you carried the empty canoes
first, leaving the lighter baggage for the second trip; but
Red had seen a series of beaver-ponds which he thought
he might use. So they reversed the procedure, left the
canoes on the spit of land and carried some of the baggage.

The mile-long riffle chattered along the base of a steep
bank on its southern side. It was easier to stumble
through the shallows than to scramble along the slope.
No one knew what Red planned, though he kept climbing
to look at the extensive ponds that clustered beyond the
bank. This high ridge declined to a low crumbling limestone scaur at the point where the riffle smoothed off into
dark water. The limestone had gaps in it which were
moist, black and overgrown with coarse plants. Poplars
grew everywhere and, like repeated gunshots, they heard
the slaps of beaver-tails from the ponds beyond.

Red chose a fifteen-foot gap, filled over the years with
roots, reeds, dead trees and black mud. This rotted debris
was built in many levels, the top one speckled with pale,
fresh-cut bolts of softwood. The beavers were still busy.

They'd soon be busier for the humans ripped a hole in
the dam big enough to ensure that the heavy flow of water
would do the rest. Calvin and Red raced back. The clear
water was now muddy and the level was rising. The

canoes floated nicely and were loaded with the long sticks hung with strips of bear-meat. The fawn was bored with these activities and disappeared for a while. When they rejoined the girls the beavers, with what seemed like admirable deliberation, were beginning to repair the damage.

They left them to it, packed their baggage and were about to set off when Calvin found he'd forgotten his writing-case. He remembered clearly the crotch of the choke-cherry tree where he had put it the night before. It was the change of plan, the hurried packing that made him forget. He wouldn't take long.

At that moment they saw distant smoke to the north – a cooking-fire, they thought.

Red offered to go with him but there was the faintest tinge of irony in his voice so Calvin decided to go alone.

Because they'd seen the smoke, Calvin was careful. He didn't splash his way downstream. He loaded Brown Bess and took a short-cut south threading the sparse forest that grew on the high southern bank.

He approached the spit of land with caution and examined it from the hill. It was as they'd left it. He saw the place where they'd slept. He saw the ring of white ashes. He saw the high tangle of blackberries with the roses pouring into them – very early, a protected south-facing bank. Growing from the shadow was the stubby trunk of the choke-cherry. He scrambled down the slope.

He couldn't be sure about the mahogany box till he was very close; it was almost the colour of the bark. But it was where he'd left it. He put it under his arm and the smell of roses was so rich as to crowd out the air.

He mustn't waste time. He regained the top of the high bank and started for the beaver-ponds. Then he looked back.

Over the tops of the trees he could see the stretch of deep water below the riffle. It curved in from his left towards the spit of land. Yesterday it was dark and clear. Now it was brown with mud. In the middle, moving quickly, a canoe with two paddlers had almost reached the place.

If he'd come to collect his case ten minutes later—

He recognised the hopping of his heart as an old reflex, to be disregarded. And the canoe couldn't be interpreted to mean that they were being followed – except that it slowed, drew in and was beached where their own canoes had been beached.

Why hadn't he brought his glass? He'd like a closer look at the two young men. What happened next was a shock and he went cold. It wasn't until two minutes later that he recognised this old familiar sensation. From the shadow under the blackberries crawled two other young men who leaned against the choke-cherry tree which had held his writing-case all last night. The young men from the canoe joined them and they chatted for a little while before moving towards the lower end of the riffle.

The figures were small with distance but they were identically equipped – shoulder-length hair, yellowish doe-skin breech cloths, yellowish headband, moccasins, stout bows and quivers of arrows. Their uniform appearance and the fact that they carried no muskets was sinister because it was unusual.

They stood in bright sunlight for some time watching the river – watching the *mud* in the river?

The question was, of course, how long the two young men had been hiding under the blackberries.

All night?

And had their friends joined them by appointment?

He must warn Red and the others. He took a quick step, changed his mind and turned back to watch the four young Indians again. The water in the riffle was already clearer and the flooding was finished. He could make better time on the high ground than they could if they tried to haul the canoes up the river which was again shallow.

The sun had swung into afternoon. He felt hungry and a mosquito had found him.

There was something really unexpected about seeing four strong young Indians, all of an age, with identical clothes and equipment. Why?

There was no doubt now in his mind. They were being followed. But why?

The four Indians piled into the canoe and Calvin heard faint sounds of laughter. They couldn't hope to paddle up the shallow water—

They didn't. They swung left and swiftly, with the current that would carry them round the loop and westward, they diminished and disappeared.

Calvin, holding his writing-case, plodded east. He could catch occasional flashes of light from the beaver ponds ahead of him. The air felt heavy and was filled with the subdued mutter of the riffle which he couldn't see.

He should, he supposed, have examined the spit of land carefully after the four young men had left. Red, or an Indian, or even the girls, might have learned something about them. Had they been there, in position and spying, all through the night? Not likely. But his thoughts were desperate because nothing seemed to make sense. Yet there must be reasons! There must be reasons unless things just happened and had no causes.

5

A Gift Given

*'Give a white man food and
you've fed your murderer'*

Longhair

KITTYPET, Moonluck and Red all found his earnest efforts
funny.

'Two of those Indians could have been there all night!'

'But why?' asked Red. 'Why should they sit all night
watching us sleep and then paddle away in the morning?'

Calvin fumbled about for a reason. 'They only had
bows and arrows,' he said.

Red wasn't impressed. 'Why didn't they steal our guns
while we were asleep?'

Calvin leaned forward and his intensity increased.
'That's what I mean. If they were just thieves they would
have. They're following us.'

When Calvin had reached the others after retrieving
his writing-case he'd found them fidgety. What took him
so long? Had he lost himself? Had he slept well? He let
them go on nagging at him for a few moments before he
exploded his bombshell. It proved to be a squib.

He was hungry and they'd saved some food for him,
but they were hard to convince. Their remarks made him
hot because of the ancient charge of being scared of
Indians. The pickerel they gave him caused interruptions
too. It was bony and he'd have to stop in the middle of a

115

sentence to keep from swallowing sharp spines his tongue had missed. Into these pauses they'd slip their foolish ripostes.

He ploughed on, however. He'd use their scorn to increase his calm. He went over the points with precision, imitating the manner of a lawyer he'd once heard.

'Those four Indians weren't the first thing. The day I met you you let me aim Martha and I saw some elder-blossom move.'

'That was weeks ago.'

'You said does were moving about more.'

'So they are.'

'Then I heard a cough or something and I went to see and it was a porcupine rubbing itself, but—'

'What?'

'It could have been a cough.'

They laughed, all of them.

'What about the ox-bow – the dandelions – the flattened grass?'

'Deer,' said Red.

'Those four Indians were too interested in our camp,' Calvin insisted.

'Then why did they turn round and go home?'

'I don't know.'

'Anyway, no tribe would waste that much time on two sour women.'

Calvin gave up, but was dimly aware of two contrary attitudes: that Red thought he was wrong, and that Kitty-pet and Moonluck protested because they were afraid he was right.

They finished their meal but made no plans. Calvin took his glass and wandered away disgusted to look at the muddy shores of the connected ponds, much of their water drained away. Kingfishers and herons were busy in the shallows and muskrats could be seen round every bend. Only two beavers were now working, but the level

116

of the water was rising and by evening there would be great activity.

Red joined him and showed him what Martha could do with a bigger charge. Calvin couldn't understand why he should waste time and powder on this demonstration, but he took out his glass, lay down behind the same log as Red and focused on a brilliant white ring round a half-cut poplar nearly a mile away. For some reason his hands trembled a little, which was absurd since he was only holding the telescope, not a gun. Also Red hadn't loaded yet.

Red used a scrap of calico to clean the barrel and let the fine powder flow into the muzzle. Then he put three measures from the primer in as well. He tore and folded the blackened piece of calico, wetting it slightly with excess oil from the lock, and made a thick wad which he rammed home, giving the lock a sharp tap between each stroke of the polished ramrod. He wanted a perfect ball and let a few dribble back into the leather bag before he found it. He pared it in two places with his knife, fitted the ball to the muzzle and was satisfied. It was a hair too large. He forced it in with the butt of the knife, then finished the loading with the ramrod. Towards the end of the stroke the ball slid gently down the rifled barrel.

Calvin was curious to see that he left the ramrod in while he lay down and aimed.

'Did you notice anything about those bears?' asked Red.

Calvin, expecting the shot, was concentrating through his telescope on the white hour-glass patch of the poplar. He looked up in surprise.

'What about them?'

But Red had uncovered the priming-pan and was filling the touch-hole. The preliminary aiming had been a flourish intended to make sure the ball was tight in the rifling. The dispensing release on the powder-horn had put remarkably little powder in the pan.

'The looser the powder the quicker the flash,' he said.

'What about the bears?'

The muzzle of the rifle was slightly raised and it took the full length of Red's arm to extract the ramrod after a final tap. It was pulled out carefully and laid aside. The stock was pulled into his shoulder, he adjusted his legs and his elbows and finally lowered the muzzle.

'Ready?' he asked.

Calvin lay down and put the glass to his eye hurriedly. He'd barely focused it on a particularly broad white tooth-mark when he heard the click, the hiss and the bang. A chip flew from near the tooth-mark. He had the absurd notion that the tree was going to fall. It didn't, but a sliver of white wood had been chipped off. The target was only about six inches across. The distance was enormous.

'My God!' said Calvin, and the remark was only partly blasphemous.

Red smiled and began cleaning up his gun. He pointed to a faintly smouldering leaf five feet along the log which a spark from the touch-hole had lit.

'The bears didn't carry that honey,' he said, slowly. 'I didn't see a honey-tree. I certainly didn't see two. But there were two trails – bears, flies, butterflies. Someone made the trails, both leading to the camp.'

'Why?'

'Well, what happened?'

'We got a bear.'

'The girls have no guns. The bears could have done some damage.'

'Whoever did it didn't know about us.'

'Or knew we were away. Or meant it as a joke. The four you saw were all boys?'

'Young men.'

118

This was different. Red was perfectly calm, but what he said made everything momentously different.

'The only thing that worries me,' he went on, with a half laugh, 'is that we've seen nobody. A hundred miles and we've seen nobody. Yet I haven't heard of any big meeting. I haven't heard of any gathering of tribes. No big parley.'

'What does that mean? What might it mean?'

Red shook his head and examined the oily scrap of calico. It was foolish to waste it. He wrapped it round the ramrod.

'I don't know. We'd better go back. Don't talk about it.'

'Why not?'

'For a while anyway.'

They went a quarter of a mile before Red spoke again.

'Neither of those girls is a real squaw. Neither of them would be happy.'

Calvin thought Red was probably right but he couldn't discover a definite reason, nor could he think of it as their business. The girls were Indians. Whatever they'd done, they'd done. Leaving a husband would be, in Berwick, a serious sin, almost worse than a criminal act, but out here—

They'd hauled their canoes to a mudbank by the biggest of the ponds and Red stopped to look at them. He was still wondering what to do. He looked along the river, then his eyes swept south.

At that moment Calvin found the final proof. All the ramifications didn't leap to his mind at once, but there was Red's canoe in front of him, he'd seen it for weeks, a hundred times, on the water, on the beach, bottom upwards – and it had no keel!

No strong split sapling was bound to the bottom to take up some of the wear of beaching.

119

The canoe used by the four Indians had a keel. Calvin began sputtering.

'The canoe – you have no keel – neither have I. The Indians this morning had a keel, and when I met you – that one had a keel.'

'What are you talking about?'

'The day I met you – I thought it was you!'

'What?'

'The canoe!'

'What canoe?'

'I thought *you* paddled along to see me while I was asleep.'

'No. Next day.'

'That canoe had a keel. I saw the mark. I'm sure.'

'Didn't you notice it then?'

'No. I thought it was you. I didn't pay attention. But the mark wasn't the mark of your canoe.'

Red thought about it. Calvin stared at him. Moonluck came towards them with a goose she'd caught on a line.

'Get the fire going. I'm hungry,' said Red.

Moonluck went, but Calvin was aware that she'd seen strangeness in their attitude. Normally they didn't stand for several seconds looking at nothing.

Another point clicked into place. Maybe it was the curious comprehending glance of Moonluck as she went away. Calvin remembered the evening, so long ago now, which he thought was going to be his last evening with his new friends. They lay in a row on the big cedar bed. It had been Moonluck who suggested that they should go with him to the south. She was supposed to be anxious to rejoin her people in the north, yet she seemed delighted with the change of plan, and they had agreed.

But the point was that the suggestion had been made almost immediately after Calvin had asked about the visit in the night and had said definitely that the mark of the canoe had been on the beach that morning. Was there significance in the timing? Had the sudden knowledge of the pre-dawn canoe stimulated the change in Moonluck's plans? He concentrated so deeply on this curious problem that, when Red spoke, Calvin didn't catch what he said.

'I think we should go south.' Red repeated his opinion decisively.

'I do too,' said Calvin, and he noted that Red's decision was based, not on speculation about Moonluck's hidden purposes – nothing had been said about these – but simply on his growing conviction that someone, for many weeks now, had been following them.

'If anyone is following us,' he said, 'they'll go on up the river. We'll gain a day, maybe two. We might lose them.'

In his relief that Red finally agreed with his own conviction, Calvin dismissed Moonluck's sudden change of plans so long ago.

They'd have to conceal the marks of the halt, hide the canoes, pack for a journey on foot; Red thought the big lake couldn't be farther away than one day's march.

Now that Red agreed with him Calvin felt grown-up, tolerant and generous. They should make their preparations without telling the girls the real reason.

'Why?' asked Red.

'They're women. It'll upset them.'

But he was wrong on two counts. The change of plan couldn't be concealed; the girls caught on instantly and were very helpful. And neither seemed upset by the reason for the change, though they still scorned the notion that they were being followed, or said they did.

While they worked that afternoon Calvin returned to the puzzle he'd not mentioned to Red. He watched Moonluck carefully. He caught her in silences out of which she broke with effort. Was there something relevant she knew that they didn't know? Was it something she'd learned recently, or something she'd known for a long time?

Calvin was wrong on another matter, and it was Moon-luck who directed them. They didn't try to conceal the marks of their temporary halt, they made new marks by starting up-river in the ordinary way. Then they drifted back and regained the beaver-pond along the bed of the diminishing stream. The four Indians had seen the flood of muddy water, so there was nothing to be lost by trampling through the tangle of the beaver-dam. When the canoes were reloaded and they floated in the pond the temporary increase in the flow of water had already obliterated any new traces and, after an evening's work by the beavers, the water-level would be raised by several inches, hiding everything.

The series of ponds took them south about a mile, where they found swampy country between them and a long low rise, dense with hardwoods. The swamp itself was edged with a thick tangle of willow, elder and sumac. At one place stumpy cedars held wide flat branches out over channels of black water and the hummocks of sedges. There'd probably been a fire. The cedars were thick, short and tangled; they would hide anything, especially if it were raised above eye-level. With much heaving the canoes were lifted, upturned and stowed where, from three yards, they were invisible. Some of their gear they cached.

They carried the sticks of drying bear-meat with them, and Calvin's writing-box. It was late when they started and they didn't get far. They were tired, and the endless rise to the south seemed endlessly the same. The ground here was clay, covered evenly with an undisturbed layer of dun brittle leaves. Widely splayed roots from fat trunks tripped them, and the trunks were not only thick but tall, lost in a green gloom. Flecks of sun might speckle the drifts of leaves at noon but at evening only the top branches were washed by direct rays.

They could hear the whine of wind in the high leaves. The ground rose and levelled off. A few saplings, incredibly thin, grew here, and a few pale plants, the leaves of which were veined with white. A family of squirrels began to follow them, chirruping in what was so obviously a language that answers seemed called for; but the language was unknown, private and peculiar to these forests.

They followed the compass south. When the ground began to incline slightly in that direction they stopped, too tired to continue. The worst, they thought, was over and the journey next day would be all down hill.

They found a great root upraised and in the hollow it left when the tree had fallen – it must have fallen decades ago since the root was clean as picked bone – brittle leaves were drifted against the flat wall to a depth of three feet. If they scraped to within an inch of the ground they would find layers of moist, black and matted leaves smelling of mushrooms, but the top layers were dry.

One fat birch provided a wide cylinder of bark which hid the light of the fire. Smoke would not be seen at night. Moonluck and Kittypet made a stew of bear-meat. Slices of brown fungus mollified the peppery flavour of some crinkle-root they found. Calvin, as usual, was distrustful of the fungus, but the smell was appetising, he was hungry, and if he died of poison the girls would die first because they ate faster.

Until they pissed on the fire to put it out there were no loud or suspicious sounds. They slept to the mewling of a wind they couldn't feel.

Next day was the same. Calvin touched the trees near his trail and when his count reached a hundred he figured he'd walked a mile. Their trail would be easy to follow.

There was no way to avoid that. One person might, for a short distance, conceal a trail over such ground, not four. The leaves floated each fall from the branches and stayed where they fell. They appeared to have been there for ever, undisturbed even by wind. They weren't easy to walk through. You lifted your feet high to diminish the noise, which tired your knees. You walked normally and no foreign sound could penetrate the heavy rustling.

At one point they stopped and Red climbed part way up a tree suitably placed to allow him a half-clear vista for a quarter of a mile along their back-trail. They were silent for twenty minutes. They heard no voices, no sound of pursuing footsteps, no suspicious flight of birds, only the creeping stillness. They went on.

Mist began to collect. By mid-afternoon it was thick in the upper branches. An hour later the whitish beech-boles could be seen soaring into it. By evening it reached the ground and they could hope to see no more than a hundred yards. When the sun dropped and the mist was no longer half-luminous, visibility was down to a hundred feet. During the long evening – it was June now – it dropped to fifty.

They must have walked for twenty miles. The air was colder and their packs were heavy. They were following a small stream of clear water which moved without sound along a shallow gutter of sodden black leaves. Sometimes a drift of brittle leaves covered the stream completely. Only occasionally a broken branch had formed a miniature dam and they could hear a pouring sound.

Moonluck had disappeared. No one saw her go. Probably she didn't go. Probably she'd just veered a little when no one noticed, and their trails diverged. Should they shout? They argued in low voices. It was evening. She'd been with them not long before. When she realised she'd wandered away from them she'd follow her own trail back until she found the spot where the trails

124

divided, then catch up. There'd been no sign of pursuers all day. They'd probably lost them – if they were being followed. But it would be foolish to shout.

'Have you no signals?' asked Red.

Kittypet said 'Ah!' and made a faint enquiring sound with her lips and teeth, exactly like a wren. She did it again. A wren answered and flew within three feet of them. They could hear it chirring before it streaked in out of the mist. Its intention obviously was to land on the stump that was Kittypet. When it realised its mistake it rose vertically on loud wings, rasping its own noisy warning, and disappeared in an instant. They'd seen it for only a second or so, but they heard the warning racing through the forest, echoing, first here, then there, for what seemed like minutes. They might as well have shouted.

No. The wren could have been frightened by a weasel, by anything. The wren, at worst, could be only a hint; a shout would have provided proof.

They continued to follow the little stream. The mist was growing thicker. Formerly, when it swirled, they could recognise trunks of trees at twenty feet. Now, on rare occasions, they could reach out a hand and touch a trunk they'd not observed. Calvin had the curious feeling that sometimes he could *hear* the presence of a tree ahead of him. They went slowly, testing each step. The light was almost gone. Before it went completely Calvin brought the compass from his pocket.

They were going north.

He stopped the others and pointed. It was the stream, of course. It paid no attention to the compass, only the slope of the land; and, in the mist, they'd followed it. It could take them anywhere. They'd better stop till morning.

They sat down where they were and waited for the long-continued rustle that would announce Moonluck's arrival. They leaned their backs against a beech. The mist seemed a little thinner. They could see for about five yards. After the roar of feet through leaves their ears were now aching with listening. Their eardrums felt cold.

Was it possible that a cloud of mist could hiss as it trailed over the leaves?

An arrow thunked into the beech bole they leaned against. The head was buried in the corky bark and the shaft hummed for a couple of seconds. When the hum was no longer audible the grey feathers vibrated spasmodically as does a shot rabbit's tail, sometimes, just before it dies.

Red quietly lifted his rifle but no one else moved. They couldn't see what they'd be moving from, so there was no point in moving. And there was no sound of movement from the mist. It was a time to wait through. They could see nothing, they could hear nothing. They were so tense they wondered if muscles would ever again respond or if they were now congealed to gristle.

The arrow stuck straight from the tree above their heads. Whoever shot it could, just as easily, have shot one of them; but Calvin read it, for some reason, not as an attack but as a signal of attack to come. The fact that the arrow was almost horizontal suggested that the bowman was close.

The pervasive grey deepened but took hours to become dark. It was impossible to tell how long they waited. Calvin noticed that Kittypet's eyes weren't focused; that she gazed on nothing, and that her face had fallen into lines of resignation he'd never seen there before. She looked much older. Red sat beyond her and he was just a shadow against the darker shadow of the forest so no expression could be seen, though the attitude was one of close and still attention.

126

Calvin was waiting for an owl to hoot, for wolves to howl, or for painted savages to coagulate from the mist. None of these things happened, but the beech trunk at his back was the only comfort. Not the only one. They had guns. He wondered if they shouldn't explore, or hide, or— He turned his head to voice his thought and saw the shadow of Red's hand rise from the stock of his rifle to silence him. He went back to the painful and pointless business of listening to the creeping mist.

Calvin felt a slight movement under his knee. A leaf moved, and then another. He couldn't see, but that's what it sounded like. Then he felt the weight of a small coin travel along his leg. The fabric of his trousers was slightly pulled. He moved his hand. The mouse squeaked once and dived into the lapping leaves. The rustle died away. He turned his head and again Red signed for silence.

He thought he heard something. It sounded like the whirr of a night-hawk's wings at some distance.

Again he waited and began to detect occasional sounds of breathing. His own? His friends'? Or someone else's? He closed his mouth and breathed more deeply and more slowly through his nose. He opened his mouth again – there was a tacky sound. You could hear better with your mouth open. Again the peculiar whirr of wings. How could a bird, even a night-hawk, see to fly in this mist? He'd heard no hooting of owls.

Was the mist clearing? Just a little? What would be disclosed when the mist did finally clear? Four young Algonquins, each with a narrow headband? It was possible that one of them had seen a movement – it could have been Red, Kittypet or himself – and had thought it the movement of a deer, a bear or— But if so, why the silence? And why no search for their arrow? The noise it made when it struck the tree would have been audible for some distance. The head was completely buried in the

127

hard wood. It was a good straight arrow, well-feathered and not to be lost without a search.

Again the night-hawk sound and Kittypet raised her head. Kittypet's lips pushed forward a little and a breath came out, fluttering the tongue. It was a similar sound. It might even sound identical at a distance.

Kittypet's flutter was answered. Red patted her knee and she pushed her face into his shoulder.

The three looked left simultaneously. Then Calvin saw Red shake his head as if in exasperated uncertainty. If the night-hawk was Moonluck – and who else could it be on a night when no real night-hawk would dare to fly? – Kittypet's answer was drawing her into danger. Or might she not, because she'd used the night-hawk's whirr, be aware of the danger already? Of this new and positive danger? Or simply of the danger they'd feared all day? What to do? How to warn her?

It was useless anyway. The silent archer who had shot their beech-tree would know the night-hawk whirr, and would probably have heard footsteps rustling in the leaves. Maybe that was it. Maybe the arrow was to pin them down so Moonluck could join them and the archer would have them all together in a group.

If so he achieved his purpose. She didn't make much noise but her approach was audible from some distance. The rustling stopped, Kittypet made the whirring sound again and the approach resumed. It was all useless; their enemy knew each move. Nevertheless they played out the game and, when Moonluck loomed, a darker patch of mist, a few feet away, they spoke in low tones. Moonluck was exhausted.

She flung the stick with the strips of dried meat on the leaves, shifted her pack and slipped it to the ground. Only then did Calvin realise that no one else had unburdened himself. He squirmed out of his shoulder-straps and Red did the same. Moonluck looked at the arrow in the tree.

128

She could barely reach it. Red took the shaft in one hand.

'Get the head,' said Moonluck. Her voice was low but she didn't whisper.

'Why?'

'Give me your knife.'

She took Calvin's knife and stuck it into the crack in the bark below the arrow. Red thrust his heavy knife into the crack above it. He hammered the knives in with the cushion of his palm but this was not enough. He took his hatchet. The sound of the blows was shatteringly loud and foolish to Calvin but the two knives relieved the pressure on the arrowhead until it could be eased out. Then the knives had to be extracted but that was easier since the blades were strong enough to stand the leverage.

'I need to see,' said Moonluck, her voice already losing its caution. 'But—'

'But—' began Kittypet.

'You two go over there; we'll go over here.'

A distraction, thought Calvin.

Red and Moonluck disappeared into the mist to the left. Calvin and Kittypet ploughed the noisy leaves to the right, then turned. They saw a light flare up briefly, then heard Moonluck laugh, a low, surprising sound.

They were together again.

'It's the Flyer's arrow,' said Moonluck.

Kittypet grabbed it and tried to see. 'He bought six iron arrowheads—'

'Your brother?' asked Calvin.

'Yes,' said Kittypet.

'I watched him make them,' said Moonluck. 'He made them very well. He bound them carefully. The shaft didn't split, even hitting hard wood.'

Red didn't understand it at first.

'He thinks he's The Joker,' said Moonluck.

Kittypet agreed and began to explain. 'He's always playing at it,' she said. 'He's only a boy. He's not very tall. He doesn't get on with my father. He likes tricks and jokes. The only time he's happy is when he's playing at being The Joker.'

And next morning, after consultations with Moonluck which were alternately solemn and hilarious, Kittypet played out the game – all mysterious to Red and Calvin. First she made a special cake of maize in the shape of her brother's totem. This was the Flying Hawk, a jagged shape, and of the three she made only one remained unbroken. She then chose a flat boulder and made a circle on it with sand. In this she placed the cake and the arrow. Then they hid. While they waited Kittypet whispered the story of how her graceless brother tricked strangers with a white man's glove. He stuffed the little finger full of moss, put the glove on and held it up as if he had all his fingers. Then he chopped off the little finger and gave the strangers a terrible shock. Oh, the Flyer was wanton and knavish, but she liked him.

At noon the mist began to clear. The fawn came back as if it had never been away. It licked Red's hand, nudged the others and lay down, panting. Strong puffs, as of steam, came from its nose.

They still couldn't see far but they heard clearly the rustle of branches and some laughter. The fawn lifted its head.

When they went to the flat boulder the cake and the arrow were gone. The Joker had been recognised and placated. The gift was accepted. The cloud was lifted.

But, before the mist cleared completely and their long time of strain effervesced into joy, Calvin gained a curious impression.

Kittypet was understandably bubbling with happiness, but it was Moonluck who seemed the more relieved. A natural fear had been lifted from Kittypet. It was as if the burden lifted from Moonluck had been close to mortal terror.

130

Why?

Especially as Moonluck must have suspected something like this! She must have suspected it because, when she rejoined them after being lost and saw the arrow, she went straight to it. She knew it was the Flyer's arrow even before she examined it. Calvin was sure of that.

And if she knew why was her relief so tremendous?

And could such a relief be produced by anything other than the removal of a terror so gruesome—

Round and round. And all foolish, all nonsense, all superstition. A waste of mental effort to try to understand.

Mr Colethorpe called them 'simple children'.

6

A Gift Received

*'Pontiac's was the strongest
Name in the Society'*

Longhair

THE RELIEF spilled over the next few days but it was
raised to a pitch of high excitement by the surprises of
that afternoon. It was to be some time before Calvin
understood – or felt he understood – the significance of
the Joker, the arrow and the gift of the cake, but he was
never completely to understand the processes by which
the world could suddenly become, quite simply, marvellous.

They thought a light wind was shifting the mist. They
couldn't see pine trees anywhere near but they could hear
them; though, in such gentle breeze, the low dry sound
never rose to a sustained and musical note.

As the sun strengthened the mist attenuated. Ragged
gaps appeared and crawled northwards, then these rifts
joined up leaving only patches and threads of vapour
snaking through a park-like valley which swung in a
perfect curve between two green hills to the south. They
followed the curve, but, when they reached it, the curtain
beyond the hills was still blank and blinding. Then the
white disc of sun burned through more often. The curtain
thinned and lifted as it thinned. They saw a silver beach
and they knew the sound they heard was not the sound of

133

pines but of little waves foaming towards them. In a minute or two the curtain-cloud trailed its torn fringe over their heads, revealing the limitless, pale blue water sparkling to its invisible pale blue south horizon. Though the line where lake met air could not be located, the mist they'd been in was the last cloud to leave that wide sky. Four blue herons laboured up, rowed a hundred yards across the wind and moored themselves again, two feet above the water.

Grass banks thinned into sand unmarked except by the herons. The little stream they'd been following cut clean curves through the sand-bar and the main channel glittered with racing schools of shiners. The four humans splashed across the stream and the million minnows poured under the floating foam-lines where the waves broke.

Four trout, each must have weighed eight pounds, beached themselves in the shallow water in their effort to reap the harvest. Three of these were pin-wheels of glittering silver on the white sand till they could slide under the gleaming curve of the next wave and flash again to a safer part of their own element.

The fourth was flapping violently from Moonluck's outstretched hand. She tied it in a deep shadowed pool, then she shed her clothes and joined the others in the limpid water. The fawn raced along the beach and back again, charged an advancing wave and butted it, leaped the next one, then grew frightened of the third and beat it to the shore by a wide margin. She then began to graze on the terrace of short grass that grew above high water mark.

The humans were far out beyond the white water. The water and the light were so clear they could lie and watch the shifting ripples on the bottom three fathoms below them. They could see their four shadows move there and a small school of whitefish came lazily to look at them on their way along the coast. An otter chased the whitefish, and they raced away like rockets. The otter saw the humans and rose to watch them. He swam all around them twice, lithe and curious, trailing a few bright bubbles when he dived, then he went about his business.

When you lay on your back you could see the water-lit undersides of the gulls sweep by, turning their heads to stare. A large flock of mallards flew over them paying no attention and making noise enough to show they feared nothing in this open place.

Turning on his belly Calvin thought he saw the six-foot shadow of a sturgeon just at the edge of vision. He could have been mistaken. Moonluck was the best swimmer and she dived beneath him towards the shadow, a flame of liquid gold adrift against the rippling sand. Then, curving, she surfaced. Calvin was thirsty. He opened his mouth and drank. He drank a great deal and, momentarily, thought that the water tasted of sunlight.

A current had moved them slowly west and when they went ashore they saw the sculptured cliffs of pale clay above the beach. The cliffs rose a few hundred feet to a lace of thin birches and, where springs had formed a crevice, the wet patches gleamed like mirrors in the sun. They felt the warmth reflected from these cliffs and the glittering drops of water runnelled down their skin and quickly dried. At a few places they saw washed patches of dark purple in the sand. Calvin was reminded of the splash of purple among the white flowers. Curious. Purple there and purple here, staining white sand—

A terrace of harder clay projected towards the water. They climbed the water-carved and rounded steps that led to it and in the middle of the small plateau there was a pool, flat and shiny as stretched grey satin. The wet surface was almost hot.

A great deal of experiment with toes and hands went on until they were in the pool up to their knees. It was like wading in lumpless porridge. The warmth was marvellous. Then, a few inches deeper, the pool was icy cold. You could move only slowly, as in some dreams. The clay was liquid but very heavy. You could lie on it and sink only an inch or so.

They grew bolder. The bottom seemed hard, although it was so slippery it gave them no purchase. You could walk slowly and forever in the same place. If you could get in up to the waist, your feet not touching bottom, the clay would support you. Then you could hold yourself rigid and see how long it would be before you toppled slowly to one side.

It was Moonluck, her hair now unbraided, who first stood on her hands on the bottom and let her weight force her into the clay head first. She came out looking sinister, and startling, and beautiful. They all followed her example. The clay was so smooth that when they touched in the small pool it was like the touch of a tongue on the inside of a cheek. They moved slowly against each other, oil against oil.

Their feet were freezing and they climbed out. They stood in a row drying in the breeze and the sun. At first the breeze was cold, then they felt the most curious sensation as the clay turned slowly paler. Their skin was being drawn. Not an inch of their bodies was insensitive. Each nerve was most subtly extended to take in rare and new sensations.

They turned in the sun to dry more evenly and soon they were four statues from some antique city. Hard shadows and highlights were moderated by the matt surface of the now whitish clay. If they moved the clay cracked. Presently they were crazed like old china and they looked, Calvin thought, less like four statues than four unburied mummies long since dead.

They raced to the lake and as they plunged a pale stain spread out from them.

Then into the clay again. And again. And again. It intoxicated them. They must sense again the extension of feeling that took place as drying clay made new and electric contacts between skin and air and sun.

The clay penetrated every crevice. They went along the shore to splash clean water on navel and nostril. They cleaned each other's ears. Both men rolled back foreskins to sluice every surface. They had new skins, but the clay they washed from their bodies took a long time to settle in the lake. The water for a hundred feet was grey and didn't sparkle.

They sat on the grass of their former terrace and lit a small fire for company. They didn't need it for warmth. The sun shone warmly, though it was far to the west along the coast.

Kittypet, sitting slightly behind Calvin, reached both arms round his waist and cupped his balls in her plump hands. Calvin started, then reached his shoulders back to contact. She swivelled round. He was erect. She lay back and he followed her. They paid no attention to the others or to the fawn. The fawn paid no attention to them. Calvin had the sensation that thrusts were instantly timed to heartbeats, that they became, first irresistible, then out of all control, that bowels, lights, heart and brains melted and bubbled to a living fluid that poured, poured, poured at its own whim, leaving him cool, still and empty. And all within fifty seconds.

Kittypet rolled like a bundle across the grass to Red, who fondled her, then heaved and laid himself with slow deliberation between her legs. She whispered, then whined like a small cat, then moaned as strokes went deeper. Their fucking was a long single slope. His left arm was under her shoulders. His right hand lifted her buttocks and she was suspended there between the earth and him till their pulsing gathered concentration, climbed in power, lifted them steadily to speed and exploded them precisely into their own new orbit of serenity. They were stranded there for a while, wheeling slowly.

She was inert and sleeping. Calvin was inert and mouthing with a lazy mind the thought that life was unpredictable and varied. Later he opened his eyes and, with no self-consciousness at all, watched the curiously formal coupling of Red and Moonluck. Each minute of that slow hour was different and intense. He didn't find himself excited watching them. The feeling was more like awe. And he loved them both, he thought. Each gesture they made, each attitude they assumed, had a fulness that crammed meaning on top of meaning – none new, but none forgotten and all created at this instant. He was watching an intensity of living which became creation. The thoughts were shapeless and cloudlike. A good was not to be clung to. Not to be retained or even sustained. It must be created. Then there was no such thing as an old good thing. All good things were new.

And between Red and Moonluck there was nothing not in its essence good. But it was a feeling, not an argument.

Towards dawn – they were now between blankets on soft sand – Kittypet took Calvin again. He was instantly alert. He'd been dreaming and was erect, which is why she took him; but she was kindly rather than demanding, and gentled him slowly. He was beginning to know the feel of her and to be more confident that ecstasy could be depended upon. Her breasts and her belly and the warm soft bulge between her thighs were worth deliberate, not frenzied, attention. The dawn light helped. It came from behind the hill on their left and was reflected from the pale blue emptiness of sky and water which contained no visible living thing. Not even the first gull was yet awake. Calvin was as brown as Kittypet, or she as pale as he. They merged in the curious light and their hands were uncertain, sometimes, which of them they

138

touched. It was a quiet fuck and very happy. They slept again.

Next day Red and Calvin were suddenly made aware of a violent quarrel. Things were going on they didn't know about. Kittypet was beating her fists against Moonluck's breast.

'It's your fault and I wish I'd never found you.' Kittypet burst into tears. 'Don't you see? It's because it's too good!'

They were unaware of the two men. Moonluck held the weeping girl by the shoulders. At each short phrase she shook her once.

'You're a baby. You said it first. You asked me to help you. You said run away, run away. You said you'd never marry. Not that man, you said. You cried then too. You want everything. You cry when you get it. You're a baby.'

'I wish you'd never come. I wish I'd never met you. I wish I'd never asked you to live with us.'

'Then go back,' said Moonluck. 'Do what your father says. Marry that man.'

'I won't!'

'Then stop crying.'

'It's all your fault.'

Calvin saw on the ground a piece of one of the discarded cakes baked as an offering to the Joker. Maybe it reminded Kittypet too touchingly of the little brother she had mothered for so many years. More probably the quarrel was a delayed reaction to the exhaustion and final terror of the dark journey through the hardwood forest. And at some time, Calvin knew, everyone regrets a decision and wants to turn back to a peaceful time when no decisions were necessary. In some ways Moonluck was right; Kittypet was a baby.

139

'You don't know what a terrible man my father can be,' said Kittypet. 'Always politics.'

'All the more reason to run away,' said Moonluck.

'My brother likes me. He's funny and he likes me. How do I know your people will like me?'

'Because I say so.'

'You never got to know my brother,' said Kittypet gloomily.

'I did, and he's silly.'

'He isn't. He likes me.'

'He's silly. He hangs on to old ways. "The Joker!" What's "the Joker?" It's a story. Bows and arrows all the time. Tricks. Games. Ceremonies!'

'He's not silly.' Kittypet was not protesting so much as indulging in gloom.

'He is.'

'Why did he leave with my cake? Why didn't he stay? Why didn't he talk to me? He could have talked to me!'

'Of course he could,' said Moonluck, 'but he's silly. His game is too important. He likes his game more than people – more than you. I don't like people who hang on to old ways, or people who live in a game.'

In contradiction Calvin suddenly remembered the night they decided to start south, the short trick arrow in Moon-luck's doe-skin bag, and the bag of blood made of red earth and duck-oil. That was a game too, wasn't it? But he kept the question to himself.

Though the former violence was guttering to an argument the girls were still absorbed in their quarrel and, since it was largely unintelligible to Red and Calvin, they decided to take a walk. If they hung about they might learn something, but curiosity couldn't reconcile them to involvement.

They suspected a cause which they didn't wish to discuss. They were always uncertain that they understood how Indians felt about things. Calvin knew he couldn't be the object of jealousy so he didn't want to talk about it. Red knew that he could be so he was embarrassed to talk about it. Or was this just the thinking of white men? Red had come to the conclusion that white people's uncertainty about the feelings of Indians was close to the root of their troubles. He recognised a sad sequence – apart from deliberate villainy – misunderstanding, then fear, then hatred, causing more misunderstanding.

Individuals might out-flank this sequence – Moonluck might – but where could they then 'fit in'? Nowhere. There was also misinterpretation. Red laughed suddenly.

'Moonluck thinks white women can do whatever they like,' he said, and Calvin nodded.

'Independent,' he said, 'very strong-minded. She'd be a handful as a wife.'

'Are you thinking of marrying her?'

'No, no, no!' said Calvin, and then more positively, 'No, no.'

They'd covered another fifteen paces before Red summed up.

'Those girls are going to have a bad time.'

Though Calvin agreed he wondered if Red were contributing to the bad time by helping them. But what else could he do? Two women alone? Savages, but women. They'd just dropped in on him but he had to help them. Why, suddenly, had they begun to quarrel?

Calvin patted his pocket to make sure he had his glass with him. They were both panting when they collapsed at the top of a narrow cleft in the clay cliff. It was cooler here on the grass among the birches. Wide cracks meandered near the edge. Platforms of turf were spotted about on the slope to the lake, some still level and carrying a single tree. They dangled their feet into a wide crack.

They were far above the faint haze that clung to the water. The horizon was clear, and many small clouds in

141

the west were waiting their turn to be ferried across the empty sky. Seven miles to the west and at the same distance to the east low headlands, the colour of sage leaves, thrust out into water the colour of forget-me-nots. Far beyond the eastern promontory they could see a vertical combing of thin lines. They used the glass. Smokes from a distant village.

But the eye-catching sight was the brigade half-way between the headlands. The seven big canoes seemed close, but must have been five miles out, maybe more.

Then the glass showed Calvin a man with no head riding in the middle of the second canoe. He focused, and the blunt lump became clearer. The man with no head became a man wearing a tricorne, only one horn of which was still pinched into shape. A unicorn. The rest of the broad brim flopped to his shoulders, hiding face and neck. Such a broad brim would protect his neck from rain but it was very old-fashioned. The man who sat facing him wore a tricorn which was neat, modern, military and British.

But the man with no head – the unicorn?

There was gossip that Mr MacBain wore his hat in a peculiar way. Probably others did too.

But how many independent traders could travel up the lake in a brigade of seven canoes? More likely a Hudson's Bay Company man. A Factor? A superintendent even? Mr MacBain?

And if it were Mr MacBain why meet him? He could travel to Montreal and miss him. He wouldn't have to deliver his letter. He couldn't deliver it. And Mr MacBain's deputy might give him another posting on the basis of his maps.

But the lazy summer was too good and there was no need to hurry.

Where was the brigade going? Detroit? Michilimacinac? Fort Pitt? Sainte Marie? Or this new, enlarged Bruce

142

Factory? Calvin was glad that the canoes were so many miles out of possible contact.

'Light a fire?' asked Red.

'Why?'

'The smoke.'

Calvin's interjections bubbled. No reason to. Important party. Interrupt their journey. Wouldn't thank him. Busy men. Who was he? And that was that. Calvin was surprised to find how little the brigade had excited him, but how relieved he was at the whole summer he saw before him.

'British hat,' said Red, closing the glass.

Maybe it was the hat that started him talking as the canoes proceeded on their way. Red *had* served in the army. He'd done a number of things. They chatted for an hour. An hour should give the girls time to cool down. Calvin felt flattered and interrupted seldom. Red spoke unemotionally, though he had frightening things to say.

He had scouted for Braddock in the attack on Fort DuQuesne. He gave details of the massacre. The mercenaries had deserved what they'd got, in a way, they were so stupid – as were most of their officers. It was that engagement that started Red's dissatisfaction. The feeling took a few years to grow. Finally he signed on no more. Oh, there'd been reason in the beginning, but there was no reason to keep on doing what he found foolish. He leaned back against a birch sapling.

'When I was a boy it never seemed to me that what I did on the farm was foolish. That was because it wasn't foolish. It made sense. We grew our food. We liked the food we grew. If we grew better food we liked it better. Nothing we did was foolish.'

Then he stopped. His lips moved slightly, as if he were counting. Calvin had the distinct impression that a rank of years was passing through his mind and his head shook

143

as the present came in sight. 'But it is foolish to think that a man by himself can feel like a boy in a family.'

Quite suddenly the dead voice became animated and Red, recollecting, went on in a rush.

'We had an uncle. He lived west. On the Ohio. I was sixteen. We heard he was in trouble. I went to help – very sure of myself, wouldn't follow the river, went across country, got sick and got lost. Some Delawares helped me. They found out that my uncle had gone back east. I stayed with them for two years.

'After two years I went home. Everything was burned, and not long before. Not a barn, not a pig-sty left. Just the chimney and the valentine carved in the stone. I found things that belonged to my small brothers and sisters. People said it was some Tuskaroras. I don't know. I went west with a gang of Virginians. We murdered a lot of Indians. Potawatamis. I took a long trip to see my Delawares. They'd been attacked and scattered. A couple of my friends were left but they didn't like me any more. Everything had changed. It was all a surprise to me because my family – and all the families – in Pennsylvania were friendly with the Delawares and they liked us. Some people thought they were a nuisance in the winter but they were no real trouble and some of them were a great help at harvest time. Everything changed.

'Then all the murders and the broken promises – I got tired of the same thing time after time. I've never had any trouble with Indians myself. Not up here and not in the old days.'

'What about this "Longhair"?'

'Oh, him! I saw him with Pontiac at Fort DuQuesne. Later, at Detroit, I heard Pontiac make a big speech. Longhair – he'd begun to grow his hair then – was one of his young men and they sat in the firelight listening and the speech made them all cry. All the trees spoke, and the earth, the sky, the rivers—

144

'I hear Pontiac was murdered last year, somewhere out west. He was a drunk by then. They're still squabbling about who murdered him. My guess is that this Longhair has gone crazy by now.

'This country was pretty empty. Some of the French had left. I figured there'd be no trouble here.'

'Don't you miss your own people?'

'I'll always miss my long-ago family. I miss friends among the Delawares. Don't miss settlers, soldiers or Indians as they are now. Everything's changed. I'm glad to be out of it.'

'You're a hermit.'

'I suppose so.'

'I wouldn't want to be a hermit.'

'I'm ten years older than you are.'

'But don't you ever mean to go back to – to—'

'What is there to go back to? My father started something. It lasted twenty-five years. Now it's gone. It's better here. Empty country. The trouble won't get this far in my life-time.'

Red picked up the glass and focused on the horizon. Calvin knew he wouldn't learn much more about him, but he was wrong. Red spoke again.

'I saw a sergeant stick his bayonet – one of the long ones they used on the long Brown Bess – into an Indian twenty times. The same Indian. A dead Indian. Twenty times. It gets silly.'

And, a moment later, there was one further curious spasm of low speech.

'Maybe I'd feel differently if I'd seen the Tuskaroras – if it was them – kill my brothers and sisters, and father and mother. I was fond of them. I was fond of my friends with the Delawares. I might have liked the Potawatamis I killed. I don't know. There are a great many mad people. I like it better if I don't see too many people. It's not that I don't like them. I do.

'But you can't get away from it; I'm mad, or they're mad. You can't have it both ways; I'm not stupid, but I'm not as bright as my father was. He could understand it. He could even understand me. He'd say you can't live on memories. Yes, that's what he'd say, I can hear him. But what do you do when the memories are far better than anything you see around you, or are likely to see?'

To Calvin this sentiment was unbearably melancholy and he suddenly thought of Red as of someone needing comfort. He felt inadequate. Comfort had to be doleful and he was diligently searching for something suitable in that mood, so he found the laugh that followed the most unexpected sound he'd ever heard.

And it was the right sound. There was no bitterness in it. The amusement was the most genuine and the wide smile the most generous he'd ever seen.

Because it was right Calvin's eyes prickled and there was even a touch of awe in the still constriction of his throat; yet it remained astonishing that he could accept the level sentences calmly but find himself deeply moved by the laughter.

His early training had instructed him that no one is perfect.

They sat for some time looking at the lake. The brigade was almost opposite the western arm enclosing the bay. Experienced canoe-men would not have ventured so far off-shore, if there'd been any but the gentlest of waves.

There was a contradiction. How could Red become at once a more considerable man and a man more in need of help?

The girls had probably stopped fighting by now. They struck inland and came to their former trail along the stream near the bend into the lake. They had great good luck. In a sandy basin they saw three great shadows. Two

146

moved sinuously about, one was almost still. They looked enormous and very dark in colour.

'Get a big piece of bark. Make a pail. Quick.'

Red sat down and began taking off his moccasins. Calvin had some distance to go before he found a big enough birch. He used long hawthorn pins to clip the corners. When he was back Red was wading in the stream not far from the shore. Suddenly he threw himself forward. There was a riotous puffing and splashing until he stood up again, both arms clutching a five-foot fish.

'Bring it here,' he sputtered. 'Hold it under.'

The powerful plated and nubbly fish was thrashing its tail in long sweeps back and forth. If it hadn't been hugged so tightly one sweep might have broken a leg, Calvin thought. A grey ooze dribbled from its pinkish vent. Its long snout was snapping against Red's left shoulder and his right hand pressed on its belly. Calvin caught the spurt of small eggs in the pail he'd made. The sturgeon grew momentarily quieter as Calvin squeezed its belly, gingerly at first, then more firmly. The lumps on its plated skin were not sharp. Calvin couldn't understand Red's excitement. In about a dozen steady strokes they'd collected nearly a pint of the slimy mass. What was it for?

Red let the fish go. The shallow pool was muddy from the struggle and they could trace her course only by the smooth upwellings of water that followed each stroke of the uneven tail. There was great commotion. The other fish were getting out of her way. She surged through the water in a circuitous figure eight and she didn't seem inclined to stop. The upper end of the pool was clearing now and she sent her scoop-shaped bony nose a little further up the shallow riffle at each circuit.

'Too shallow,' said Red, putting on his moccasins.

They didn't wait to see whether she left the pool or not. Calvin wondered how such a big fish could flounce over the sand-bar where the stream entered the lake. He eyed the grey granular jelly in his birch-bark pail and asked aloud what it was for.

'To eat,' said Red. 'Rich people pay three shillings a pound for it.'

'They do?'

'A Russian in Philadelphia told me how to fix it. "Ikra" he called it.'

The sturgeon wasn't the only luck they had that day. When they rejoined the girls they were dragged with great excitement to see a large snapping-turtle helpless on its back. They'd attacked it with two strong branches and it was unwise enough to fasten its beak to one of them, held by Moonluck, who pulled it to shallow water where Kittypet had levered it over.

So they planned the feast.

A feast none of them would ever forget.

First, to deal with the turtle, Moonluck needed Red's hatchet and the large pot, but only a small fire. She put chunks of the half-dried bear-meat in the pot with the remnants of the goose-bones. She added green fat and flesh from the turtle, stalks of mint and yellowish roots of wild garlic. The pot bubbled away all afternoon, the odour growing hourly more appetising.

Next, a big hole in the sand, a big fire in the hole and big stones in the fire, some of them cracking with dangerous explosions. Moonluck went to the clay pool and made an enormous pancake, not too damp and not too dry. The clay and the fire in the hole were for the big trout. It was cleaned, wrapped first in a layer of wild parsley, then in the clay. It made a large, heavy bundle which was placed among the ashes, the hot stones and sand on top.

Red was the only one who knew about 'ikra' and

148

Moonluck protested at the amount of salt he proposed to use.

Kittypet found a patch of small, brown, conical mushrooms with jet black gills which she said were very good. Calvin hoped so, for she put them in the stew. She wandered a long distance hoping to find raspberries but they weren't ripe enough. She did find dozens of mayapples hiding under their individual umbrellas. Only a few had turned colour and were sweet enough to eat as fruit. The green ones were thrown in the stew. The seeds were a nuisance but they'd give flavour. She found one hillside where she picked about a cup of wild strawberries.

The prospect of the feast was so good it was treated with unusual ceremony. Nothing was to be eaten till everything was ready. So they wandered about. They swam. Calvin worked on his map.

He and Red were gradually made aware of how the quarrel had started. Neither of the girls was shy about discussing it. Kittypet was defensive but cheerful. Moonluck was scornful but amused.

Very early in the morning Kittypet had been seized with terror. Immediately afterwards she'd been seized with a sad resignation. Both moods irritated Moonluck.

It was like this:

Kittypet was nibbling at what was left of the broken maize-cake she'd made for her brother. Suddenly she was sure that if he knew where she was, her father must know too. She ran to Moonluck. They must leave at once. They were too close to Detroit here. They must go. They must go north.

Moonluck became judicial – an infuriating attitude since she was a year or so younger than Kittypet – and proceeded to point things out, one after the other: that the Flyer liked to keep secrets, that there'd be no joke in the business of the arrow and the cake if the Flyer had been merely scouting for his father, that he didn't get on well with his father anyway, that scouting for him would be the last thing he'd be likely to do, that he liked Kittypet, that he'd want her to be happy, that if her father had been following them they'd have known it and she'd have been taken home.

Moonluck was urgently out of breath, so she was infuriated when Kittypet made a complete about turn.

'I've always been a good daughter,' said Kittypet. 'I'm going back. I ought to do what my father wants me to.'

'Goodbye!' said Moonluck.

'You don't care,' said Kittypet.

'It's your life.'

'You hate me. You're deserting me. I'll have to go back. You want me to marry that dull man.'

'Nobody's deserting anyone.'

'It's your fault!'

And so on.

One final argument persuaded Kittypet: no one could hate her now because the Flyer had accepted her cake.

And now the quarrel was forgotten and the feast nearly ready. The heap of sand over the trout wrapped in clay was warm. The stew smelled of all its delicious ingredients. The ikra was piled on birch-bark and Calvin was mixing a batter for pancakes. He used a little of the white flour he had left and two partridge-eggs Kittypet had found. Red said you wrapped a portion of ikra in a small pancake.

The shadow of the high cliff was advancing over the beach when the girls announced that the stew would be ready in an hour. They went into the water again, warm from the walking and cooking; Calvin's legs sent messages of intense pain. The day had been brilliant and the flames of the fires invisible. Calvin was startled that invisible flames could sear his skin to such a sore redness. The lake was warm except for the layer of water next to the clean sand bottom. In this cooler water the pain evaporated. They floated idly till the shadow of the cliff enveloped them and the temperature of the air began to fall.

They dried themselves in the still warm sand and brushed it off carefully. Sand could diminish the pleasure of fucking. The sun still shone on the land above the cliffs so the cool air still flowed from the lake. They put on their shirts.

Red was the only one who really enjoyed the blinis and caviare. The others found the salty-fishy taste pleasant but— Did people really pay three shillings a pound for it?

Next the big trout. The clay was baked hard and cracked away in heavy potsherds with crisp patterns lining the hollows. The smell of trout and parsley that steamed up at them was so strong that each of them had to swallow a rush of saliva while the pink flesh was filleted for them by Kittypet. It was overdone – the flakes fell apart – but the flavour was better than the smell. They finished half the fish – nearly a pound per person – so they waited a bit before they tackled the stew.

They were comfortable and cheerful. All Kittypet's gloom had vanished, and Moonluck's impatience, and Red's melancholy.

Dissolved in well-being, Calvin's curtain of secrecy and shame wasn't there any more, but he was surprised when he found himself in the middle of a confession. He had once been terrified of Indians. That's what he found himself saying. He stopped. Then, light-hearted, he went on. He told them about being fired and why. It didn't seem so important now. He said he was sure the whisky jug had had its stopper in. He talked in snatches because the others interrupted so often, finding it funnier than he did. He still remembered terror at the ambush, but he was beginning to remember, with some amusement, Mr Cole-thorpe, and how no expression could settle for long on the red face, how glee changed to disgust, disgust to fury and fury back to triumph.

They asked questions. The whisky was merely incidental. Mr Colethorpe should have taken more satisfaction. His joke proved his point; at once and conclusively.

Suddenly he connected the word joke and the idea of the Joker. It was an interesting notion.

'Maybe the Flyer wasn't chasing Kittypet at all. Maybe he was chasing me. The Indians laughed and howled and split themselves at my wet pants. The story must have got about. They might try it again – or something different. People despise cowards. They love scaring them.'

They considered the idea but shook their heads, Moonluck most definitely.

'That happened hundreds of miles away. Kittypet's father and the Flyer live in the other direction. How could they have heard?'

'Stories travel fast.'

'Stories about important people.'

'Mr Colethorpe's important.'

The others thought this interpretation improbable. Calvin thought of another point—

'So far the scouting, leaving out the signs that we're not sure about (the canoe-mark, the patches of pressed grass), have been jokes! The two honey-trails could have been a joke. The arrow was a kind of joke. The ambush certainly was a joke. Maybe it's me they're after, not the girls at all.'

It was Moonluck who pointed out that no one would waste all that time and travel to plague a poor, young and unconnected stranger.

Somehow it didn't seem very important so they started on the stew. It was triumphant, but they'd made far too much. The pot was too big. Or maybe they'd already eaten too many pancakes, too much caviare, too much pink trout. They had second helpings, of course, and patted their distended bellies. They burped, and lay back, and sat up, and dug more comfortable depressions in the sand.

The sun had set and the sky was dappled with rose-coloured clouds to the zenith. The breeze had stopped. A narrow burning line of orange stretched from the dark cliff southward over the lake, and the lake sent back golden reflections.

They gave Calvin the ripest of the may-apples because he'd never tasted them. It was full of seeds but the juice had a flavour more delicious, he thought, than any fruit he'd ever eaten. They gave him more. He broke the skin and pressed the fruit with his tongue, collecting the seeds between his cheek and his jaw, then he spat them, one by one, into the fire. A few seconds later each one that landed accurately in a hot place exploded with a tiny pop.

They tossed strawberries in the air and caught them in their mouths. A game developed until their fingers were pink with juice. They were too full. One by one they jumped up and stretched. Moonluck went off to pee, then lay down on her belly and drank from the stream. Kittypet went along the beach and Red followed. They had a pee and waded in the little waves.

'It's good to eat too much sometimes,' said Moonluck. Calvin agreed and they were quiet for a moment looking at Kittypet, at Red, and at the sunset.

'You should have pissed in that man's face, not in his whisky,' said Moonluck, moving to the big stew-pot and picking out a mushroom with the stirring-stick and her fingers.

'I didn't like him,' said Calvin moving off into the dusk. But you had to be fair. He remembered that Mr Colethorpe didn't like him either. He felt peaceful as he found a tangle of wild roses. He didn't pee right on the roots but a foot away. He hoped idly that the roses would benefit.

Kittypet and Red were too far along the beach to hear Moonluck's whimper. Calvin only heard it when he lifted his head from the stream. He'd tried to drink at the place where the stream poured into the lake, but the water was fast there and carried too much sand. He was drinking at a pool up-stream and lifted his face, still dripping, from the water. It was dusk now and a weak warm breeze was moving from the valley to the lake.

The sound wasn't terrifying till he realised what it was. Moonluck wasn't like that. She wouldn't whimper—

The whimper continued, gaining strength. She was near the fire so she was more than a silhouette against the lake. Calvin began to hurry.

Her chest was a nervous bellows, jetting out small high cries that increased until it seemed a great scream would come, but she swallowed and the convulsive heaving began again. Calvin was close enough now to see her face, which was a mask with a shuddering open mouth and wild wide eyes staring at what she held suspended on the stirring-stick.

This was – the shock was extreme and took seconds to penetrate—

This was a human hand, severed at the wrist. The end joints of three fingers were tight hooks that curled round the stick. The hand was shiny with dark gravy which dripped, slowly now, from the protruding wrist-bone back into the pot.

'Don't tell Kittypet,' said Moonluck.

7

The Right Trail

*'When I saw a white man hanged
everyone behaved with dignity.'*

Longhair

BUT it was Moonluck who told Kittypet.

Rose-coloured sunset deepened into purple night as
they sat there, knowing constantly that every move was
watched. It wasn't possible that every word was heard
but they spoke quietly, even Kittypet, until she was
reluctantly told where they'd buried the hand. When she
dug it up and recognised it she screamed. That issue of
pain was the second most terrifying sound Calvin was
ever to hear.

She washed it in the lake, being careful to get all
the sand off the still-white cartilage of the joint, and
dried it on the bear-skin. The flesh had not fallen away
from the bones. In a private voice she muttered phrases
like—

'It hasn't shrunk – it didn't boil for long—'

Sometimes she addressed it as though it were a blind
kitten. She stood for a moment wanting to put it down
but unable to find a suitable place, then she brushed dust
off a smooth stone and set it there. She moved her hands
as if to apologise, as if to say the place was temporary.
She cut enough from the bear-skin to wrap it into a neat

155

parcel, fur on the inside, which she tied with a thong and hung round her neck. She sat near them. Tears made her cheeks glisten. She shook her head violently.

'It isn't my father,' she said.

'He's a stubborn man,' said Moonluck.

'It's not my father,' said Kittypet again, with some anger, 'it's your husband. It's Speechmaker, your husband!'

Moonluck rejected this idea just as violently. 'Why should he tease me with your brother? He doesn't know your brother!'

'It's not my father, it's Speechmaker!'

'No,' cried Moonluck, 'it can't be! I'm not – I'm worth nothing to him. He's had ten months. He's done nothing. It's your father!'

Calvin thought privately that any father who could cut a son's hand off for any reason would be as monstrous as that legendary Longhair they talked about. It wasn't worth looking round. Whoever was watching them was good at hiding. It wasn't worth throwing another branch on the fire so they could see better. Whoever was watching them could see better too. They sat.

But Moonluck's mind was still plodding along the same trail of thought and Calvin found her ruminations both complex and hard to follow.

'He took the gift. It could be because the Flyer accepted your little cake.'

'No,' said Kittypet.

'When he accepted that he accepted you.'

'No.'

'Your father could think that puts him under obligation.'

'No!'

'And in a way, it does. Though to feel under obligation to someone you don't approve of—'

'It isn't my father.'

156

'They've never liked each other. Why should they like each other now?'

Kittypet looked up.

'You think he's alive?'

'The Flyer?'

'Yes.'

'Why not?'

'Oh!'

Which was worse, to be dead or to be a boy with a stump instead of a hand? Tears again ran down Kittypet's cheeks and she put up both her hands to caress the parcel. Moonluck reacted harshly.

'You're not a Carrier!' she said with disgust.

'I'm carrying this.'

(Calvin learned later that the Carriers were an Athapascan people in the far north-west among whom it was thought proper for a widow to carry the ashes of her late husband in a basket on her back for the period of mourning. Moonluck's people found reports of the custom unbelievable, or, if true, foolish. It must be, they thought, at best a kind of self-indulgence and, at worst, hypocrisy. 'It's either one or the other,' said Moonluck, positively.)

Red hadn't said a word, even to comfort Kittypet. He'd gone into the same sort of sadness Calvin had become aware of that morning on the clifftop.

Kittypet was making smudges of her tears.

Moonluck was staring at the fire with a grimness Calvin would not have thought possible on such a pretty face.

He felt a surge of impatient energy flood through him. He jumped to his feet and glared at the lake, the little valley and the cliffs. Then he bethought himself and sat down again doing his best to appear casual. But there was nothing casual in his tone when he said, 'We must go. We must find him. Or them. Or we must lose them.'

Moonluck looked up slowly.

'Yes,' she said quietly, though in passionate agreement. 'And now!'

It was Moonluck's plan they adopted after a discussion which was thorough but very hushed. Moonluck behaved like a person twice her age. At the prospect of action Kittypet stopped crying and Red's melancholy fell away. All the practical problems he solved quickly. He could do more in five minutes than Calvin in an hour.

Along the lake to the west was Detroit and the village where Kittypet's people lived. To the east were the Indians Red and Calvin had seen from the clifftop. Their only safety was to go north – their original plan – and try to join Moonluck's people.

So the canoes must be recovered.

Their pursuers might know where they'd hidden them and be waiting for them. They might not. They had to take the risk.

They'd have to leave most of their supplies. The only disagreement arose over Calvin's writing-box. Moonluck was the most vehement that he should leave it. Calvin didn't argue. At the last moment he'd take it with him. It was an awkward thing to carry, he knew that. Kittypet and Red might be exhilarated by the plan but Calvin, after his surge of resolution, nursed a feeling of impending disaster. He clung to the writing-box because the feel of it gave him momentary sensations of security.

The purple light had gone and they were helped by the layer of cloud coming in from the west. They got ready for sleep. It was possible to conceal the preparation of their packs in such casual action.

The fawn, they realised, would be the real problem. She was grazing somewhere up the little valley. They hoped she would stay away but she didn't; she came back and lay down near the dying fire. Red fondled her head

158

and scratched her ears. She seemed to be sleeping peace-fully. The fawn could be a test. They might be able to get away without disturbing her when it was dark enough. If they didn't disturb her they might escape the attention of other eyes too.

Two and a half hours after the Flyer's hand was dis-covered the fire was dead, the night was black, and, with-out speaking, they set out. It took great self-control on Moonluck's part to refrain from objecting aloud when she felt the sharp corner of the writing-case on Calvin's back. She glared fiercely. The camp was left as it was, the fawn sleeping by the ashes. When they were really careful their footsteps made no sound in the sand.

Red led the way. They followed the stream for a few hundred yards till they came to the great curve from the west. They turned sharply east. If they were being followed the men trailing them were expert; they heard no sound of pursuit. They climbed the high bank and entered the hardwood forest, still moving eastward. Shortly after one o'clock they'd covered two miles and the first diver-sion occurred.

Moonluck had planned well, though the exercise took six days. It depended first on making their pursuers un-certain, then on dividing them. One by one, Moonluck first, they were to stop dead in the darkness, letting the rest pass on. Each was to stand where he stopped for an hour, utterly still. If he heard no sound of pursuit in this hour he was to select a hiding-place, conceal his trail to it and disappear for a specified number of days. Pursuers following their tracks or the noises of their progress would thus pass by. One by one the hares would vanish.

Calvin was to be not a hare but a red herring. This was simply because he was the noisiest. He was to travel the farthest. He didn't like the idea but he was excited into agreement by the carefully planned evasions he was to perform. These involved timed stops for listening and six

159

ninety-degree changes of direction, three on the third night, three on the fourth. He would cross his own trail three times, once at sunset, twice at dawn. He would thus be able to detect traces of pursuers. Moonluck assured him that by dawn on the fifth day he would have lost them. She regarded it as a ritual that never failed. So it proved to be.

His total route covered seventy miles, the last thirty by daylight. Six days on a diet of last year's nuts, raw eggs, the odd mushroom or handful of berries and two frogs left him utterly exhausted.

He reached the appointed place – near the camp where they'd shot the bear – at two in the afternoon, and he concealed himself for a long wait. Exhaustion and anxiety kept him awake. At four o'clock the marvellous moment came. Red and his canoe swept into sight, having picked up first Kittypet then Moonluck, each at her assigned place.

In the interest of speed he'd brought only one canoe. They chose a place to camp and dined on a large bass which they ate raw. (Why risk spoiling a six-day effort by a puff of visible smoke?) They wondered what had happened to the fawn. She was getting wilder anyway; she'd have left them soon. They whispered their adventures. Moonluck had heard distant sounds of pursuit from her hiding-place on the first day, but nothing since.

A sound sleep revived them. There'd been rain up-river. Many rapids were easier to negotiate. In two days they were sixty miles to the north. As Red's farm was a known point they made a circuit to avoid it, which carried them round the difficult country near the hot springs. Deductions from Calvin's maps gave them hints on this route.

They worked hard and ate innumerable fish, eggs and ducklings. A hidden fire at night was possible. They came to the ox-bow where Calvin had found patches of pressed grass. They carried the canoe over the neck of land instead of following the river. Grass, shrubs and trees were lush now and fully grown. For two nights they heard wolves howling but there were no signs of human enemies. Moonluck's plan had worked but they didn't relax their speed. Two more days, forty more miles. The girls were surprisingly efficient – meals seemed to be ready by magic – but they were silent and uncommunicative. For some reason Red was silent too.

Calvin couldn't understand it. They were safe again and you'd think they'd be extra cheerful. He himself felt no oppression, no fears. He felt, in fact, better than he'd ever felt in his life. He woke every morning with an iron cock but the aching distention did not fill him with hopeless longings any more. It didn't mean he was deprived and lonely, it meant he was ready. He was confident. The iron in his cock had a purpose and, at a suitable time, it would be achieved. Doubts had all vanished.

He recognised later that his astonishing sense of wellbeing could have been the principal cause when his mind, one evening, suddenly slipped a cog. A secondary cause was the unexpected compliment Red paid him. Compliments in Calvin's life had been infrequent.

He and Red were swimming that evening in a deep pool of the river. The girls were preparing food a hundred yards away where the dense canopy of hardwoods and a faint evening mist would conceal the smoke of a small hot fire. Calvin came puffing up from a dive so deep he'd brushed his chest on the tawny sand. He hauled himself to a turtle-back rock and gulped air, flicking water from his scalp and fingers.

'You're filling out,' said Red, and his frank pleasure in noting the fact was expressed with an admiring friendliness that made Calvin look at himself.

It was true. His arms were thicker and his legs had lost their scrawny look. He'd never be like Red, each of whose shoulders reminded him of the hard haunch of a racehorse, but he had hints of muscles now in unexpected places. His skin was tightening over a more grown-up shape. He could lift more, swim deeper, jump higher.

'You're filling out.'

If there'd been a high branch handy he'd have leaped to grab it and demonstrate his new muscles. Instead, and half in earnest, he struck a pose that bunched his biceps, which he examined. He relaxed them. He tensed them. They merely twitched, however, they didn't flop about like Red's. Then he sat down to watch the constellation of expanding rings where fish were rising for miles along the black mirror of the river.

This hypnotic Utopian image of complete peace had a deeper influence than health or vanity. Whose mind wouldn't slip a cog in such serenity? They say women don't re-live the seizures of childbirth once they've finished.

'These two girls would make good wives,' he said, after a moment.

'Yes,' said Red, curious.

Then, a moment later, Calvin continued, 'I'm not scared any more.' And Red couldn't comment because he was puzzling out the train of thought.

'I've been scared of Indians ever since I came to this country but these two – you couldn't find a white woman who'd make as good a wife as either of them – they're just like us!'

The impetus of his thought carried him incoherently forward. 'I mean they are! I've been scared of stories. Just stories. They're ordinary people. They're the same as us. Just as reasonable. What are we running away from?'

Red's face was a curious mixture of understanding and surprise.

'I mean they'd be very useful to a man. We could buy them. If they've done something why shouldn't we just buy them? Why don't we meet their people and buy

162

them? Their husbands, or fathers, or whatever, are probably just as reasonable as they are. All this running away is a waste of time.'

It may be that Calvin spoke more words than usual because he spoke in English. 'Don't you want to buy them?'

'I don't know.'

'They're very nice. Why've you left your farm and wandered all around if you don't like them?'

'I like them.'

'Then why?'

'If I bought them I'd have to look after them.'

'You're looking after them now.'

'I might change my mind.'

This seemed silly to Calvin and he shook his head in some exasperation.

'If I were still with the Company I could buy one of them. I could borrow the money and buy one.'

'I think you should,' said Red.

'I'm not with the Company.'

'You will be.'

'Why do you say that?'

'Oh – the Company won't let you go. They haven't all that many useful servants.'

This was a direct statement of his secret hope.

'You think that?'

'Yes.'

Calvin considered his next comment for fifteen seconds before he made it. When he did so he was dissatisfied with it.

'I think those two girls are wonderful.'

But Red seemed to detect no inadequacy and answered quite seriously.

'Yes. I'm sorry for them.'

'Why?'

'They aren't suited to be ordinary squaws.'

What a curious thing to say. Colethorpe's dismissal phrase echoed in Calvin's mind. 'I'm not suited to the north,' he quoted aloud.

'Neither am I.'

And this was the most surprising statement Calvin ever heard from Red. It was so surprising he found himself fumbling his way back to the main trail of the conversation. The fumbling may have been another minor cause of the slipped cog. He spoke in a rush.

'Anyway we ought to meet their people. We should, shouldn't we? They're women. Women get nervous over nothing. I used to be scared of Indians too. Shouldn't we find out? Shouldn't we make sure? Maybe we're running and no one's chasing us. There's been plenty of time; anyone could have caught us if they wanted to. The girls are all right. Neither of them's hurt. Nothing's happened—'

Red interrupted with a half angry incredulity. 'What about the Flyer's hand?'

Calvin was stopped in full spate. He couldn't believe his own lapse of memory and his jaw waggled. They sat on the turtle-backed rock hugging their knees while the battalions of old fears rushed in on Calvin with the late sun. He felt exposed. He shivered. Moonluck came down the opposite bank. She waved, dipped some water from the river and went back into shadow. Red was speaking slowly.

'It's all mixed up and odd. It's not normal. Nothing's as it should be. There's something we don't know about. Something going on that we don't know about. I've talked to the girls, trying not to scare them. They don't know. I've tried to puzzle it out myself. I get nowhere. It's so odd I wonder if White men are up to something – not Indians at all! Two things mainly—'

But he stopped and Calvin had to ask him what the two things were.

164

'The country's too empty.'

'You said something about a big meeting.'

'It would have to be a very big one. We've met no one. No one at all. I think people are scared of something.'

'What?'

Red shrugged and went on. 'The second thing—' he turned and looked at Calvin. 'When they saw that hand which of the girls was most upset?'

'Kittypet.'

'You think so?'

'It was her brother.'

Red nodded, but was not convinced. 'For a minute Moonluck looked as if she'd seen the Devil himself.'

This was true. Calvin had noticed.

A bubble was spinning in the centre of a new expanding ring where a small trout had taken a fly. Calvin thought he could hear it when it burst. There were three, bubbling, enquiring, silky cadenzas from a thrush behind them. A large moth was drying its wings and brushed against a flimsy fern. The evening was so serene it was suddenly uncanny. Mr Colethorpe would say anything, but old wives' tales had a curious power.

'Old Colethorpe used to go on about the Devil,' reminisced Calvin. 'He said the Indians are the Devil's children. "They're red aren't they," he used to say. He said he saw one with a tail once.'

'They've tails and hooves and horns. This Longhair's eyes are supposed to be yellow and to shine in the dark. I've heard all the nonsense.'

'You don't believe any of it?'

'I've seen Whites do worse things than any Indian.'

'You can't say that!'

'General Amherst – this is five years ago – told Colonel Bouquet to send a bale of blankets to a big family connection of Potowatamis—'

'What's wrong with that?'

'Every blanket was rubbed all over a whole platoon of men dying or dead of the smallpox. They did them up and sent them quick, while the pus was fresh.'

'I don't believe you.'

'It's the meanest thing I ever saw, I think.'

Red was dry enough now and he began to dress slowly.

'If we do talk to their people,' Calvin asked after a moment, 'which of the girls do you want?'

'Both of them,' said Red.

'Oh!' said Calvin.

'They're fond of each other. One's no good without the other.'

'I thought – I thought maybe—'

'I'll see them safe with Moonluck's people, then I'll go back to the farm.'

'By yourself?'

'Yes.'

'You said you wanted both of them.'

'Not enough.'

'You're crazy!'

'No, just lazy.'

'Moonluck's—'

Calvin couldn't find words to express the attractions of Moonluck. He began to sputter. 'And she – and she—' He was trying to say how completely she turned to jelly when she looked at Red.

'Get dressed,' said Red. 'Aren't you hungry?'

Red crossed the river. Calvin couldn't understand the later part of the conversation. He was grimly startled again at having forgotten the Flyer's hand. His mind went back to Red's solemnity when he talked about the country being too empty, and about something going on. He saw a fantasy of yellow eyes.

His clothes were on the other bank and he circled to wade across in shallow water. There was a threat, he was sure of that. But they'd evaded pursuit.

166

He stood dead still in the middle of the stream when the thought struck him that, though they might be in no immediate danger, they were being nudged, waved, beckoned or steered towards a particular destination.

The whole pursuit, even the hand, had produced no direct attack; only terror and the need to escape it.

And if they had an unknown destination what would they find there?

They travelled fast and northward. The gunwale was within two inches of the water when they were fully loaded but portages were easier with only one canoe. There was now a luminous wash of paler green over the dark spruces but hardwoods were fewer. Moonluck admitted grudgingly that Calvin's maps helped them to guess at two useful shortcuts. They risked a ten-mile paddle to the west along the verge of a lake wide enough to have been dangerous had there been any wind. They came to the mouth of a small river flowing in from the north. Along the vista between its dark banks Calvin thought he recognised the top of the gravel hill from which he'd first surveyed this empty country. They followed the river which took them west of that high outpost.

There were now three unanswered questions which cropped up many times a day. Were they being followed? How many days' journey before they reached Moonluck's people? How safe would they be when they got there? Only the second question had an answer and that was far from definite. About two weeks' travel now, Moonluck thought.

The gravel hill was now north-east. They portaged over a long groin to a deep slow stream flowing north, which Calvin marked on his map.

Kittypet thought too many flocks of pigeons were flying north. They wondered if they could smell smoke on the south wind. With one mind they decided to try to answer the first question. Moonluck organised the operation. Red was increasingly taciturn and she was increasingly in charge. She selected a hump on the pine-covered slope of the hill where it levelled off into the flatter country. It was five miles from the river. They went through an elaborate back-trailing exercise which placed them by the next evening fairly high on the long south-west slope. They lit no fire. They took turns watching – for smoke or movement while daylight lasted, then for the glow of fire or moving blacknesses on the glinting surface of distant water.

After midnight Calvin woke. He crawled to where Moonluck kept watch, her elbows propped on a moss-covered boulder. There was a chilly wind from the west and he put his arm across her shoulders. She was very slender, really. She turned her head and rubbed her high forehead against his neck. Large clouds were passing. Pools of light from the hidden moon moved over the empty country and in those patches it was possible to see far and with surprising clarity.

She whispered softly, asking him questions; but the sound was little more than the warmth of her breath on his ear. The others wouldn't wake. He was surprised by the questions she asked because they had more to do with him than with their present situation.

Was it good country around Berwick-on-Tweed? Were there big lakes there or just rivers? Had he been scared by Indians or by the stories told by White men *about* Indians? He answered, and found the conversation veering towards more general experience, common to them both. He told her how he was beginning to believe that most of the things he used to accept as true were – not lies exactly, but—

She felt the same. She remembered how simple every-

thing was when she was a little girl and how, without her
being aware of the change, everything was suddenly
complicated. She said she hoped everything might be
simple again when she grew old. Then, after a moment,
'If I grow old,' she added, and suddenly clutched his left
arm with both her hands and hung on.

The gesture was unlike her. Not knowing what to do,
Calvin stayed still. Once before, in the field of white
flowers, Moonluck had gone back to see if they were
being followed.

Then an apt recollection came to him. 'Life is a fishing-
line,' he said.

'What do you mean?'

'When you're ten it's long and straight and lined out
before you. When you're twenty you're in the middle
and it's all a tangle. When you're a hundred it's
long and straight again, but it's all lined out behind
you.'

There was a half-ashamed smile on his face, and a tone
in his voice suggested he was quoting someone.

'Where did you hear that?'

So he told her about meeting the three old men, and
how he shared the two rabbits with them.

'It sounds like a talkative old man. Do old white men
talk like that – as if they know something no one else is
bright enough to know?'

'Just the same.'

But her next question was a surprise.

'Do you think one of those old men sent you the rabbits?'

'Sent them to me?'

'Yes.'

'How?'

'Told them.'

'Told them?'

'Yes. Told them to sit there and be shot.'

169

'I don't know – why?'

'To save himself the trouble of shooting them.'

'That's silly.'

'Maybe.' She spoke as if she believed he was right. But she disregarded this consideration. 'What else did they say?'

'One of them said "a white man is just a scared Indian".'

'What else?'

'I can't remember.'

'Maybe those old men were having an important meeting and you interrupted them,' she said. 'They don't eat, they take a steam-bath, they go through the ceremony to clean their minds, then they talk. Tell me more.'

'I remember a story. The middle one told it. He said this was the first land, an island. Just made. A Garden of Eden was what he meant. He must have heard about it from some white man. The first two people lived here. Then, later on he said, "Any man who's any good thinks he's a first man".'

'What do you think he meant?'

Calvin was in difficulties. After all it was just the talk of an old Indian, but— 'He didn't mean Adam, or the first man like that. I don't know. I think he meant a man who enjoyed himself like Adam, finding things out. Everything is a first time to a man like that. If it isn't a first time he makes it a first time. I don't know. He was talking about being happy, I think.'

He rather expected Moonluck to be sharp, but she wasn't. She was gazing forward but not at anything physical. She nodded her head. A little later she dropped her eyes and said – so low he could hardly hear it: 'Red is a first man.'

'But he's so sad,' protested Calvin.

Then Moonluck did answer sharply, 'He's the only

170

man I've met who could be a first man!' And a second
later she added, in a sort of burst, 'That's what makes it
so wicked and mean!'

'What makes what wicked and mean?'

For days Calvin was to wonder if what followed was
because she feared she'd said something that might hurt
him or something that too clearly revealed some secret
knowledge. Or, possibly, both.

She turned and faced him, stroked his hair and
smoothed his beard. This beard was just long enough
now so she could hold a tuft of it with her fingers and
thumbs.

A cloud moved and they were flooded with light.

She put one hand on each of his shoulders, held him
firmly, looked him in the eyes and smiled.

Once, he remembered, her eyes had scraped the inside
of his skull. Now the smile went deeper and embraced
him completely, touching and warming individually every
pore, every string of muscle, every drop of blood – almost
as if she herself were capable of providing a calm glow, a
still radiance, that could penetrate to and illumine the
darkest dungeon.

She was a remarkable woman, he decided. He could do
nothing but look at her, which struck him as being
curious, even uncanny. He'd have known what to do if it
had been Kittypet yet, at that moment, he felt closer to
Moonluck than he'd ever felt to Kittypet. But, for the
time being, he'd forgotten his question.

Moonluck insisted on hiding for a second day. The
loom of the gravel hill cut off the landscape to the north-
east, but all other points of the compass were clearly in
view, from the loam and hardwoods of the south to the
granite and pines of the north. On the second morning
the air was crystal for about an hour and they could see a

deep blue horizon – the Lake of the Hurons – to the west. How far? Twenty miles?

They watched with care. They could identify many points along their trail from south to north. The place at which they'd doubled back was clearly visible five miles to the north. Their trail south from that point threaded pine forest up a gentle rise and ended in an open meadow. In all the empty country they saw no suspicious signs except two vast flocks of pigeons that rose, circled and settled.

By noon on the second day Calvin had decided that their pursuers were non-existent or inexpert.

They were neither, and the event that proved it was, at first, charming and utterly unexpected. Trotting openly along their trail from the north, where they'd doubled back, came a fawn. It was limping slightly. They thought it was a wild fawn and wondered at its boldness.

Then she saw them, crossed the meadow, entered their circle and danced sideways about Red, taking time to make light-footed charges towards the other three and back again. She was shyer. Only Red could touch her. Her excitement was extreme. She'd pause to graze a little and dance back again, tossing her head and stretching her nose to nuzzle the big man. She was just beginning to lose her spots. She was thin and her skin was cut in a few places. Her journey was, of course, impossible, as they realised quickly. Their trail had been much too long and much too devious, some of their travel too fast, and no scent could be followed over miles of water. She'd been captured and carried. They knew this even before they saw the plaited thong round her stick-like hock. The end was frayed. Had she broken loose, or been let loose deliberately? Red had some trouble cutting it off and found it was decorated with a small tassel of beads, yellow and black. Kittypet drew in her breath sharply. The probability was that it was made by her people.

The fawn had approached from the north, so the band that had carried her was just waiting there, somewhere close to their trail, and their elaborate exercise was useless. The band had one canoe at least. They'd need that to carry the fawn. There was no way of telling how many men there were.

A paralysis descended on the four of them and they said little during the long afternoon. The fawn made no allowance for Red's mood and, when she would suddenly trot up to smell him again, he would have to force himself to play with her.

Towards sunset, far to the south, they saw a line of five big canoes approaching. The light was grey but it allowed them to see the long shapes nose in from the lake and beach themselves. There was no attempt at concealment. These five canoes were new and very white. There seemed to be no tribal or family markings but they were too distant to be certain. Watching through the glass Calvin said he could see no women.

'How many men?' asked Moonluck.

'Forty or fifty.'

'Painted?'

'It's too far to tell. One might be painted.' He closed the glass. 'I suppose they've been seen by the others.'

'Yes,' said Moonluck.

'Then they'll know where we are in a couple of hours.'

'They may not be—' but Red didn't finish the sentence. 'I don't understand it.'

Calvin found Red's bewilderment extreme and even pathetic; yet Red had had more experience than any of them. There was a contradiction here. Calvin couldn't solve it so he turned to practical matters.

'They'll expect us to go east along the slope and turn north round the summit – near the place where I first met you,' he said.

'Yes,' said Moonluck, and made up her mind. 'We'll

go straight west between the two troops and then head north.'

'What about the lake? The big lake?' asked Calvin.

'Too exposed. We couldn't hide.'

'Hiding hasn't done much good so far,' said Red.

'It's too far and the canoe's too small for lake waves.'

After a curious, half-pleading glance at Red, Moonluck made decisions. Their preparations were quick and desperate. Would they take the fawn? No, they'd desert the fawn as they did last time. Their former evasion was successful – their trail must have been picked up later – so they'd separate again.

Hard and decisive, Kittypet said she wasn't going anywhere if she was to be by herself.

'It's me they're chasing.'

Moonluck yielded. Then she began a fierce argument over the writing-case.

Calvin yielded. They – or he – could come back for it if—

If?

There was no point in waiting. The night was clear and the moon bright. They reached their canoe without incident. It had a large hole cut neatly in the bottom.

They hurried further west and came to deep still water, too wide to cross easily. They could detect no flow. They turned right along the wide and treeless shore. The going was easy. By dawn they were ten miles to the north and in the shadow of the gravel hill. By the time it was far southeast of them the sun came out from behind its shoulder and the chill vanished.

It was not a lake but a river they were following. The area of black water narrowed and a gentle northward flow nearly kept pace with them. The water was deeper and as they moved forwards the speed of flow increased. By mid-morning the water was moving faster than they could walk. The cliff forming the other bank was higher, the right bank more tumbled. Calvin noticed that the rock seemed different. The high cliff was one smooth wall of granite. The bank they followed was a softer rock, all pitted and chunky. No trees grew close to the river, which flowed north straight as a ruled line.

Then, just before noon, they thought they saw the beginning of a curve in the line of cliff and Calvin climbed a deformed but well-placed spruce where he might see their forward trail. The curve was there, and it enclosed a wide and impressive horse-shoe of surprisingly open land. At the apex of the horse-shoe curve the cliff rose to two hundred feet. To his right the height diminished though the curve continued. The land they stood on was a peninsula enclosed by the powerful river and the high smooth cliff. A mile and a half to the east, across the base of the peninsula, he could see where the river curved east again, breaking through the granite cliff, and emptied into the end of a long lake. Except for this one vista the landscape was enclosed and still, an amphitheatre bounded by the smooth bowl of granite with its delicate fringe of spruce and birch.

The sun, behind him, filled the bowl with heat. There was no wind. He smelled smoke. Against the highest and most distant curve of the cliff the sun shone brilliantly but there was a shadow there too which disturbed the boy; a long narrow shadow which sometimes cast the shadow of itself. It was a motionless pall of smoke.

He swung down and told them. Moonluck climbed the tree. Calvin fidgeted and wished he knew where Moonluck's people were supposed to be. She rejoined them slowly, and her uncertainty decided him. He suggested they move directly towards the lake. After a second she nodded, her face without expression. Calvin and Red checked the priming of their muskets.

A shallow valley of three curved terraces scored across the base of the peninsula. They followed the nearest and highest level because it was also the most thickly forested. The lowest level, they could see, was sandy and open, with tufts of young trees growing at odd angles where spring torrents had stranded them. Beyond this curved spillway to the eastern lake three parallel terraces rose in low steps to a height of twenty feet or so. This mound extended to the tip of the peninsula, where it was cut off by the swift hidden curve of river and the bulging cliff.

Far to the south-east they could see the loom of the gravel hill. They moved quietly. The village – if it were a village in a place so ravaged by spring floods – must be small. They were all tired. They trudged along paying attention to nothing but the cautious placing of their steps. Red and Calvin were leading and Calvin, his mind wandering, was suddenly thrown back in memory to a moment when he and Red had arrived in another camping place. He saw three bears crouched over their packs. Then the bears rose up and became three tall Indians wearing bearskin hats which trailed a short sort of cape of the same skin.

There was a wild scream from Kittypet behind him, which diminished into sobbing.

Calvin and Red lifted their guns. A shot would be suicide. At least a dozen Indians with bows in their hands – their headbands were made from yellow and black beadwork – stepped quietly from the trees on each side of them.

An important older man was approaching, accompanied by two of his soldiers who carried muskets. He wore a blanket with yellow and black beadwork at the edges. Kittypet sobbed more loudly. The chief stood and looked at her for a moment, then came back to stand in front of Red.

His dialect was identical with Kittypet's. He was curiously nervous, Calvin thought, for a man surrounded by two dozen of his own soldiers.

176

He spoke only to Red. 'Speechmaker wants to talk to you.'

Then, quite suddenly, wild commotion began. Calvin didn't see everything. There was a scuffle behind them. He turned to look. At that moment Red shrugged off the two men who were guarding him and dashed for the trees. A few tried to stop him but he was unstoppable. No one put an arrow to a bow-string.

Calvin ran the other way. He was quickly taken and held firmly by the arms. He recognised instantly the smell of rancid bear-grease, wintergreen and wood-smoke, the aura of prosperous soldiers. Since they'd made their capture easily and quickly they could interest themselves in what was going on elsewhere. They held the boy but watched Red disappearing into the forest.

Kittypet stood still, sobbing steadily. Where was Moonluck? Calvin searched carefully. Then, towards the river, where a rounded rock projected twenty feet or more above the water, he saw wild running. His guards, as well as he, wanted a closer view so they moved together. They saw Moonluck with a bow in her hand aiming arrows at her pursuers. How had she got it? The bow was much too heavy for her and the arrows went wild. She backed to the edge of the big rock and threw the bow away with her left hand. The pursuers were closing in.

She screamed and screamed again. Her right hand, covered with blood, was trying to pull an arrow from between her breasts. About eight inches of the feathered end projected. Now she fought the arrow with both hands, screaming. Quite suddenly the screaming stopped, the eyes became fixed, the mouth open, and she fell back slowly. Two seconds later they heard the splash. The two young men who held Calvin by the arms weren't much older than he was but they were at least four inches taller and much heavier. They were impetuous and curious. They half lifted him as they rushed towards the rock to join more of the young Ottawa soldiers, stripped for action, who peered at the half-submerged body, its small hands still clutching the arrow. Calvin was astonished at how wooden the body looked as it surfaced, sank again, rose and rolled slowly in the current that sucked it steadily towards deeper water.

An enthusiastic outcry turned them to see Red, doubled up and tied in a loose bundle, carried jerkily by six running soldiers towards the place where Kittypet and her father stood in silence. Calvin was promptly led to the same place. The old chief beckoned and the procession headed across the lower level and down the smooth granite bank to the wide, sandy spill-way so curiously spotted with driftwood.

Calvin could now see a small huddle of wigwams and teepees on the terrace which rose beyond this open plain and must extend to the end of the peninsula. Above the second-growth trees loomed the great bowl of grey granite carved out by the curving river. It seemed to lean over him though it was half a mile away. The whole amphi-theatre was humid. The fringe of trees at the top of the curving cliff moved constantly in a breeze which never penetrated the deep-cut bowl. These delicate fronds put Calvin in mind of the seeking tentacles of a sea-anemone. One morsel was already engulfed. Three more were still struggling.

The band of sandy plain was wider than he expected, and the procession took five minutes to cross to its north-ern boundary, a long curving roll of granite varying from five to ten feet high. At one point, set back a few yards from the top of this wall, was a curious square frame.

The trunks of two young spruces, standing twelve feet apart, had been stripped of their lower branches. Con-necting them, at a height of ten feet, was a five-inch beam – a length cut from a maple sapling – and the cross-lashing at each end was neat and firm.

178

Directly beneath the beam, and in line with it, were two posts four feet apart and four feet high. The tops of these posts were not hacked off by an axe but cut cleanly with a buck-saw. Where would the Indians get a buck-saw?

The ground about the frame was cleared. Calvin was so apprehensively curious about this scaffolding on its higher level that some minutes passed before he noticed three simple structures on the sandy plain below the escarpment. They stood in a cleared area surrounded by a ring of stones. There was one ordinary round hut made of bark, a hut for living. The other hut was a square box made of poles which were draped with bearskins. It was just large enough for a man to sit in. Around the base was a ring of human skulls, some with the jaw-bones still attached. This box was sheltered by a wide canopy of birch-bark, supported by tall saplings. The edge of the canopy was fringed with dangling white leg-bones and switches of horse-hair. The leg-bones did not stay still and Calvin began to hear a faint clicking sound as they touched. He changed his mind about the switches. They did not come from the tails of horses.

The last object he noticed was, in a way, the most startling. A few yards in front of the canopy, with a reed mat spread before it, was a windsor armchair, empty.

Four men stood by, chatting in Algonquin. They were young and powerful. Their hair was shaped into a bristling crest. They didn't wear breech-cloths or leggings, only small embroidered aprons that half-covered their privates. They carried no guns but the staves of their bows were unusually thick. As the prisoners were brought forward they turned and Calvin was relieved to see that their faces were not painted.

No one was particularly rough with Kittypet, who was left standing there alone while her father joined the council group. She sniffed constantly. Red and Calvin were thrown to the ground with great violence. Calvin's face struck stones. Blood shot from his nose and his mind began to spin towards nothingness. Before it got there he became aware of someone on his back tying his hands together. Someone else was tying his feet. He had recovered a clearer consciousness by the time they had him securely trussed and turned him over. He struggled to sit up, but it was difficult. When he managed it he saw that Red had been treated the same way. The empty windsor chair was ten feet in front of them. On the escarpment behind it, a few yards from the scaffold, grew a wild apple tree, small apples already visible.

Calvin and Red saw every head turn left, and they looked in that direction. A tall man was approaching carrying a bundle on his left arm. He wore a heavily embroidered apron, nothing else. He was a lean man with strong muscles. It was difficult to see his features because they had been painted black, except for a white streak across the bridge of the nose. His body was unpainted.

He sat in the windsor chair. He undid the bundle from his left arm and nodded. The old chief, Firepouch, went over and kicked Red who had slumped forward with his eyes closed.

'Look at Speechmaker,' he said.

Red raised his head and Calvin saw that his temple was badly cut and blood dripped from the red beard. Speechmaker looked at him, then at Calvin. Calvin, even in his dazed condition, felt his heart miss a beat. He peered closely. The bundle Speechmaker carried was the long tangled skein of his own hair. He was unrolling it slowly. He flicked the hank over his shoulder, hooked it under the arm of the chair and brought the black tress across his knees. The tip almost reached the ground.

Calvin was too dazed to think very clearly but he was conscious of complete bewilderment. Speechmaker – Longhair – Speechmaker – Longhair. The same man?

180

Longhair reached out his hand and a fat woman in a full cotton dress rushed forward to hand him a curious flat object and a steel knife which gleamed in the evening light. The object was a piece of heavy rawhide roughly triangular in shape and eight or nine inches across the long side. This long side was not straight. Two lugs projected from it, each with a hole pierced through it. The rawhide was damp and flexible. It was heavy enough to have come from the shoulder of a buffalo. Longhair proceeded to bevel both short sides of the triangle so that they could be neatly sewn together. He examined it and bent it in his strong, long-fingered hands so that the tapered edges overlapped and the two pierced lugs were opposite each other. It appeared to be a sort of cone-shaped cup with no bottom. The hole where the bottom should have been was less than an inch in diameter. The two lugs at the top, like the sturdy grips of a wooden firkin, were stout enough to take a rope handle far too thick for the miniature pail, if that's what it was.

Longhair held the object up and looked at Red speculatively. Firepouch tottered to examine Red's clothing. The shirt was badly torn so he ripped it off, cutting the sleeves away. The moccasins were easy. The socks were obviously much valued. Red's legs had to be untied to get the trousers off, but he struggled very little, either because he was groggy or because he knew it was useless. Longhair leaned forward to look at him.

Then he looked at the miniature pail he was working on and nodded. The fat woman gave him a small knife.

Firepouch began to busy himself again. He made gestures and two grave young men carried in a square open structure made of two-inch hardwood saplings bound together with spruce-roots or leather. Longhair examined the bindings and the four six-inch rawhide loops at the sides and nodded.

Red saw the cage and staggered half-way to his feet. Firepouch tapped him on the side of the head with his blunt stone tomahawk and four young men caught Red before he collapsed. They carried him to the cage and dropped him in. The top was put on and two stout poles were run through the loops. Red was curled on the saplings that formed the bottom. These were spaced at five-inch intervals. When the young men stepped aside two women trotted to pull up a couple of tall thistles which they did by clutching them near the roots. They came back to the cage and poked at Red, who didn't move, so they sat and waited.

The fat woman stood by Longhair and handed him an awl, or a thong, or a knife, as he needed it.

Calvin gazed at this curious activity, his mind wandering. He could make nothing of it. He was gloomily oppressed by the concentration of the legendary ogre in the windsor chair, by his complete silence, and by the unnatural quietness of the people round him. But maybe this quietness contained no threat. He'd seen Indian men sewing things on occasion, and making articles of leather, though the women did most of this work. Moonluck was good at it.

Moonluck! He glanced around him. His mind was working better. It was a trick, of course. He didn't know how she managed to do it so well, with the liquid blood and the slow collapse backwards into the river. He didn't know either what she could hope to achieve. But Moonluck was both clever and resourceful. If he were to take it that she had escaped he felt sure she could get help somehow. It would be foolish to count on it but— Her own people couldn't be very far away, and the Hudson's Bay Brigade they'd seen on Lake Erie must have been headed in this direction – might even have arrived in this area by now – via the Lake of the Hurons. And there was no doubt Moonluck was a remarkable woman.

So Speechmaker is Longhair – the legendary ogre, Longhair. And Moonluck didn't know! He kept blanking out repeatedly, but the thought was persistent though there was something wrong with it.

Speechmaker, Moonluck's husband, is Longhair and he's sitting there in a windsor armchair making a leather cone with his long hair across his knee. Why does he look at Red so often, and then at the piece of leather?

Well away from this clear place – almost as if the clear place was somehow special – a few Indians stood to watch. They were, most of them, southern Ottawas. There weren't many women. Then Calvin saw the concentrated malevolence of the glance the fat woman occasionally directed at Red. What was the connection between her and Longhair?

Kittypet was silent and he could see that she was trembling – constantly trembling. He wished his head would clear.

And there he sat, this legend, shaving with a small sharp knife at the edge of a piece of leather. He tried to see the features through the paint. His eyes grew dry with looking, though the concentration was partly the result of dizziness and a headache. Once, through the noon-time shadow of the bent head, he thought he saw the black lids lift, disclosing, first, the whites of large eyes. Calvin knew he should stop looking, lower his gaze; he was being examined. He should be humble. He shouldn't stare. But he couldn't tear his eyes away.

The eyes of most Indians were dark brown. The irises of these eyes that glared at him so steadily seemed to glow as they floated between the crescents of white and the black brows. The pupils were small and the irises were yellow.

The head turned. Longhair glanced at Firepouch and nodded towards Calvin, then the work was resumed.

As Firepouch moved towards him Calvin was so numb

as to be without interest until the old man cut the thongs that bound his hands and ankles!

Calvin was so surprised he just sat there. Then he began to wonder idly if he should thank Longhair. He got to his feet. His mouth wagged but no words came. Longhair's complete silence unnerved him. He couldn't speak from where he stood so he took a step towards the powerful figure in the windsor chair. He was hauled back roughly by Firepouch who said 'No', in a firm, quiet voice.

Firepouch was at least capable of speaking to him. He even seemed rather nervously human.

'Why?' whispered Calvin, since Longhair appeared to be paying no attention.

'He's going through a silence and he's beginning his fast tomorrow. In a few days he hopes to dream. He hopes it will be an important dream.'

Calvin heard a groan from Red's cage and he began to stagger towards it. Red moved and one of the women thrust the thistle between his legs. Calvin broke into a run.

He didn't get far. One of the young men swung the heavy stave of his bow round in a wide whistling arc and it smashed into Calvin's chest, almost breaking the arm that tried to stop it.

Kittypet began to whimper.

Through the trees came four men, two of them naked except for moccasins, two of them with soaked leggings and aprons. They held Moonluck by her hair and arms, and hauled her, still struggling, into the circle. Her skirt and tunic were gone. She was wet and stained with mud. When she saw the figure of Longhair she became still and the expression on her face was ghastly, Calvin thought. Longhair looked up and beckoned. She was taken closer. She looked at the cage where Red lay, and she gazed fiercely into Longhair's eyes.

Longhair made a light gesture to the men who had brought her and they turned damply away. He held up

184

the piece of rawhide, not to show it to Moonluck – he didn't look at her – but to examine it in a different light. Then she saw what he was making and she screamed and screamed and screamed again, till echoes from the granite walls across the river volleyed back at them. She rushed forward and Longhair raised his hand and swung the palm accurately so that it smashed into her face and knocked her down. He still held the piece of rawhide in his other hand. Almost before she touched the ground she grabbed a little knife from the fat woman and was leaping for the seated man. He dropped the piece of rawhide, held the girl's wrist and took the knife, throwing it into the ground. Then he slapped her again and once again. After a moment she began crawling towards the cage where Red was slowly coming to, helped, possibly, by the poking thistles.

Two young men stepped firmly to bar her way and she lay there, her face pressed to the trampled ground.

Longhair took up the knife, and the piece of leather, and went on with his work.

Low conversations began among the Indians. Some of the women went back to the wigwams to prepare food. They paused to look at Red in his wooden cage. A low muttering came from the men, who sat in a half-circle round the windsor chair and its busy, concentrated occupant.

8

White Man to the Rescue

*'An Indian might kill my uncle,
only a white man would steal his totem.'*

Longhair

CALVIN spent a restless, sick night. He woke often and yearned for sleep again. Once, in the dark, he smelled a smear of vomit on the grass near his face and he rolled away. The movement sent growls of pain through his back and legs; but the pain in his chest, where the swung bow had smashed him, was fierce. He noticed that Moonluck had disappeared.

Later he woke to hear a muttered conversation between Firepouch and two older men. He didn't open his eyes but his precaution didn't help him to learn much. They expected Chippewas, Northern Ottawas, Wyandots, Tionontatis, Lenapes, Potawatomis, Crees and Roundheads. Only a small party of Miamis had arrived and Longhair took exception to their highly ornamented dress. Their leggings were fringed with white fur, their capes lush with fox-tails, and they tinkled with shells as they moved about.

'He' was supposed to have arrived yesterday. (Calvin didn't discover who 'he' was.)

Longhair couldn't be expected to remain silent much longer.

Plans intended for ten tribes couldn't be executed by

one or two. Longhair would be furious if no conference assembled to hear his dream.

The old men appeared to be as worried about Longhair's reaction to the facts as about the facts themselves. They had some hope that this red-haired man would take his mind off the conference.

'Think, think, think!' said Calvin to himself as the old men moved away. But it was hard to think; his mind wouldn't stay clear. But he had to think, to figure out what was happening, because – because there might be a way out and unless he understood what was happening he'd never find it. There were no interruptions except an owl and a night-hawk. Yes, he'd think, and he'd set about it now. He went to sleep instead.

Then, later, he was awakened by a voice which he recognised as belonging to the fat woman who had held the knives for Longhair. She was behind him. She sounded disgruntled. The night seemed very dark. He never discovered whom she was talking to.

'He saw a hanging by white men,' she said. 'That's why. He thought it was good. It was very slow. Very formal. Very solemn. He likes it that way but the people won't.'

After the voice stopped the valley was suddenly filled with moonlight and inumerable small bats chased the silver gnats.

He woke again with a raging thirst a few seconds before dawn. Longhair, fast as a racing hare, swept past him and leaped to the upper terrace where he joined fifteen naked young men. They went through some sort of ceremony as the sun rose. Longhair was silent but his lieutenant, whose hair was tied in a heavy queue, and whose fine face was uplifted in the level light, led a low ritual speech so clearly that Calvin could catch all the solemn phrases.

188

'Each enemy I fail to kill will kill a friend.
Pain is the seed of joy.
War is the seed of peace.
Death is the seed of life.
I welcome pain,
I welcome war,
I welcome death,
To follow our father—
Pontiac.'

Pontiac was dead! He'd been killed a thousand miles away in the south. Nothing made sense.

There was a faint smell of wood-smoke from the encampment. He remembered Red and looked towards the wooden cage. Two guards sat beside it and they were alert so they must have been recently posted. Red was sprawled on the bottom saplings, brown blood in great smears over his face and shoulders, one large clot plastering the hair to the side of his head. The guards looked up and Calvin heard a low whimpering behind him. If he stayed still his chest hurt less, but he turned. It was Kitty-pet, her face dirty with tears and her expression more doleful than Calvin would have thought possible.

'Have you seen Moonluck?' She wiped her face.

He made his voice as harsh as possible but it wobbled.

'No, I haven't.'

'My brother's very ill.'

'He's one of them. He shot the arrow. He followed us.'

'He didn't know.'

'Stop crying!'

'I can't.'

'He followed us. Stop crying!'

Her low continuous sobs were unbearable and jammed all the channels of thinking. 'These are your people. That's your father. Can't you do something?'

'No one can. My father won't talk to me. He's one of Longhair's friends now.'

'I wish I'd never met you,' said Calvin. There was a long pause while his heart began to flutter. He clenched his jaws to choke sick rising sobs and muttered weakly, 'I don't know how to get out of this.'

'You won't,' said Kittypet. 'Nobody will.'

'They haven't tied us up.'

'They don't need to.'

'We've got to do something.'

'What?'

Calvin was silent, strangling hysteria.

'You must have known,' he said finally, and fiercely.

'Known what?'

'Who was following us.'

'I didn't!'

'You're useless. Get away from me.'

Kittypet's sobbing grew to a loud wail and she ran towards Red's cage. The two young men, who had watched the scene with detached interest, rose to their feet and Kittypet realised there was no help there. She wailed again and ran off a few yards to throw herself on the ground and put her arms around a flood-washed, stranded log.

Kittypet's uncontrolled crying had attracted attention. A few people paused in their work to see what was going on. The thought crossed Calvin's mind that a number of these people must have known Kittypet from babyhood. Now she was cast out from any friendly contact. He felt a surge of sympathy for her, but he suppressed it.

There was a movement on the terrace above. One of Speechmaker's young men, now wearing an apron, was leaning a ladder against the top bar of the curious frame. The ladder was made to the white man's pattern. Now why was that?

A procession of Miamis left the upper terrace and approached the cage. Calvin knew they were Miamis by their resplendent clothing. Their necklaces of wampum

190

didn't rattle on bare chests but on soft doeskin jackets heavily embroidered with beads. Some of the feathers upright in their headbands were dyed red and yellow. Their capes were flowing and ornate. The leggings of several of the men had a startling fringe of white hair down the side seam. From the manes of white horses?

He heard a series of hoarse groans. Red, usually a little too late, was avoiding sticks poked at him between the saplings. A couple of people poked viciously and Red writhed away. The groans came when they poked at his belly. The two guards were interested but lofty. There was nothing Calvin could do. His brain, he knew, wasn't working properly. And it was useless to go on saying 'think, think, think!'

Kittypet had been quiet for some time. Suddenly she was on the ground beside him and put her arm across his bruised waist.

'Calbn,' she whispered.

'Get away from me!'

He rolled towards Red's cage and Kittypet let her face fall to the trampled earth.

Then there was a long gasp from Red and a burst of laughter from the Miamis. Suddenly Firepouch appeared and the two young guards, fearing his arrival, began shouting at Red's tormentors to leave him alone. Firepouch reinforced their shouts with vigorous protests of his own and the group around the cage slowly dispersed. The Miamis were goodnatured. They caught sight of Calvin and moved to examine him instead. Calvin raised himself to one elbow and did his best to appear at his ease. In as firm a voice as he could manage, he said, 'I've always been friendly with The People.'

'Hudson Bay Company,' said one of the Miamis – he wore a yellow feather – in an accent which was just understandable.

'If any harm comes to me the Company will be angry,' said Calvin.

'I'm frightened,' said Yellow Feather, and began asking riddles. In other circumstances Calvin would have found some of their riddles funny.

Question: How many white men are too many?

Answer: One.

Question: When will we see the backs of the white men?

Answer: When have we seen anything else?

Question: Why are a white man's tongues like his feet?

Answer: They point in two directions.

Question: How can you tell when a white man is dead?

Answer: When he stops telling lies.

Question: Where was the white man who was helping the Indian?

Answer: Dead and buried in his corn patch.

A young man with a white fringe on his leggings had supplied most of the answers. He went on, as if telling a familiar story, 'The white man tied the Indian's feet together. He tied his hands behind his back. He put a blindfold over his eyes and a gag in his mouth. He leaned him against a tree and used a mile of rope to tie him there. "This is what I call a fair fight," said the white man, and shot him.'

The young man made sure that Calvin heard the end of the story before he moved to join his friends.

In his cage, Red was leaning on one arm trying to stop the bleeding from his leg with the other hand. He pressed the flesh above the long gash in his thigh. Firepouch finished scolding the two guards and went back towards Longhair's hut. Calvin wondered. They stopped people from hurting him. Hopeful, or sinister? Red might know something. If he could speak to him—

Calvin climbed to his knees but knew he'd get dizzy if he rose further so he crawled slowly towards the cage.

The two guards didn't move. Calvin continued shakily until he saw in the distance the fat woman of the previous evening carrying a couple of objects in their direction. He stopped while she was still far off. He thought he could risk a question, which he voiced with a low, clear intonation.

'Why did they put you in a cage?'

'I don't know,' said Red, and Calvin was convinced he was telling the truth. There was a flicker of helpless irritation in the reply which was convincing. Red didn't know.

He didn't know. Who might know? Moonluck. She'd disappeared. Why? She'd disappeared before. She'd know. She'd know. There must be some explanation.

The fat woman had no expression on her face as she shoved a bowl of warm stew into the cage and placed a leather flask outside it. Red fumbled for the flask and drank till Calvin thought he'd burst. It was awkward because the cage was low. To get the last of the water Red would have to lie on his back. Calvin licked his own cracked lips.

The bowl of stew was eaten more deliberately, with many pauses and much hard swallowing as if the throat were swollen or the stomach unwilling. Calvin's awareness of his own thirst became frantic.

When Red put the bowl outside the cage the fat woman, still expressionless, emptied what was left on the ground and padded off. Calvin inched a little closer.

'I'm a fool to eat, or drink,' Red said in English.

The guards heard but paid scant attention, possibly because they didn't understand.

'Why?' asked Calvin, gathering himself for another move. 'What's going on?'

Red's answer was almost inaudible and took a long time in coming.

'I think there are two conferences, this one of Longhair's and another one. Ottawa Walker. Somewhere near.'

There was a pause before the weak voice went on.

'Hudson's Bay Company wants a new Factory. Bruce Factory. Ottawa Walker wants it. Longhair's against it.'

Calvin was now close enough to the cage to hear quite clearly. He was also aware of the intense effort Red was making.

'There could be a war,' said Red.

'Why are you in a cage?'

'Longhair thinks I killed his uncle.'

'Who?'

'I didn't. I was nowhere near, but – Longhair's not in his right mind.'

'Killed who?'

'Calvin, if you can—'

A request was coming, but the voice stopped, then resumed on a puzzled note.

'There's something about a totem. That's what they searched for. It's important. It's a stone thing. They searched – everywhere.'

'What is it?'

But Red evidently had some important message he wished to get across. He sweated and trembled.

'Don't blame the girls. Don't – and Cal— If—'

Calvin heard Kittypet behind him. Her hand stroked his shoulder.

'Come with me,' she whispered. 'I'll find you some food.'

He was suddenly lost in fury. Why was she so stupid. Groaning he raised himself and pushed at her till she fell and he beat her with his fist, roaring hoarsely, 'Get away from me! You've spoiled it! Get away! Get away! Get away and don't come back!'

She crawled hopelessly away. Calvin turned back to the cage. He had to find out more about—

194

But the two guards were angry and a couple of others nearby. Maybe it was because they were of the same family as Kittypet. They came towards him with purpose.

Calvin rose. He heard Red trying to say something more.

'And Cal, please, if – please, if—'

But the four Indians were knocking Calvin down and kicking him. He was conscious enough to be glad they wore moccasins, not boots. Red was still trying to speak to him when he heard Firepouch shouting and the two guards tucked him under their right arms by the knees and chest and ran off with him. They dropped him heavily a couple of hundred yards closer to the south forest and then went back to their duties. All the time they ran with him, and while he lay there, all the breath knocked out of him, Calvin heard Red's voice. It was unsteady, it was spasmodic, but an unmistakable cry for help. It was shocking to know such desperation came from Red. The voice repeated his name time after time, and in between the repetitions came the two wild words—

'Shoot me!'

Like echoes the shouts grew weaker. 'Cal. Shoot me! Cal. Shoot me! Cal. Shoot me! Shoot me! Shoot me!'

In and out of consciousness, Calvin was convinced that the quietness immediately around him – except for the limpid lyric of a thrush – was a threat. Also a threat was the murmur, which emphasised the quietness, of many voices sounding from a distance, possibly from the place where the young men were working at the curious frame.

There was a threat too in the fact that the murmur was bass; there were few women present and no children.

He ached intolerably and eased his head round towards the taller trees where the thrush sang. Few women, but here was one woman coming towards him. He didn't know that any of the people were camped in that direction. This woman wore an undecorated, sleeveless garment that almost reached the ground. Half the time she was screened by shadow, tree or shrub. Maybe she wasn't coming towards him. He lost sight of her.

But Red's hoarse cry was the most frightening thing because he knew Red understood far more of what was going on than he did. His cheeks were wet and his throat was raw. He couldn't stop his muscles twitching. He was cold. His whole body trembled. He was powerless, and Red was the best friend he'd ever had, the best man he'd ever known.

He must think. He must think!

The big canoe he'd seen from the cliff that day was probably a Company canoe. It might have paddled north in the lake of the Hurons. Company men *might* be closer than he thought.

Even an individual trader from Montreal would help if – if—

Even French traders. Red said there were a number of them about—

There was a burst of shouting and Calvin eased his head round again. Two young men with bundles, accompanied by three with heavy bows, were moving towards Longhair's private clearing. Longhair came forward and met them in a patch of sunlight where Calvin could see clearly. The bundles were thrown down and Calvin was certain one of them moved slightly. He watched closely.

Longhair stopped, selected something and held it high so everyone could see. White sheets of paper fluttered to the ground. It was Calvin's writing-case. When the examination was finished Longhair gesticulated and all the papers were gathered up and carefully replaced.

Other pieces of their baggage, including the bearskin, were examined. The bundle that had moved was, of course, the fawn. The coarse rope wrapped about her hooves was cut, though she was still tethered by a thong on one hind leg. She didn't rise immediately and when she

196

did she staggered. Her head drooped and her feet seemed, somehow, in an awkward position for standing.

The meeting took some time. Every item was carefully searched before it was distributed; Longhair kept the writing-case and its contents himself. The fawn couldn't be persuaded to move so she was lifted and carried towards the frame. She didn't struggle.

With the scattering of their baggage Calvin's summer – even his life – seemed also scattered. He felt quite faint. Berwick, his youth, were rushing away from him. There were no more cries from the cage. The two guards sat beside it. Red, in spite of the blood and dirt, was pale behind the bars.

Calvin rolled to his back. The woman in the long dress was kneeling beside him, holding a birch-bark vessel full of clear water. He reached and tried to lift himself. His lower chest and diaphragm seemed cut in two. An arm went round his shoulders and raised him. He drank like an open drain until the vessel was raised high and his eyes met Moonluck's.

He stopped drinking, hurled the water in her face and rolled to his right away from her. She said nothing.

He was on his elbows, his head drooping. He examined a perfect skeleton of a maple leaf resting lightly on the moss. It was incredibly delicate. The least breath could tear it to pieces. Easily broken – easily broken— He looked at it for some moments—

'I want you to listen,' began Moonluck in a soft clear voice.

'It's your fault,' said Calvin.

'Listen. Can you walk?'

'You knew all the time.'

'Can you walk?' The question was quiet but insistent.

'You knew. You knew it was Longhair.'

'Try to walk. Move slowly.'

'All the time! You knew all the time.'

197

Moonluck shook her head impatiently and glanced across to the terrace. There was a brief pause before she spoke.

'I suspected from the time of the arrow. I knew from the time of the hand.'

'You knew long before. You knew when you started south with me. That night. The canoe. The keel—'

Against her will Moonluck was drawn into argument. 'Suspect?' she said. 'Know? I tried to find out—'

'What?'

'Who sent him.'

'Who sent who?'

'Flyer. He wouldn't tell me.'

This was an admission utterly unexpected by Calvin. Finally he blurted out, 'When you were lost?'

'Yes.'

'In the forest. The mist—'

'Yes.'

'You disappeared. We thought you were lost. You found the Flyer then?'

'Yes,' she said.

'Talked to him?'

Moonluck grabbed Calvin's shoulders desperately and spoke with great intensity.

'We've no time. We can be safe. We can get away. If we move slowly. If we're quiet.'

Calvin tried to shake her off. 'Why is Red in a cage?' he began.

'We've no time, Calvin.'

'Why is Red in a cage – and not you?'

She took her hands from his shoulders. 'I'm not important,' she said. It was both a resigned discovery and a resentful admission. The tone stopped Calvin for a moment. She went on urgently.

'If we go now, if we hurry Calvin—'

'Why is Red in a cage?'

'Speechmaker thinks he murdered Pontiac at Cahokia.'

'He didn't.'

'A red-head fought him at Fort DuQuesne. A red-head fought him at Detroit. A red-head was seen at Cahokia. I run away. He hears I'm with a red-head. These four wolves make a pack. He howls, roars, makes no sense, his dreams deceive him so now he thinks he knows. Red will never get away.'

It was hard to follow and she spoke in a brittle, sharp manner which discouraged questions. 'Can you walk?'

'Not with you,' said Calvin. 'Bitch. Bitch.'

'Try to walk. Try—'

'You knew. *And* about Red. You led us here.'

Her low voice now throbbed in an effort to convince. 'No!' she urged. 'No, this is where my father makes camp. Always. My father. He must be somewhere near—'

'You knew, and about Red too. Red liked you—'

'I was trying to get him to my father.'

'You led him straight here.'

Calvin's rising hysteria was caused only partly by pure weakness. At that moment he was suddenly aware of seeing clearly – the keel, the arrow, the hand! And at each point of decision Moonluck had been both decisive and insistent. And straight to this place they had marched—

'Go on away. I don't know. If he dies you've killed him. Go away. Go away and leave me alone. Bitch!'

He babbled on into slobbering silence.

'You're stupid,' said Moonluck. 'You know nothing.'

'Bitch!'

'Stupid! Gutless! Why do I bother?'

'Get away from me.'

'Listen—'

'If Red dies—'

'He's dead already.'

Calvin peered back at the cage, saw an arm move awkwardly.

'He isn't dead,' he said.

'Stupid,' said Moonluck, sputtering, incoherent.

Calvin was the same. 'Best friend – good man. He—'

Then he saw that a group of four of the strongest young men had detached themselves from Firepouch and were moving deliberately towards the cage. They carried a length of the coarse rope. He watched them as if hypnotised, muttering disconnectedly over his shoulder, 'Run if you want to. Bitch. All your fault. You knew. You never told us. You knew. Longhair once sharpened his hatchet and— What'll he do?'

He waited a moment for an answer before his wild stammering continued. 'The stories. Old Colethorpe. Yellow eyes. What'll he do?'

She'd know. She'd known all along. The four young men were close to the cage now. Why didn't she answer? He must demand an answer. He turned back painfully. His sight was bleary and he couldn't see her. He blinked, pawed at his eyes weakly and blinked again. She was nowhere. Not a branch swung, not a shrub sprang back into place, not a leaf trembled. Calvin remembered the startling disappearance of the three old men. The three old men – pleasant, smiling, gone in an instant. Were they real? Was she? None of them existed. Dreams. In a dream land.

For an unfathomable reason this desertion was worse and less expected than anything that had happened; and for a couple of minutes he couldn't take it in. The thrush behind him, like liquid bells, burbled serenely of some world he had glimpsed briefly. Then, slowly, he began to accept the desertion as part of a pattern. It was a pattern which he could still hardly believe but the facts, like plugs of mash down a goose's gullet, forced themselves into his consciousness. Facts were facts and had to be believed, a bitter medicine that had to be swallowed and digested before it could do you good. Moonluck's disappearance

200

added desolation to the emptiness that was now exhausting all resolution from the whirling capsule of his mind.

When Calvin clawed himself back to facts, Red had been hauled out of the cage. His arms were bound but his feet were free. Four of Longhair's most muscular disciples jostled him across the glade towards the terrace where the frame stood. When he was half-way to the low granite rampart, Red made a surprising effort. His thighs and waist were suddenly convulsed. As he lurched and swung violently left, the two who grasped his right arm were almost lifted from their feet and hurled against their pivoting companions. One went down, the rest scrabbled with slippery moccasins for purchase on the sandy ground.

A stoop, a powerful butt with the red head and a heaving lift with the shoulders to the right and he was free of his captors. Before they or Calvin were aware of how he'd done it he was five yards away, racing east through shafts of sunlight. The four were after him but he was widening the gap. The big legs were not only powerful but they lashed the ground fast as whip-cracks. One thin young Indian with a white zigzag painted on his chest kept pace and closed on him, angling from his left. Red swerved towards him, lowered his shoulder a fraction and bowled him over. The Indian rolled, somersaulted backwards and regained his feet, but Red was ten yards nearer the trees and still accelerating. He thrust out his neck, leaned on the air and lengthened his stride.

The glade was full of shouts and echoes. The trees were fifty, forty, thirty yards away when two of Longhair's young recruits appeared and raced, half-stooping, not directly towards him, but so that he would run between them. Calvin saw the rope they dragged. He watched it tauten and rise. Red leaped. One foot was over. They lifted the rope, caught the other and Red crashed to the ground. The crash opened the cut in his head. The tribe cheered and six young men, panting, lifted the inert body.

They carried it till they reached the low bulge of granite. Then Red was flung to the top of the first terrace, lifted again and carried towards the 'frame'. Calvin wanted to see. Then he decided against it. He didn't want to see. Red would die. He hoped it would be quick.

Suddenly, dizzyingly, he felt himself lifted. He hadn't sensed anyone near him. One young man held his ankles, one each arm. He was slung low and face down. A few thistles raked his scalp and ears as they ran with him. They dropped him in the cleared area between the 'frame' and the terrace wall.

He could see the tops of a couple of teepees through the trees on the next terrace. There weren't a great many people and they were scattered in a wide semi-circle, seated on the ground, several of them eating. The shadows were short. It must be noon. The fawn, dirty, thin and weak, stood centrally, her head hanging.

Most of the Indian women wore moccasins, a skirt to the knees and a tunic that fell just below the top of the skirt. Their hair was in two braids. Some of them, because it was warm, had left off the tunic. Some wore a short cape instead of the tunic. A couple of the old women wore both. They liked to be warm. But, as Calvin had noticed, there weren't many women. The soft garments – very few were made of fabric – were extensively decorated, as for a party.

The young men of Longhair's own army wore nothing but thong, breech-clout and headband. A few had a quiver of arrows on a band over the shoulder. All these young men were strong enough in the shoulder to use the heavy bows they carried.

The rest of the men were more conventionally clothed with moccasins, leggings, breech-cloth or apron and some added a shirt, jacket or cape. Firepouch himself was wearing a fine cloak of some light glossy fur, probably mink. Underneath he wore a wide decorated coronet with a fountain of black hair cascading from the top. It was made from the mane of a black bear, a narrow strip, doubled over to increase the display of hair. The headband was embroidered at the lower edge with dyed porcupine quills. This stiff band helped to keep the hair springing upright and bending over. It was more dignified than his own hair which was sparse and grey.

The square 'frame' was the centre of the semi-circle. A long coil of coarse twisted fibre was slung over the high bar and a ladder leaned against the centre point. The individual rungs were bound, not dowelled or nailed, to the uprights.

Work was still going on below this structure, but Calvin was unable to discover what was being done.

He lay on a slight rise, so when the crowd turned to watch the arrival of the band of Miamis, he could see them as they threaded their way through the seated Ottawas to a place reserved for them. Their bright and somewhat fantastic clothes made the others look drab. Some of them carried curious net bags with chunks of corn-bread, or meat bones, in them. The net seemed to be spun black hair, neatly knotted. There were a few questions from the Ottawas. Some of these Miamis came from quite far away and their village was called Chicago.

Calvin didn't retain a consecutive story of what went on; his attention wandered but he noticed some things that happened near him when his eyes were not too blurred or too unfocused.

Kittypet was dragged in by two women. When she was flung to the ground in front of him Calvin saw that her face was grey and her legs scratched as if she'd run through brambles. Firepouch asked where Moonluck was, and the women said she'd disappeared.

'Where is she?'

'I don't know,' said Kittypet.

Surprisingly an old man in a grey blanket came by with a few roasted quail in his hands. He tore one in half and gave it to Calvin who grabbed it and began to chew at the breast. The old man looked familiar.

Suddenly the scattered semi-circle went silent and stayed that way as a procession of three appeared, led by the fat woman. She directed her young men to place the windsor chair they carried directly in front of the frame and she put a pottery bowl of water beside it on the ground.

A little later she came closer to Calvin and gazed at the forest on the far side of the open terrace. Yesterday she'd been stone-like. Today she was agitated. Firepouch joined her and Calvin gathered what he could from their low, quick conversation.

Everything was wrong. It wasn't traditional. It was too slow. The people were bored. And it was peculiar to find Speechmaker, of all people, adopting the ways of white men.

Nor would all this preparation help his dream.

'If he wants to be invited to join the Society he ought to behave like a member. He should leave a killing to a war chief,' said Firepouch with finality.

Calvin fumbled about in his mind for the name of the 'Society'. He found it at last. Medewiwin. He wondered what it signified. Longhair didn't want the Hudson's Bay Company to build Bruce Factory, but he wanted to join this society. Were these things important?

Then he wondered about the fat woman. It occurred to him that she might be Longhair's mother. She seemed almost as influential as Firepouch.

Later there was a sound of subdued cheering from the crowd around the frame, and as they dispersed Calvin could see someone holding up a shallow basket which had just been completed. It looked more like a sieve than

204

a basket. The willow twigs were far apart though neatly woven. It was nearly four feet in diameter but only a foot deep. The rim was made of thin split hardwood and neatly bound. Two thongs of braided leather were fixed by both ends to the rim. The basket hung level when suspended by these strong handles.

Firepouch went towards Longhair's hut.

Just at that moment Calvin was conscious that the fat woman was again coming towards him. Two young men rushed from the valley and met her ten feet in front of him. One carried a spear with a small, bristly, ragged animal impaled on the tip.

'Quickly. Quickly,' she said, pointing to the ground at her feet. They lowered the dead thing carefully and she covered it with her doe-skin cape. She glanced around with some signs of nervousness. Some of the people may have seen the incident but not many because they were watching for Longhair.

Calvin was close enough to recognise the grey and black quills of a porcupine before it was covered by the cloak. The thought of the quills shocked Calvin into closer attention.

When, with some ceremony, Longhair arrived he supervised the filling of the flat basket. He was still maintaining his silence, but his gestures were clear and commanding. Nearby was a pile of dried leaves, brittle from a year of wind and sun, and another pile of feathery moss faded to a pale grey. Calvin recognised the moss as being the same, though more carefully winnowed, as mothers used to pack around their babies when they were carried on a black-board. First a layer of the trailing moss was lightly spread over the bottom of the basket, then a layer of the dry leaves. Alternate layers, as light as down, were tossed into place until the basket was filled. The final layer, longer strands of moss, took more time. These were tucked in and tangled so that a wind would not carry away the layer of brittle leaves. The filled basket was placed between the two four-foot posts directly under the high cross-beam. The braided handles were freed.

Then Calvin saw where Red was. He'd been dropped near the frame. He was still unconscious but the coarse fibre rope was passed over his chest, under his arms and lightly knotted at his backbone. Longhair made a negative gesture when someone offered to revive him with a bark bucket of water. The young men tossed the two ends of the rope over the high cross-beam and Red was hauled upright. He revived a little and, by a reflex, tried to stand. His legs sagged, however, and he was carried to the ladder. As he was pulled up by the ropes, the young men held his feet so they would not touch the basket. When he was high enough one foot was placed on each short post and tied there securely. He was leaning forward at quite an angle till his knees sagged again and the weight was taken by the rope. His head clunked back against the cross-bar and the accident made Longhair angry.

The knees were straightened by main force and the young man on the ladder stretched Red's heavy left arm against the cross-bar, and tied the wrist in place. Then he leaned but couldn't reach the other wrist. The ladder would have to be moved. He finished tying the left arm, binding it round and round with inch-wide strips of rawhide.

Only the fibre rope round his chest kept Red in place as the ladder was moved and the other arm secured. They'd been forced to hold his knees, his thighs and his waist to keep him upright. Once the arms were secure he could sag if he wished. A band was placed around his forehead and tied tightly. The ends of this band dangled behind the cross-bar and when they were pulled the head was drawn back across the bar and the throat stretched tight. Red was in such a position that he could stand on the two posts, his feet wide apart or, if his legs gave way, he would be supported by his bound arms. The chest rope was removed and the young man climbed down from the ladder.

The basket had to be moved back a little so the windsor chair could be conveniently placed. Longhair stood on it. He needed both hands, so he loosed his hair which fell nearly to the ground. He put a thorn through Red's fore-skin, lifted his cock up and pinned it to the skin of his belly. He drew very little blood, but the sharp jab was enough to make Red shake his head and open his eyes. Longhair held out his hand. The wet triangle of rawhide with its dangling laces was taken from the bowl and handed to him. He placed it as high as possible round Red's testicles, then the laces were adjusted.

Longhair tested the top of the cone. It compressed the skin of the scrotum a little but not too much. He tightened the laces a little. In doing so he caught a few hairs and Red jerked upright, taking his weight on his own legs. The laces were firmly tied.

A strong round plaited leather line was knotted and threaded through each round hole in the two lugs at the bottom of the cone. As the cone was five inches long Red's balls were completely covered, but they were not yet compressed. Longhair gathered his hair round his arm and stepped from the chair which was removed. The basket was lifted by two young men. Each handle was tied to one of the lines from the cone and Longhair judged the length with some care. When the knots were made firm he stood back.

He moved his right hand gently up and down and the young men, by almost invisible degrees, lowered the basket. Longhair wanted the braided lines to take the weight evenly, and a sudden shock was to be strictly avoided. When Red became sufficiently conscious again he would undoubtedly provide his own shocks. The basket, at present, was very light. The cone didn't slip more than an eighth of an inch. After tense moments the young men succeeded. The basket swung back and forth slightly as their hands came away. Its twisting motion was negligible.

Calvin was ripped out of a region of unbelieving horror by a curious sound. A handful of the people were giggling. To Longhair the giggle was an affront, and he stopped it by slowly turning to identify the source. Calvin was not surprised that most of the levity came from the Miamis.

Longhair obviously decided the process must be finished quickly. A young man was sent up the ladder to jerk the thorn out of the fold of belly-skin and out of the foreskin. As soon as this was done another young man tied an apron round Red's waist.

A third, carrying a birch-bark vessel of water, now climbed the ladder and jerked Red's head back across the beam. The water was poured into the open mouth and a reflex against suffocation forced Red to swallow some of it. What he swallowed, Calvin knew, would tend to revive him. The rest dribbled through the dirt and blood on Red's shoulders, down his sides and along his legs. What was not soaked up by grime dripped on the dry moss in the basket.

Calvin saw that this moss could absorb a considerable weight of water. He saw also that the cone would descend, that Red's balls would be compressed and that, as the leather dried, the cone would shrink.

Red now supported his own weight, though he blinked slowly in the sunlight.

Longhair nodded. His chair was picked up and he strode back to his hut. A few of the men came close to look, and some of the women. Calvin wondered idly if the apron were intended as a gesture of modesty. He was surprised that most of the people just sat there finishing their meal. A few, having finished, were wandering away. The pain of a foreigner isn't really pain, he thought.

208

The fat woman's sharp eyes were fixed on Longhair. As soon as he disappeared in his hut she muttered to her helpers who ran to bring the squeaking ladder round to the front of the frame. They leaned the top against Red's arm.

The fat woman was coming towards him, and Calvin didn't take it in for several seconds. He moved his head weakly and rose to his knees.

But she wasn't interested in him; she stopped beside the doe-skin cape she had thrown down earlier. Calvin forgot her and began to crawl towards Red. He didn't know why. No one stopped him. He passed Kittypet who lay motionless and without expression. When he passed the fat woman she was on her knees and he saw her select four quills from the porcupine – not the longest, but the stoutest. He'd heard enough of the chatter around him to realise that she was important. She claimed she was Pontiac's wife for a time. Now she was claiming to be Speechmaker's mother. Speechmaker – Longhair – whatever his name was – paid little attention, but tolerated her because she was a link with the great man.

Calvin's hand was on what was left of the pile of moss. He looked up. Red's eyes were closed but he was supporting his own weight. The fat woman was on the ladder and the concealing apron was swung to the side. She held the four quills by the thick ends between her teeth and she was rolling back Red's foreskin. In a line with the axis of his cock she pricked the purple glands lightly to a depth of no more than an eighth of an inch and left the quill to hang there. She used three and spaced them evenly. She hesitated and glanced over her shoulder at Longhair's hut. Calvin knew what she wanted to do with the fourth quill. She decided against it and the fourth quill fell into the basket. Very slowly, adjusting the quills to lie straight, she brought the foreskin down to cover them and hold their microscopic barbs in place. A drop of blood hung on the butt of the longest quill protruding from the foreskin.

Calvin went faint and his open mouth, when he came to for a moment, was full of sand and moss. Firepouch and the fat woman were quarrelling in hushed, vicious voices.

'He'll be angry,' said Firepouch.

'He won't know,' said the fat woman.

The ladder had been taken round to the back. There were two weals on Red's arm where it had leaned. The apron was in place again. Red's eyes were open and he was looking down. He didn't see Calvin. His head lifted till it hung just a little forward and he seemed to be looking at the horizon.

Calvin knew that when they lifted Red down from his high perch he would be meat, already partly decayed.

The sun shone warmly. Calvin heard, faint and pure in the distance, the incredible clarity of the notes the thrush poured out – curious at noon when most birds were quiet. Was there someone near that thrush, disturbing it? From far away came a shout. Like an echo it was repeated from a nearer point. Everyone paid attention though Calvin couldn't make out the words. The distant and the nearer shouts betrayed excitement. Longhair and Firepouch were together by the time the closest sentry ran in from the east and called out the message clearly.

A Hudson's Bay Company brigade was on the eastern lake. It was approaching at speed, would enter the river in an hour, and the proudest canoe carried centrally a white man in a floppy hat.

There was great activity. Calvin saw Longhair's lieutenant race up the ladder and put a gag in Red's mouth, holding it there with a leather strap.

Several young men were cutting saplings. They began to prop up a screen of these in front of Red. Then he saw Kittypet rise slowly to her feet. Instantly she was rushed

210

south across the open spillway. Evidently she recalled Calvin to their minds because more young soldiers searched for him, found him, and rushed him in the same direction. They went through a jumble of rocks and into the low mouth of a cave in the wall of the southern terrace. Two guards stayed with them, but neither Kittypet nor Calvin was tied up.

The Hudson's Bay Company?

MacBain?

Calvin's mind was moving far too slowly but—

MacBain was a powerful man. They'd get Red down again.

Calvin looked round him. The cave was narrow but it went a long way in, and it seemed to slope downwards.

The sun was bright outside. Across the open valley they'd almost completed the screen around Red's scaffold. They'd get Red down.

It was cold, here in the cave. Calvin shivered as he waited.

9

One Dream

'All skulls smile.'

Longhair

BUT MacBain didn't come. The guards stood attentively at the entrance to the cave, watching preparations to receive the white man. Calvin was able to haul himself to a curved shelf on the limestone wall. He could see, over the shoulders of the guards, that for some time there was great activity. Firepouch kept running back and forth from a cleared space on the lowest terrace to Longhair's hut. His agitation may have been caused by the difficulty of communicating with a man who refused to speak. Calvin saw the last sapling put into the screen which now hid Red completely. A group of soldiers disappeared to the east, towards the point where the river curved into the lake. They were intended, Calvin presumed, to welcome MacBain. The windsor chair was brought in and placed in the cleared space Firepouch had selected. About ten young men, now fully armed with bows, spears and hatchets, sauntered up, one by one.

They'd been waiting for about half an hour when there was a renewed series of shouts from the distant sentries. Firepouch became even more agitated and conferred with three older men, one after the other. Then the four of them moved off towards Longhair's hut.

Calvin understood enough of the sentries' shouts to

213

learn three things: that MacBain's brigade had been joined by a small canoe, paddled by one person; that there had been a brief conference in mid-lake; and that the whole convoy had put in to the north shore, not far from the 'other camp'.

What other camp?

Three times the name of the Ottawa Walker had been mentioned.

Mysteries: the lone canoe, the other camp, and the Ottawa Walker.

And Calvin found his brain too dull. Single thoughts remained like lumps in porridge. Time passed at two different speeds, unbelievably fast and glutinously slow – always mysteries. He was very tired.

The two guards were getting impatient, uncertain whether to stay or go. As inconspicuously as possible Calvin slipped down the curve of limestone and crawled further back in the cave. His vision took a few seconds to adjust to the darkness. He stopped when he saw Kittypet sitting with her back against the opposite wall, her eyes low and half-closed but in a fixed stare. Her hands lay limply on the sand at her sides. Calvin watched her dully for some minutes then his eyes closed, and suddenly he slid sideways till his left shoulder and face hit the sand, and there he slept.

He didn't dream of Red's torment or of his own chancy situation. He was in the flume of fast water again and the large slow trout gazed at him as he raced by. He was tantalised by the rippling girls as they flowed into sunlight and out again. Red was secure, heavy, powerful, a hero; though even in the dream he was a vague hero. He hadn't done anything, he just was. He was, and there was no possible betrayal in any nerve, cell, or fibre of his being.

The dream turned pages in random order. Everything Calvin had ever longed for was already accomplished.

Moonluck's eyes, which understood everything, were lit by gold from Red's hair. Kittypet's breasts were warm and heavy on his belly and chest, yet he was lying in the channel of her thighs. They lifted him into all the wonders of creation. There was no darkness, no pain, no fear. Eden, without a serpent, was achieved. Warm air, cool water, health, ravishing foods, silk skin, the hero's muscle, smooth strength and enveloping softness were to be his – and he was to have quick nerves that would always savour them.

In his dream the four of them were one. Each inhabited the other. It was a world of total joy.

Then he stopped dreaming and his breathing became slow and even. He continued like this till late afternoon.

Longhair, Firepouch, the guards and two other soldiers woke him by taking off his clothes. They removed everything, even his ragged moccasins. The attack was sudden and it took Calvin some time to take it in. Everything was searched by Firepouch. When he failed to find what he was looking for Longhair searched each garment a second time.

'Do you know where it is?' asked Firepouch.

They looked enormous in the one-sided light from the cave-entrance. They were supernatural and could take what they wanted.

'A small stone figure on a string. It was taken by the man who murdered Pontiac.' Firepouch was trying almost desperately to make himself understood.

'Pontiac's— Pontiac's totem. His name!'

'I haven't got it.'

'Have you hidden it?'

'How could I?'

'Have you seen it?'

'No.'

Things happened, thought Calvin – frightening things, and you didn't really grasp them. Suddenly the six men had gone, though Calvin didn't see them go. He'd been manhandled during the search and dropped on the sand so that Kittypet was quite close. He reached out slowly and took her hand.

Curiously, all the threat of the startling search was less frightening than the touch of the girl's hand. It was almost cold, a little damp and seemed quite lifeless. The lowered eyes looked at him and didn't see him. This was a cool, deadly place.

His hand twitched away from Kittypet's as he thought he saw movement far in the black gullet of the cave. But he didn't pay much attention. He lay on the sand wondering how long Kittypet could stay inert, unseeing and unresponsive. Almost deliberately he tried to slide again into his dream.

He slept, and awoke in utter darkness. He was shivering. As some slight protection from the cold, he groped about for his clothes and struggled into them awkwardly.

Mr MacBain was close. He'd be bound to enquire. News travelled. He'd arrive. Maybe unexpectedly. He'd do something. Calvin didn't go into the problem of what he could do, but he could do something—

And the old man who'd given him food, and whom he'd thought he'd met before—

And the imminence of the Ottawa Walker, the powerful chief of the Northern Ottawas—

And those three old men who had been interested in his writing-case—

And who was paddling the one canoe that met Mac-Bain's brigade?

So he slept again and didn't care whether these encouraging thoughts were deceiving him or not.

Someone was shaking his shoulder. The light was very faint but he could make out two eyes in the shadow of a head. It was a young Indian who whispered, 'Pancakes.'

216

Then a hand guided Calvin's hand to a pile of pancakes which were still slightly warm.

'What's happened to her?' asked the whisper, and Calvin knew he referred to Kittypet, leaning, as before, against the cave wall.

'I don't know,' said Calvin.

'Give her some pancakes.'

Then they heard the beginning of a faint drum-beat from outside and both listened.

'What's that for?'

'Speechmaker will begin his dream tonight, tomorrow, the next day.'

'Why is he doing this to Red?'

'Pontiac's orders,' said the unknown Indian.

'He's dead.'

'He had a ceremony. "What do we do to white men?" he asked, and the answer was "Rip their balls off".'

The drum-beat was suddenly loud, then it diminished.

They spoke very quietly, then the young Indian left him and Calvin heard his soft progress over the sand. He didn't go towards the mouth of the cave but into the deeper blackness in the other direction. Was there another entrance to the cave?

Was it the Flyer? It was a real hand that guided Calvin to the pancakes but he thought he'd seen another arm that ended, a little short, in a round bundle of fur.

Calvin waited. The drum-beats finished. The quietness was absolute. All sounds of the retreating visitor had ceased. The light was a little less grey when he heard what seemed like the ghost of a sound – a light stirring in the still air. He couldn't tell where it came from. It seemed to be all around him. What was it? He didn't know whether to laugh or cry when the notion occurred to him that the sound was made by the wings of angels.

The pancakes rested on a basswood leaf. He ate one. It was soft and delicious. There were six of them so he took one more before he slid the leaf closer to Kittypet. Maybe it was the pancakes that put him to sleep for the last time that night. The visit had been no dream. The pancakes proved it.

Calvin's visit to Red's scaffold could do Red no good. Maybe his decision to pay the visit was foolish but in a way, his self-respect depended on it and it wasn't foolish to preserve that. He'd made the decision when he stood blinking in the sunlight at eleven o'clock. The guards had left the mouth of the cave. Why? Was he a prisoner or not?

Anyway, he struggled across the valley, taking nearly ten minutes to accomplish the short trip. When he reached the place he stopped and didn't move. He was a lump of rock, unable to influence what was going on.

Longhair held the fawn by the hind legs. Her throat was cut and the blood was draining into a bowl.

Red had his jaws clenched. Longhair's lieutenant hammered a stick with his tomahawk. The jaws were forced open and he tied the stick between them. There was still enough room for liquids to trickle past the stick into Red's throat. Water was poured in. If Red wouldn't swallow his nose was held. Feeding him with the bowl of blood took some time. Much of it was swallowed. The rest ran down his neck and shoulders making long streaks in the grime already there, and disturbing the wandering flies. Red didn't see him. It was still right for him to come, but – but to stay – to stay, and to watch?

Calvin took a long time to reach the cave again, and when he did so he was shivering violently. He went a long way in and lay in the dimness half awake, half asleep. Kittypet had disappeared. He didn't know how long he lay there. The bouts of shivering became less frequent.

His time sense was being disturbed. The order of events

was all wrong. Had the fat woman been killed today or yesterday? Or the day before?

Where was Moonluck?

Where was MacBain?

Each morning he crossed the little valley. Each morning Red seemed weaker. Each morning the Indians were more nervous and their behaviour more threatening. Each time he returned to the cave he went further in, till he sat in a constant twilight. Yet food was left for him, and a blanket.

Some events stood out in the muddle. He'd looked away from Red once to find Longhair beside him. There was something sad in his expression as the yellow eyes moved and recognised him. The glance was like a blast from a hot oven but Calvin couldn't look away. The eyes were hypnotic. Calvin found his need to understand almost as strong as the impulse to turn and run. Longhair, he was convinced, almost spoke to him, almost asked him something, almost broke his so-important 'silence'.

Maybe in this muddle of days he'd visited Red more than once a day. It was when he saw the broad green-black line curling up the side of Red's pulled in belly that Firepouch had approached him and quietly advised him to stay out of sight. Red, Calvin was convinced, was dying.

'Too quick,' said Firepouch, and slipped away. The green-black network had spread up the hollow between the flat muscles of Red's belly and the heavy vertical muscles of his side. The pulling in of the belly was intolerably pathetic – a hopeless reflex to avoid pain. Red was there, Calvin here, doing nothing. The dogs, catching the horrible smell from the basket, would put their paws on the edge and set it swinging. Red was flushed, and Calvin could see the fast pulse at neck and ankles.

A half-erection lifted the light leather apron away from his groin. Calvin knew the erection would pull back the

219

foreskin, which would catch the minute barbs of the quills, forcing the points further and further into the glands. The pain reduced the erection and the apron went down slowly. Drops of blood formed on its lower edges. Suddenly a spurt of urine washed them off. The urine would splash on the rawhide cone, stretching it a little so it would slide down a little.

Longhair was there, saw what was happening and grabbed a spear with which he lifted the apron and looked under it. A cloud of blue-bottles whined out angrily. What he saw explained Red's weakness to Longhair who dropped the spear and looked grimly around, holding his stone-headed tomahawk.

If the fat woman who had used the quills had stayed still – but she didn't, she turned to sneak away. The tomahawk flickered after her like a stick-thin dwarf doing cartwheels in the air and the stone head made a cracking sound as it struck. She fell instantly, and curiously slowly. Her heavy body made no sound. Her skull was shattered and the haft of the tomahawk stood out like the handle of a spoon from a boiled egg.

Calvin had hardly reached the cave again when there was great excitement. MacBain was arriving. Time again passed at two speeds. The proud ceremonies were drawn out endlessly and compressed confusingly. The guards were back and Calvin was threatened with a gag, so he stayed quiet. MacBain wouldn't have to be told. There was no secrecy. The news must have travelled.

He saw how formally his telescope and his writing-case were presented. There was an argument, maybe about his musket. That was not handed over. MacBain, standing in his floppy hat, handed the two articles to one of the white men who came with him. The rest of his party consisted of six tough-looking Indians who were canoe-men, as suggested by the heavily muscled shoulders. Longhair approached and the group sat on the sand.

Quite suddenly, and for no apparent reason, the guards took it into their heads that their prisoner might be visible so they hustled him farther into the cave and returned themselves to watch. Calvin waited. These conferences sometimes took a long time. He listened for a variation in the sound coming from the outside but the murmur didn't seem to change. He saw the two guards move a few yards towards the conference, chattering. Would they chatter if important men were meeting? He crawled back to his ledge slowly.

The conference was ended. Longhair was going back to his hut and MacBain was just disappearing into the trees to the east.

Calvin was, by now, incapable of thought and he staggered after MacBain, calling loudly. The guards and the young men gathered around him, imitating him, calling out in what they thought was English. Calvin was stronger than he thought and he began to run. He remembered Red's desperate dash for freedom but the result of that attempt didn't stop him. He was hysterical and senseless with disappointed hope. He didn't realise before how much he had hoped. His speed increased but the young Indians had no difficulty keeping pace. A couple preceded him, staggering and weaving, calling out, and occasionally falling to the ground.

The effort was, of course, unsuccessful and, when his hysteria steamed off his energy, the Indians dragged and carried him back to the cave. This disappointment was too much. He went on crawling when they dropped him, back, back into the darkness, farther back than he'd ever gone. It wasn't completely dark even here. A drift of sand, curiously bumpy, rose in front of him. It was almost high enough to touch the roof of the cave but not quite. Cold air flowed over his sweaty body. He crawled part way up the slope before he lay still, panting. He closed his eyes.

After a moment he felt a round stone under his hip.

He pulled it out, and then another. He didn't pay attention at the time to the lightness of these stones. He realised he must have slept when he opened his eyes a little later and found the cave quite dark. He was still bothered by the boulders and hauled out a few more to make more comfortable hollows for his hip and shoulder. All the stones were round. This was curious. Had the cave once been the bed of a stream? He slept again, and through his sleep came the distant growl of thunder.

He woke, shivering, and uncertain about what had awakened him. He was in a blaze of light. The moon was rising and it was enormous – the disc filled completely the entrance to the cave and its light poured over the round stones he'd pulled out to make himself comfortable. Each stone was a human skull and some of them stared at him with great black eyes. He felt a hand on his forehead, stroking it, and heard a voice whispering.

'I've water here, and his rifle. We can get away, I think.'

It was Moonluck. She sat behind him on the sand and Calvin threw his arms around her waist and buried his face in her belly.

'We'll have to wait for Kittypet and her brother. They're stealing some food.'

Calvin took a long time while he moved his face up to nuzzle her breast.

'Red's rifle?' he asked.

'Yes.'

'Where's Red?'

'He's dead, Calvin.' Moonluck was still whispering but Calvin read a hundred meanings into her intonation.

'Thank God,' he said, and clutched her more tightly. Then he began crying and couldn't stop. Whenever he closed his wobbling jaws, clenched them and thought the weakness gone, more tears would gather in his eyes and he'd burrow into her body, wiping them off.

The glare of light showed him that Moonluck's eyes were dry and that she was looking into nothingness, her face a mask of grief which she had already accepted. Her hands wiped the tears from his cheeks and she said, 'You were his good friend.'

Then they were quiet for a time.

'You didn't kill him,' said Calvin.

'No,' she said.

Soon the moon rose higher and the cave was dark again. Moonluck had brought water and a little food which they ate.

'Kittypet and the Flyer won't be able to get here till nearly morning. We may have to wait till tomorrow night. Big things will be happening tomorrow.'

Calvin nodded, knowing he didn't understand and wasn't in control. Grief and hysteria were very close. He lay back and stared at the darkness of the roof. Tears came again and he put out his hand for Moonluck and clung to her. When he'd clung for a long time it seemed as if the contact might have no end. She laid him slowly back.

It was strange. It was unexpected. It was awful and it was beyond wonder. They were both crying.

It was Moonluck who did everything. She hovered above him and he was concentrated and enclosed. He was a germ of life deep in a pit of hell and his eyes were rolling in his head, then he was raised from that deep place, lifted, gathered up. Moonluck could tilt the world and make rivers run up hill. He didn't know how she did it because he paid little attention. He was idle. He was light. He was floating and he was free. All hopes and fears became tenuous and were being gathered from him as the sun draws mist from a swamp. Without effort he swam through sensation to utter faith. How could she turn him inside out, renew him, and make him and the world, for a moment, whole again? And there was a promise in the simple, tender and sensitive caresses that she could work this magic again and again. Smooth skin and incredible sensations were a hardly-noticed stairway to contact on a rare but not precarious height. When he reached it with long and full-lunged exhalations there was, in that rainbow-dreamy place, a tiny diamond of hard knowledge. She was a remarkable woman, and possibly unique. (The voice that kept repeating, 'Think, think, think,' was faint and distant. What absurd advice. There was nothing to think about. There was only – Moonluck.) Peacefully, in the fraction of time before he slept, he thought of himself as tied to her, not for a day, a year or a life-time, but for ever. He despised mediaeval superstition but he luxuriated in the notion that if he had a soul, she'd taken it. And it was right that it should be so. And sleep and heaven and Moonluck were one. And he would look after this girl who loved his friend.

Moonluck leaned against the high drift of buried skulls, holding him round the shoulders. She liked this unexpected, emotional boy. He behaved very curiously. He was a baby but he had great passion. Was he brave? She must think carefully about the next day.

And the phantoms and notions which it was better not to formulate into thoughts or hopes were firmly buried more deeply where all dangerous spirits must be buried – to be taken out and recollected at only the rarest moments of security. Moonluck knew how rare such moments were. This was such a moment but likely to be a very short one. She thought her thoughts grimly yet resignedly. This one she cuddled in her arms thought such moments came often and could last for ever. Silly. It was strange that a man, a year older than she was, should be so child-like. Of course, he was foreign and ignorant. She must remember how far he was from home.

She felt one throb of horrid grief when she remembered that Red, too, was far from home, yet in spite of loneliness, he used to be able to do for her what she was now doing for this boy.

On the next day they waited for hours. They couldn't get away. Something had delayed Kittypet and the Flyer, who were to bring blankets and supplies of food. Moonluck stayed in the deepest part of the cave and never showed herself. Calvin thought that with the whole valley a scene of great activity it was just as well not to attempt flight. It might not be prevented but, with the tribes gathering, their flight could not be concealed. He still didn't understand what was happening, or why. What did Longhair really want? Why was the dream so important? And why did Red have to die?

He hid himself near the entrance of the cave and was amazed at all the pomp of the occasion. He wanted particularly to see the Ottawa Walker.

He did find out one thing: Longhair had told MacBain that there had been an accident. MacBain was supposed to believe him dead. He wondered if MacBain accepted this explanation. Possibly he appeared to, thinking himself in some danger.

Since there was no one there to prevent him he climbed to a higher point above the cave to watch the tribes arrive. He could see the lake silver in the distance. By afternoon he was beginning to realise that the other camp or conference was much larger than Longhair's. Potawatomis and Tionontatis arrived together in what seemed to be a new alliance, they were so friendly. They were also undisciplined, which offended Firepouch. There were about seventy men, and, since their normal range was close, they brought more women. They'd barely begun the cheerful preparation of their camp when a larger and more splendid group arrived – Lenapes. Twenty canoes, eight men to each, moving with military precision in a 'V' formation. Their clothes were as well-made as the jackets of the Miamis – the sleeves were sewn on, not attached by thongs – and all the bead-work was precise and brilliant. (Beads stayed bright longer than quills.) They wore their hair at shoulder length and the long tails of their head-bands fluttered behind them.

The most boisterous party and the largest were Chippewas from north of the biggest lake. They wore a great mixture of clothing and their language was very familiar to Calvin since he'd known many family groups during the winter. What were they doing here?

The arrival of the Ottawa Walker was grim in a curious way. Calvin had never seen such speed. He came in a large flotilla of canoes and it passed two others on the lake. The canoes surged like horses at the gallop. When they ultimately marched across the valley Calvin could see why. The men who grouped themselves around the chief were almost deformed. He knew they were traders and spent much time in canoes, but he had not expected such spindly legs to support such hard, thick shoulders.

The Ottawa Walker – there was no doubt because of the shouts he heard by way of welcome – was the old man he'd met so long ago, the middle one, the one who wore the two small soap-stone otters round his neck.

A couple of other facts clicked into place as he watched. He'd been stupid. He should have guessed. The Ottawa Walker was a joker name. This man was Coppertooth, the magician, a Master of the Medewiwin, Moonluck's father!

Why hadn't he come before? He hurried directly to Firepouch, who took him to Longhair and a long conference followed. How do you have a conference with a man who won't speak?

Calvin felt he should go back to the cave. Kittypet and

the Flyer might have arrived. He climbed down from the rock. A group of the Ottawa Walker's heavy-shouldered paddlers, armed with muskets, was marching by. In the middle of the group, disarmed, were MacBain and his two white men! They seemed to be on friendly terms with their guards. Calvin was badly shaken. He wondered whether to shout or not. He decided against it. Possibly MacBain was not a prisoner but was being protected.

Following MacBain, and guided ceremoniously by others of the Ottawa Walker's men, came two small groups from very far away. The first group was composed of Chippewyans – they wore pointed jackets, like some Eskimos – and they must have travelled a thousand miles. The second group, only half a dozen, were Crees from the plains, the tallest, calmest, most impressive Indians Calvin had seen. He was astonished at how many garments they wore. The day was not cool.

All the valley rang with shouting and conversation. The camps were quickly laid out and the different kinds of huts erected. Firepouch, exhausted now, seemed to be everywhere.

Calvin went back to the cave. Kittypet and the Flyer had not appeared. He couldn't find Moonluck. The light was dim but he climbed the drift of skulls. There were far too many signs of ancient fury, he thought. Far, far too many – and in the sand at the top, wrapped in a blanket, he found Red's rifle, powder horn and sack of bullets. He whispered softly. There was a curious rustling sound in the dark, but no answer. The acrid smell he'd noticed before was stronger here, and a cooler air blew it into his face. It wasn't the skulls. They were all old and dry. He climbed back down the drift.

Presently Moonluck joined him. No sign of Kittypet.

'I wish I knew what was going on,' said Calvin.

'It's simple,' said Moonluck.

'Is the Ottawa Walker your father?'

'Coppertooth.'

Calvin nodded. 'I met him once.'

'I knew that up on the hill. You told me things he'd said.'

'He doesn't seem as cheerful today as he was then.'

'He isn't.'

'You've talked to him?'

'If you can call it talking. He speaks to me through an elder. I'm not his daughter any more.'

'Was it you who persuaded him to come to this place?'

'This is his place and Speechmaker shouldn't have come here. I persuaded him, but he doesn't like it.'

'What's their quarrel?'

They spoke in whispers. Moonluck waited before she answered. 'Men!' she said. 'The adders may be murderers but sometimes they listen to their women.'

Calvin insisted. 'What's the quarrel?'

'There are two quarrels. One is simple: Speechmaker thinks he's Pontiac and wants to drive all the white men out. My father wants the Hudson's Bay Company at Bruce Factory. On that one my father's right. This is his country and Speechmaker should stay in the south.'

'What's the other quarrel?'

'A quarrel between children. Speechmaker wants to be invited into the order of the Medewiwin. My father refuses. He says Speechmaker is a crazy man and believes in dreams.'

'Doesn't your father believe in dreams?'

'Proper dreams. Official dreams. Not just anybody's dreams. He resents being invited to hear a dream by a beginner, especially this one.'

Calvin remembered the frenzied searches Longhair had carried out and asked for an explanation. Moonluck found this more difficult. 'It's true,' she said. 'It's known that Pontiac tied his power to his totem and promised his

228

totem to Speechmaker. It would be hard to keep Speech-maker out of the Medewiwin if he had the totem.'

Calvin found the conversation enlightening. 'Which quarrel is more important?'

'If my father could send Speechmaker back to his own country he'd care less about the Medewiwin. Other members would have to deal with him there – a thousand miles away.'

The light dimmed suddenly. Moonluck looked up and moved quickly into the darker cave. She snatched her little cape to brush out her footprints as she went.

Then, bewilderingly, the Ottawa Walker was marching down the cave with his two advisers. Following him was MacBain.

'Mr MacBain!' Calvin began, but the white man, looking harassed, gestured for silence.

Three Ottawa soldiers carrying guns came with the party and took positions as guards. The Ottawa Walker sat down, so Calvin sat opposite him.

'You are willing to marry those two women?' asked the Ottawa Walker.

Calvin was so startled that he couldn't answer for a moment. The old man was changed. He still spoke in that deep, memorable voice but it was no longer calm and reasonable. The voice was now quick, decisive, commanding, even a little nervous.

'Well—' began Calvin.

'Will you pay?'

'I—'

MacBain interrupted. 'He'll pay.'

'I want him to tell me.'

'I'll pay.' Calvin didn't really know how, how much, or with what.

MacBain began to say something as if in explanation, 'The maps are very good indeed. I want to go over the stock-lists with you and—'

'Later, later,' said the Ottawa Walker. 'If there's a war there won't be any stock-lists.'

In the silence that followed this warning Calvin noticed for the first time the impressive clothes the old man wore, the necklace of enormous bear-claws, the embroidered jacket, the bands of wampum, the head-dress of black bear fur; at their former meeting he'd talked to a naked, kindly old man in a blanket.

'Your totem – you've only—'

But the old man had finished his discussion and rose to his feet.

'We must talk to Onatekta quickly. Stay here young man.'

Onatekta was a Chippewa chief, Calvin knew, but he was still interested in the ornaments worn by the Ottawa Walker. He peered closely.

'When I saw you before—'

'Forget when you saw me before. Stay here. The less you're seen the better.'

And the whole party marched quickly towards the entrance. Calvin noticed that MacBain tried ineffectually to delay the exit but was almost bundled into step by the dominant Ottawa Walker and could say nothing.

Calvin was astonished that a man so distinguished in the Hudson's Bay Company could be so treated, but he was far more astonished by the whole visitation and by the radical change in the old man.

'War,' he'd said, and 'Stay here'. Why was he so agitated? Calvin wished he could understand. The two things Moonluck had told him didn't seem like a reason for war. Or did they? If you were an Ottawa—

He tried to find her. He climbed the sand-bank. Red's rifle still lay there in its blanket. Moonluck was gone. She might be looking for Kittypet.

Marry those two women?

Then he wandered to the entrance of the cave. The

230

tribes were settling in. There was less activity on the lowest terrace. He was sore and tired but it was important for him to understand. The dull, self-admonitory 'Think! Think! Think!' came back to him and he tried, he really tried—

Then the cry rang in his head long after the sound had stopped. It came from an open, wide, clean wind-pipe – a not-too-far-off brazen bellow of pure pain. Red.

Calvin raced. He reached the place behind the screen. He didn't see the interested crowd, he saw only the manikin high on the frame. The heavy muscles were vicious now, and acted independently of will. They swelled and strained at the bonds. When these refused to break the muscles wrenched the figure into joint-dislocating deformities and grievous distortions. He could hear the clicking of bones in and out of their sockets.

The scene was phantasmagoric. Red's belly pulled in till it was in the shadow of sharp ribs. Hips were up-tilted forward and the basket swung. The muscles of his shoulders swelled and knotted till the two trees shook. The big thighs below the apron were hazy with quivering. Calves pulled up till the skin grew shiny – weight on the balls of the feet – knees bent – toes lifted and held straining apart.

Any movement increased the pain but a wrench would convulse the muscles of one side, hips would go sideways, the basket would swing—

And it couldn't stop.

The sun, when it raced across a rip in the clouds, seemed high. Was it only noon? There were people coming and going. The group of brightly dressed Miamis were gossiping fifty feet away. It was all mindless—

Longhair was standing beside him. How long he'd been there Calvin had no way of knowing. A gust of wind brought a reeking cloud from the basket which nearly caused the boy to vomit. A mist of flies and mosquitoes sometimes obscured Red so that outlines became diffused.

231

The smell had attracted many dogs. One of them put his forepaws on the edge of the basket and snaked his head and tongue forward to lick the fouled moss. The basket swung back.

This caused the second sound Red made. It was deep in his open throat and was the breaking of glutinous bubbles there, half-coughs repeated till a young man took a swipe at the dog, which scuttled off, silent and vicious. The weight swung back. The young man made water on the stinking moss.

Firepouch came close to Longhair and spoke to him. Calvin heard the words but didn't hold them in his mind.

'He's very strong. He'll last longer than I thought. Five days? A week? Will that interfere?'

Longhair indicated a negative and took a half-step forward. The basket seemed to slip a fraction of an inch lower.

'He's very strong,' repeated Firepouch, but Longhair didn't hear. His concentration was as intense as Calvin's.

When it happened, the sound of tearing was sibilant and indescribable. The basket didn't have far to fall. The cone was sustained by whitish filaments for a few seconds. There was a rush of blood. Then the cone too subsided.

Longhair, like a flash, dug the pressed tissues from the cone and flung the bloody mess to the dogs, which snarled, snapped and ran.

A thin stream of blood ran down the threads of dangling tissue.

Calvin was rooted. The third cry, which accompanied Longhair's action, was a brief rising whine – lips pulled back, teeth bared, mouth open, rigid – and the pitch of the sound rose so high you couldn't tell when it stopped. The tongue could be seen quivering in the middle of the wide mouth. Was the sound still issuing, a pitch of agony too high for hearing?

232

Suddenly the body sagged and the heavy head – hair now grimy and dull – lolled sideways and forward.

Longhair moved back towards his hut and Calvin staggered away. Back – the cave – darkness – escape. No reason to stay. With Red dead there was no reason now to stay. No reason to stay? That thought had made Moonluck lie to him. He blundered into a couple of men who looked at him and shrugged. Escape! Escape! Escape was being prepared—

He went into the cave and walked as steadily as he could up the drift of skulls. He unwrapped the rifle and it felt familiar. The light was dim but after a few moments he could see. He selected a ball from the sack of shot. He tore a tattered remnant of shirt to make a wad. His hands were trembling but he loaded the rifle with attention to every detail, as he'd seen Red load it.

Colethorpe had deserted him. Kittypet had deserted him. Moonluck had deserted him. MacBain had deserted him. Red had deserted him.

He heard sounds. Some of the people hadn't deserted him. He worked meticulously, though his thoughts whirled wildly.

Kittypet, Moonluck and the Flyer came towards him with a torch and guided him through the dark cave. The floor was spongy with the droppings of bats. They turned two corners. They climbed. They seemed to climb for ever. They came into the open. The light was blinding though they were among trees.

Calvin went the wrong way, towards the valley. He was so high the people looked short. The others hissed at him – they couldn't call out – but he didn't hear them. He leaned against a parapet of limestone. He was escaping, but Red had already escaped. He just wanted a look. He was high enough to see over the screen of saplings.

Then he found he was wrong. Red hadn't escaped.

The fourth cry that rang across the amphitheatre and

pinned Calvin to the rock was utterly unlike the others. This cry was loose, like slipped bowels, uncontrolled, raw, the man behind it gone. All that was left was a body floundering out of life.

Calvin leaned on his belly. His hands trembled. He sucked in on every nerve and the trembling miraculously stopped. He would have time to load again.

He waited with patience till Red's head stopped wagging and shot him accurately between the eyes. He died instantly.

The three others stood behind him with their mouths open.

'Go back into the cave,' said Calvin, 'and quickly.'

He looked into the valley again. Longhair was there.

He took time to swab the barrel properly. As he measured the powder he heard a scrabble of retreating footsteps. He made a wad and rammed it home. He picked out another of the small lead bullets – so small.

He finished priming and put the horn aside. Longhair was, of course, gone when he was ready to take aim.

Calvin heard the thud of many racing footsteps. Longhair's guards, he thought. He was still looking for Longhair when he was hit on the head.

He was naturally unaware of how close the incident had come to causing Longhair to break his silence and thus ruin the preparations for his dream.

10

Another Dream

*'An enemy has painted his
dream over mine.'*

Longhair

PREPARATIONS for the dream, he could see, were well advanced. The tribes seemed to be divided into two main groups but it was difficult to see clearly because, repeatedly, he found himself reeling off into a dizzy spell. It seemed to him he was on a fairly high platform. It was dusk. Two drums were being played antiphonally. A dance was in progress. Twelve small fires were being kindled in a half circle. Every now and then – suddenly, and without apparent reason – his head would clear completely and he could see things sharply, but the sharpness would blur and the sick throbbing would return and his eyes would close again.

The saplings which had formerly screened Red were being taken down and used to feed the twelve fires. It was this fact which first seemed important to him. Why was concealment no longer necessary – concealment from other tribes, the Ottawa Walker or MacBain? Why was everything now out in the open. Why did it seem less the disappearance of a challenge than the acceptance of one?

Though he could see things, he took them in slowly and he had no real feeling about them. He seemed to have no feelings at all. Emotionally he was numb. But his eyes were getting clearer. He could observe. The faint Presbyterian voice revived – 'Think! Think! Think!' – and seemed as absurd as ever.

Next time he came to he saw that he'd been right, and that everything was now out in the open, including himself. They'd put no apron on him and the wind was cold. The dizzy spells were growing shorter, and a few recollections became graspable. He'd regained consciousness once on the rough journey to the frame, but he remained limp as there was no point in struggling. The frame didn't fit him; it had been made for Red. His legs were long enough to reach the two posts but his shoulders were inches short of the beam. This meant that his arms crossed it at an angle and it was only the binding at his wrists that was effective. As a result he sagged more than Red had done and his head didn't lie across the beam but bumped it.

He remembered he'd come to, dimly, while Longhair was fixing the cone to his balls. He saw how earnest Longhair was, how he was concentrating, how rigidly he tried to control the fury that made his hands tremble, and how close his face was. Longhair had fine teeth. Calvin thought of a shepherd on the slope of Cheviot biting the balls off a tup lamb. He thought of the wolf and Red Riding Hood, a child's story, something to giggle at.

An enormous black cloud was rising slowly in the south and faint thunder underlay the drum-beats which were catching more of his attention. Two rows of men, naked, were dancing beyond Longhair's hut. Longhair's young men. There were twenty. Each had a white line painted on back and breast. The fires were burning more brightly. Longhair's lieutenant stood at the end of the two lines chanting, his face to the sky. Calvin could now see the glint of firelight in the upraised eyes. Between the lines of the chant and in the same rhythm came a double throaty sound from the dancers. It reminded Calvin of an

236

'amen'. The second line of the chant made him listen more closely than he intended.

> 'Our chief is asking
> Swimming Otter
> To be his guide
> Into the country
> Of all the spirits.
> He swears to open
> Both his eyes,
> To meet them all—
> Friends, Enemies—
> And then to bring
> Back to this meeting
> Only the truth
> Of what they tell him.'

While the chant was being repeated in all four directions Calvin saw the famous carved green-stone Lenape pipe carried smoking to Longhair who sat alone in front of his hut. Out of a small medicine-bag the old chief took three pinches of powder and put them in the bowl of the pipe. Longhair smoked deeply and with due ceremony.

It was interesting. It impressed the tribes. They were paying more attention. Longhair's people and Firepouch were isolated on the left. All the rest were crowded behind the Ottawa Walker and some other chiefs on the right. The semi-circle of fires which lit the central space was surrounded by hundreds of faces and glinting eyes, all intent, concentrated and serious. It impressed Calvin as well as the Indians. And there was something in all this that could be important to him—

But concentrating for a long time was hard. He was putting his weight on the two posts now, partly to relieve the strain on his wrists. The wet leather cone felt cold in the wind and caused a prickling sensation. Then he felt dizzy again. Then the headache, then sudden wakefulness.

It was at this point of real and full return to consciousness that Calvin grasped one inescapable fact; he would never get down from this place. His feet would never touch the ground again. A blankness followed the realisation.

Suddenly it was night. The half of the sky not obscured by the single monstrous cloud was an incredible web of brilliant points. Calvin had heard that some men knew how far away they were.

Kittypet was like a small dead girl. Where was she now?

Moonluck, he now knew, had lied about Red for a kindly reason. She'd told him Red was dead so he could escape without feeling like a deserter. Where was Moonluck now?

He heard dogs snarling some distance behind him. It was in that direction Red's body had been flung.

And dully, dully, 'Think! Think! Think!' was gnawing at his mind.

The chanting was loud, almost a shouted demand. The dance was heavy, tense and violent, the syllables were driven through the throats of the dancers by the same convulsed muscles that made the feet beat earth. A dozen new drums joined in and the sustained sound rose in volume as Longhair rose—

Just at that moment the bright flickering in the southern sky began – reflected lightning, the sound of which was always on the edge of hearing. The circle flickered orange to white and back again.

The chanting suddenly became a series of hoarse, shouted commands delivered with intense feeling:

'Joker
Wander
Elsewhere
Joker!'

238

Calvin felt a weird sympathy for this man, prepared to go alone into a world of spirits. He had the sensation that the whole amphitheatre was crowded, and that the ghosts were massed even to the edge of the granite cliff. There was a concentration of energy in the bursts of words and the stamping feet. These people, if they could, would help Longhair on his journey, and keep him safe.

Two young men rushed forward and held aside the buckskin curtain. Longhair, his hair trailing, addressed his body and his raised hands to the south. Then he paused. The flickering light seemed to make him uncertain and he had to draw himself up with a great wrench of will before he turned himself abruptly and entered the hut. The curtain swung to behind him and the young men looked at each other. There was a groan from many hundreds of men and women. Calvin had the feeling that some omen was unfavourable but he didn't know what or why.

The silence after Longhair's retirement only seemed like silence. The drums became continuous and soft, the chant continuous but on the breath. Quiet, so the dream should not be disturbed. The dancers sat on the ground and maintained the rhythm with their hands. They did not clap but brushed tough palms together with a sound that made Calvin think of a million weightless ghosts walking on dry grass – *wheap, wheap.* Absurd. How could a weightless ghost make any sound at all?

His mind was working on two levels. He must concentrate. The practical level. The practical level—

The Ottawa Walker wanted Longhair out of his country. Longhair wanted Pontiac's totem. If Longhair had Pontiac's totem what would he do with it?

When he asked himself that question and almost got an answer Calvin felt a thrill run up his spine that ended in a tingling of his scalp as if each hair were waving, not in terror but in triumph.

But he was being absurd. It was impossible – what with the headache, the dizziness, the exhaustion—

And more – it had been going on for so long. The skulls in the cave, and killings without number, and people burned, and all the ghosts, and heads split open by hatchets in the dark, and balls pulled off, and knee-caps chopped, and time after time after time after time, for ever and ever. Amen.

Face facts. He'd soon be out of it and the sooner the better.

How threatening this soft chant had become. How long would it continue? He could see weapons now he hadn't seen before. He heard a faint sound like a bow being strung. There were spears, some with heads of honed steel which gleamed in the firelight.

Then he saw there was a big change. Both the Lenapis and the Miamis were now with Firepouch. The Lenapis, being the richest, had the most firearms. The two main groups were evenly divided. Calvin shook his arms, raised himself and tried to see. The beam continued to shake as if moved by the ponderous thudding of thunder that bounded and rebounded from black cloud to curving cliff.

He felt – he thought he felt – not exactly a pain, but a warning twitch from his balls. He knew he shouldn't move – any move could start the knife of agony – but he couldn't help it. Fear hitched his hips aside, pulled up on all his bowels, sucked in his belly. Fear tried to isolate his private parts; to hold them out and away as if they were a doggo mink about to have a fit.

There was a slow, sliding tension as, gently, one testicle pulled down, in, and under the other, which – just as slowly and as gently – eased upwards.

At once the greasy leather cone slipped off. The basket, which was still light, had only a short distance to fall. It made very little sound, not enough to alert the guards, no more than the plaited cords that collapsed so softly on the moss.

But Calvin made a sound. His laugh was cackling, loud, and loon-like. The guards and a few other Ottawas turned their heads; but such hysteria was natural and they turned back to more important things.

The high, loud laughter stopped, started and stopped again, his whole body quaking. The recurring image that kept re-starting the laughter when he thought he finally had it under control was of a cork drawn from a bottle. He was still waiting for the 'pop'.

He shook, heaved and twisted. The column of his breath shuddered as it moved in and out of his open throat. Finally he hushed himself, his mind raced and he screwed the lid down tight on his hysteria. There was nothing to laugh about. They could easily hitch that basket to his balls again. Why had no one noticed? They'd notice soon enough.

In some way the irresistible hysteria had cleared his brain. He would do something. He accepted now, as unalterable fact, that he had nothing to lose. So he would do something. Anything. The caution based on preserving what safety he had was swallowed up in the freedom or confidence injected into him by the knowledge that safety was now so tenuous it wasn't worth having.

There was a thing he could do. His mind fingered it lightly. As if it were purely academic he asked himself the question: 'If Longhair had Pontiac's totem what would Longhair do? He'd take it and show it to the angry tribes in the south, the Sauks and Foxes. He'd—

He glanced down. The nearest fire was close to the terrace wall. The wall threw a shadow which lapped across his belly. The farther fires gave less light. It was unlikely, therefore, that anyone could see that the basket had fallen.

He began to giggle again but it was weak, sad and

silent. Red's balls were as big as hens' eggs; his own were marbles by comparison. If his sensation had meant any-thing – if one testicle had aligned itself above the other – Longhair should have made a smaller cone. Presbyterian maxims swam up from his childhood: if a job's worth doing it's worth doing well.

Anyway here he was. Was the beam moving? There was a treble yelping from the dogs behind him, which drowned the chant for a moment, then it continued again at its even pace. The concentration on the black square hut was intense, as if a silence glowed from the centre of it. He bumped his head. He wished the beam were steadier. The air was chilly. A moth was under his left arm and walking down his ribs. He tried to see but bumped his head again.

It crawled to his diaphragm and tickled so that he fluttered his muscles to scare it away. It wasn't a moth, it was a hand; and it crept past his navel, and lower, and lifted his genitals. He heard a faint gasp behind him. (Surprise that the cone was gone?) He strained again to turn his head. Moonluck was on the ladder and she looked up at him, her mouth open, her jaw trembling. Her black eyes were unbelievably bright in the light of the fires. She must stay in shadow. She held his balls so gently that his eyes prickled.

Then, with great caution, she was out of sight behind him, a little higher on the ladder and, he hoped, com-pletely in darkness.

In spite of the fact that he felt warmth from her face on the side of his neck her whisper was almost inaudible.

'You're a brave man,' he heard.

He answered, breathing the words slowly, 'So are you.' That was far from correct but she'd know what he meant.

Again time passed at two speeds. She untied his wrists. She should have done his feet first. He nearly fell, and grasped the beam convulsively. He could be seen, but the arms were roughly in the same position as before.

She hid behind the posts to do his feet.

There was a long pause. He knew she was waiting for him at the foot of the ladder. She'd get impatient. He made a tiny gesture with his left hand and was glad to feel the beam sway a little as she climbed. He felt the warmth on his ear again.

'Come down.'

'Moonluck,' he whispered.

'Come down!'

'Tie the straps again.'

'No!'

'Not me. Just the knots. Tie the knots in the same places. The same places.'

'Come down Calvin!'

'Too much running away. Not any more.'

'Calvin!'

'Can you get a message to your father?'

'He won't listen.'

'No.' He accepted that; but unless the Ottawa Walker could be warned it would be tricky. Very tricky. How intelligent was the Ottawa Walker? Mr Colethorpe thought Indians were stupid children.

'Tie the knots again.' This time his voice was a little too loud because he was trying to be insistent. There was a long pause, but eventually he felt fingers near his wrists, then he felt the beam shake and the fingers worked at the straps which had attached his feet to the posts. While this went on he flexed and shook his wrists and ankles one by one. Longhair had been angry. The knots had been tied too tightly. His fingers and toes ached and tingled as the flow of blood returned.

He hoped desperately that Moonluck would tie the knots exactly as they'd been tied before – as if they'd never been untied. He wouldn't be in this trouble if he'd done some thinking earlier in the summer. Running away discouraged thinking. The politics were always the important thing. Now that he had a better notion of the politics—

The Ottawa Walker wouldn't be protecting MacBain if he hadn't a use for him. MacBain wouldn't have paid him a compliment about the maps if he hadn't a use for *him*. Longhair wanted white men out of the country. He wanted the new Bruce Factory destroyed, but he wanted Pontiac's totem more. That meant power. To give him that power the totem would have to be seen. Where? In the south. Far away from this country.

The chant suddenly became faster, though just as soft. Had there been some sign from the hut? Had he missed something? He must pay attention. The words of the chant were more muddled as if each person began to utter the thought that seemed to him most valuable at that moment:

'Wander elsewhere.'
'Guide him safely.'
'Watch and guard him.'

Events didn't give Calvin long enough to finish his calculations or satisfy his understanding of the increased pressure in the mood of the people.

The chant, the soft drums, the wheaping hands and the tension were all shattered in an instant by monstrous twin fangs of whiteness which struck, froze, flickered and buried themselves in the hiss and smash of thunder.

Calvin tumbled to the ground. Dogs raced choking from Red's corpse, some of them trying to howl, chew and swallow at the same time. Blackness held and waited while the heavy sound trundled east, west and away. The light from the fires took effect again very slowly. The air was hot. No rain fell.

Speechmaker was screaming uncontrollably as he crawled from his hut. He was a five-year-old in the grip of abject terror. His long hair tangled his feet, his knees and his hands. The screaming changed to sobs which so cramped and jolted him that the two young men knelt down and tried to comfort him. The lieutenant tried to re-direct the chant to drown the sobs, but words were now forming themselves out of the agony and Calvin listened, fascinated.

'I've failed,' said Longhair. 'I was alone. No guide came. I have an enemy. I've failed!'

The chanting stopped completely and the silence was absolute. The young men helped Longhair to his feet then cowered away and crouched to listen.

'I didn't see my enemy though I saw his shadow. His shadow held the shadow of the totem that was willed to me—'

Calvin had never heard such passion. Longhair's voice was trumpet-like and throbbed with intensity. His body pulsated in the same frequency. The emotion was enveloping and over-riding. Crouched in the shadow of the terrace-edge, Calvin felt a compulsive and ridiculous sympathy for this transported man. His audience was motionless as stone.

'No guide. No guide. And I've wrapped myself in cloud, and I've floated in a circle and I've crossed the circle. The circle touches Philadelphia and the British, Chicago and the Miamis, Quebec and the French. I've seen nothing, brought back nothing. Seen no one, talked to no one. Nothing and no one attacked me or befriended me. No one and nothing is there. I know the smell of nothing, the sight of nothing, the sound of nothing, the taste of nothing and the touch of nothing. My journey was full of death and useless.'

Calvin heard a sibilance hinting at laughter. Longhair, instead of sagging with his grief, became defiant and drew himself up.

'But I recall the great man my uncle and I'll cram you

full – I'll cram you full of the nothing that I saw. I saw what I have known. But all the hills, once blue, were grey heaps of the shit of a man fed only on meal. The valleys I've known, once green, were the same grey. All trees and little plants were wrapped in shrouds by small grey worms. The waters of all the rivers and all the ponds, and lakes both large and small – how brightly those waters once sparkled – were the milk-grey piss of an old woman about to die. The air was grey. The air was the winter-vapour of a fireless house crowded with old dead men whose lights were full of worms. The grey air was the grey breath of the last dead worms.

'I met no spirit of an animal, a tree, a hill, a bird, a river, or a lake. I met no spirit of a man. All these were dissolved in the grey slush of nothing. You too were dead, and so dissolved, and so at the end was I.'

He paid no attention to the tears that poured over his cheeks, into the runnels by his nose and dripped from his chin. Some of the black paint came with them and streaked his hairless chest. In spite of the tears his voice was firm and musical.

'All colours have gone, all darkness and light. Not a wave moves on the water, which will glisten no more for ever. No bird flies, no insect. No beast runs on the grey shit-hills, no worm crawls. Not one fish moves through the grey piss-water. Then I too was nothing and I'd taken the world to nothing with me.'

There followed a racking pause, but Longhair was tensing for some last effort and the circle of glinting eyes remained fixed on him. The moment stretched.

To Calvin it was a most curious moment in which occurred an illumination which he was never really able to remember accurately. He was a white man. That was how it began. But, in that moment he saw quite clearly that the Ottawa Walker, wise, rational, objective, full of common sense, was, in the long run, utterly wrong and

246

that this crazy man, packed as he was with haunts and hates and cruelties, was, in the long run, right. How could that be? Yet blindingly, suddenly and briefly, it was so. He didn't understand.

Longhair was shaking like a pennon in a high wind and there was foam on his lips.

'My dream is death,' he screamed. 'A totem was willed to me and it's been stolen by my enemy. The totem I should have is gone. My power is gone. My enemy is here. My enemy has stolen my totem. I – I—'

The screaming broke down into sobs, as at the beginning, and the firelight flickered on a writhing figure, wild with grief. The body wrenched about as Red's body had wrenched about.

It struck Calvin later that what followed was possibly the cruellest incident of all that doom-filled day. The cruel thing was just a statement, and very brief. The terrible old Ottawa Walker rose and said in a loud, slow, impressive voice, heard by everyone:

'Dreams by beginners are always dangerous.'

And there was general assent to this thought until Calvin, trembling – he was still naked and quite cold – walked to the edge of the terrace where he hesitated. Here he stood in the full glare of the fires, and if he made a sound the eyes would swing from Longhair. Then he admonished himself in whispered words: 'Be hanged for a sheep as a lamb. Be hanged for a sheep as a lamb—'

So he made what he hoped was an expansive gesture, pointing at the weeping Longhair, and he shouted, 'That dream was not your dream.'

For some seconds, until Longhair recovered from his surprise, Calvin had his attention.

'In your dream you found your totem. The dream you have told was put into your head by your enemy.'

Calvin could see MacBain and the Ottawa Walker whispering together. A little closer he could see Moonluck and Kittypet clutching each other, staring at him, isolated. Longhair had recovered. He leaped to his feet and rushed towards Calvin, yelling, 'Who cut him down?'

'You did!' roared Calvin.

Longhair stopped, spurts of sand squirting ahead of his feet.

'You did!' Calvin repeated, thrusting his neck forward and trying hard to stare at Longhair as blindingly as that distraught man was staring at him. Calvin bawled his short sentences as loudly as he could.

'You fought your enemy. I saw you. You beat him. You had him by the throat. He told you where he'd hidden your totem. I know because you told me. You told me before you lifted me down.'

This was as much startling and bellowing as Calvin thought it wise to do. He decided that he must not compete with Longhair on a prophetic level.

Arrows were fitted to bows and most of Longhair's soldiers rose, but Calvin scrambled painfully down the granite bank and walked towards the tall, wild, hopeless leader.

'I slept up there,' he said in a more confidential voice. 'In my sleep I dreamed too. I dreamed – this was in the quiet, long before the thunder-clap arranged by your enemy – I dreamed that you came out of your hut, you walked here, and here you fought your enemy and took his secret. You told me the words. "Press the metal button," you said. I saw all that. I saw all that and heard it in my sleep. No one else saw it because it was in your dream.'

'Who cut you down?'

'The straps aren't cut. You didn't have to cut them. After you choked your enemy you just had to raise your hand and the basket fell from my balls. The lacing is as you left it. The straps are still knotted.'

'Go and see,' said Longhair, and his lieutenant raced away. 'What is this metal button?'

'Could the Ottawa Walker – could Coppertooth join us? He's the only one besides me who knows about the metal button.'

There was some shouting and as the old chief, wary and disgruntled, came towards them Calvin was scratching at his private parts. They itched intolerably. He stopped when he realised how many people were looking at him.

Coppertooth was hesitant. Calvin was encouraged when he saw this. The tension was mounting and he wasn't sure how long he could keep the necessary strands in his own fingers. He wished he'd had clothes on. He didn't know why, but clothes helped you to think.

Coppertooth was about to speak. He was always persuasive. Calvin mustn't give him time. He interrupted, turning to Longhair.

'After your enemy was beaten you told me you must take your totem tomorrow and show it in the country of the Illinois. You told me Sauks and Foxes and other families among the people would stop killing each other and many terrible wars would end. In your dream you mentioned a beautiful coloured country – you mentioned no grey country to me – and you said you would be very busy in that country, and that you came into this country only to find that important swimming otter—'

'Have you seen it?' asked Longhair grimly.

Calvin turned towards Coppertooth, wishing he had long probes for eyes. Finally the old man looked straight at him and Calvin answered, 'I've never seen it.'

Coppertooth nodded very slightly as if in approval.

'But the red-headed man – it was his spirit that you fought – knew about a secret place in my writing-case. "Press the metal button," you told me—'

Calvin's eyes were chained to Coppertooth's. 'If I'd known where the totem was I'd have told you.'

'The red-head was your friend,' said Longhair.

This was the hardest part. Calvin had to start his sentence twice.

'Is it – is it like a friend to land me in the trouble I've been in?'

The faintest of smiles flickered over old Coppertooth's features. Calvin, still desperate to grapple the old man's eyes, ploughed on.

'If Mr MacBain could bring the writing-case we could press the metal button. Maybe we might find—'

'My people have taken charge of Mr MacBain's things,' said Coppertooth.

'Then if they could bring the case – if Speechmaker's dream is true it will be remembered as a great dream and he will have accomplished all he came to this country to do.'

The group was larger. Longhair's lieutenant had joined him. The Ottawa Walker was backed up by the Chief of the Chippewas, by his own two advisers and by MacBain, who knew enough of the language to understand. He whispered to the Ottawa Walker. The old man was sulky. MacBain took a step. The Ottawa Walker stopped him.

'I'll fetch the wooden case myself,' he said, and strode deliberately into the darkness beyond the ring of firelight.

The rest stood like statues. Dizzy as he was, Calvin tried to imitate them, but his eyes flicked constantly from the two tense lines of ready men to Firepouch, dour and suspicious; from Longhair's wet face and flame-coloured eyes to MacBain, whose relaxed position was almost convincing. Calvin knew that, if it came to war, Coppertooth, in his own country, had far more men to call on. MacBain had some reason for confidence. The real unpredictable was Coppertooth. How strongly was he averse to a war he would probably win? How clearly had he caught Calvin's intention?

Nothing at all was said till the deliberate old man came back. Though he didn't look at Calvin he was behaving very pleasantly. He opened the case.

'Which is the metal button?' he asked, his expression utterly innocent. Had he taken his opportunity? He must have. He knew, and he knew Calvin knew he knew. Calvin could play innocent too.

'I forget,' he said. 'Speechmaker told me but I forget.'

The Ottawa Walker presented the open case to Longhair. 'There are only two buttons. Speechmaker will press the right one. Press it, and that will prove there is no magic, that it is as the boy has said, and that your dream – your real dream – was productive.'

It was incredible to Calvin how convincing the old man could sound when he wanted to; at least, when he decided on a course of action he held nothing back. Calvin even suspected that the case was so presented to Speechmaker that the pressing of the correct button became inevitable. Speechmaker really had no choice.

A doe-skin bag was found in the little drawer. The totem, smooth and delicate, was inside it. Longhair examined it. 'I think – I think—'

'May I examine it?' asked the Ottawa Walker. 'I carved it. I presented it to your Uncle-Father when I invited him into the Society forty years ago. Those were wonderful days—'

He took the totem and there was a soundless pause while he examined the object with care, the object which he had slipped into the drawer two minutes before. He handed it back.

'This totem is the most powerful I have ever handled. It belonged to your Uncle-Father. It is now yours. I hope you will use the power it gives you for the benefit of The People.'

Longhair's delight became a tribal triumph. Feasting went on all night. Longhair prepared to go south in the morning. Coppertooth told him that when everything was peaceful in the Illinois country it was very probable that a deputation from the Medewiwin would wait upon him. Coppertooth couldn't guarantee it, but it was probable. Then Calvin heard him mutter under his breath, 'A lot can happen before that day comes.'

Mr MacBain caught Calvin.

'Get some clothes on,' he said.

It was arranged that Calvin was to take charge of Bruce Factory till a man could be sent from Montreal. Calvin was stubborn about his rank. He was much too young to be appointed Trader. MacBain would try to have him classed as 'acting' Trader. The work on the maps was approved, but far more highly approved was the stock-list he'd prepared and which MacBain had examined carefully.

'What about Mr Colethorpe?'

'He's retired, though he doesn't know it. The old fart's still in the North looking for the Ottawa Walker.'

The Ottawa Walker was said to have sixty bales of fur. Calvin would have to be very sharp.

He also, he found, had to be sharp when he argued with Firepouch and Coppertooth about the two girls. They were in considerable danger. His only advantage was that the two men wanted to be rid of them. Mr MacBain allowed him to draw on future stipend but both chiefs drove hard bargains. While bargaining the Ottawa Walker had to be addressed by his proper name.

Long after midnight they buried what the dogs had left of Red. On the advice of both chiefs this was done secretly. Both ignored their daughters completely. As the Ottawa Walker pushed the last heap of sand over Red's body he leaned back to relieve an ache and examined Calvin for some seconds. Calvin felt that every nook and

252

cranny of his mind was being ransacked and he began to resent it. Finally, straightening, the old man spoke, as if meditating aloud—

'I supported your absurd story.'

'You couldn't do otherwise,' Calvin shot back.

'Oh?'

'You had the totem. All I had to do was say so.'

Calvin spoke belligerently and caught the briefest flicker of amusement on the old man's face. Then the impressive eyes composed themselves into solemnity and Calvin prepared himself for a more devious attack. The old man's voice took on an intonation very familiar to Calvin, more in sorrow than in anger. He really was a wicked old man.

'You say that red-headed man was your friend, yet you shot him. You helped blame him for a murder he could not have committed. And you threw dirt on his spirit when he was dead. When you're twenty-one the fishing-line is very tangled.'

'I'm seventeen,' said Calvin.

'Oh,' said the Ottawa Walker, nodding his head. Then, after a moment, he shook it. Then, slowly, he walked away.

All Calvin knew was that Red wouldn't have blamed him for anything he'd done. He wouldn't. Everybody's beliefs were apt to be foolish, apart from kindliness. He thought, for instance, of Colethorpe and of Longhair. He decided idly, in spite of all that had happened, that he preferred Longhair.

Calvin never did discover how the Ottawa Walker had obtained Pontiac's 'name' in the first place. Moonluck told him it probably had to do with the rules of the Medewiwin, never revealed to women or strangers. Some-one had secured the totem and returned it to the Ottawa Walker.

Kittypet and Moonluck, still cautious as mice when

near the chiefs, brought Calvin food and blankets. Towards morning, when conferences and arguments were all finished, the three of them huddled together near a dying fire, arms around each other. The girls watched all night but Calvin slept. Moonluck was delighted to see that Kittypet, little by little, continued to emerge from her frightening dopiness. She knew they were fortunate girls.

A day later Calvin inherited Martha along with the beautiful powder-horn. Firepouch also gave him Red's fife, which was not to be played again for some years. The Flyer decided to travel with Calvin rather than Firepouch or Speechmaker. No one objected. The journey was unbelievably swift. The paddlers were the Ottawa Walker's superb and sardonic crew-men, and the Flyer began to joke with them. He was recovering. Calvin became convinced that neither he nor Moonluck had known of Longhair's dangerous intention to pre-empt the Ottawa Walker's traditional camping ground in order to trap Red. Finally Calvin, addressing the mutilated boy by his grown-up name, asked him directly why his hand had been chopped off.

'That man must have found the finger and liked the taste,' said the boy. Then he grew more serious. 'I'd accepted her offering. The red-headed man wasn't scared any more. He wanted the red-headed man scared, and running to the north.'

When they reached Bruce Factory Calvin, foolishly, built a very large bed. Then he found that no Hudson's Bay blanket would cover it. He'd have to use furs sewn together. 'Bears are best,' Moonluck told him.

254

Kittypet's first son had red hair. Two weeks later Moonluck had a baby boy whose hair was, if anything, redder. When Calvin's children began to come along their hair was dark in both families. The three parents were, however, pleased that all the younger children liked, looked up to and confided in their oldest brothers. The two boys were energetic, strong and cheerful. The feeling of all the later children for those two boys was very similar to the feeling that Calvin had had for Red.

Occasionally Moonluck would take off on a long trip by herself. When she returned she always felt better. She told Calvin that women had thoughts that men couldn't know about.

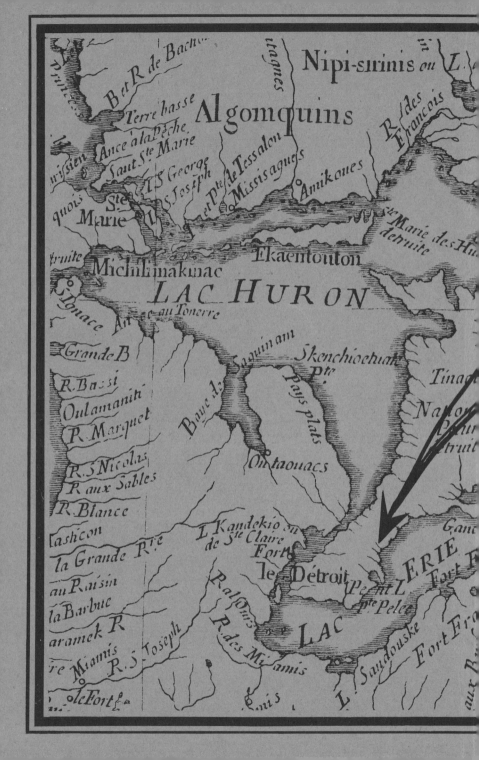